Helena Close was born in Cork but grew up in Limerick. She has worked in journalism and public relations but now writes full time. Helena has co-written two previous novels under the name Sarah O'Brien. She lives in Limerick with her husband and four children.

Pinhead Duffy

HELENA CLOSE

THE
BLACKSTAFF
PRESS
BELFAST

Thanks to my family and friends for putting up with me; to my agent, Faith O'Grady; to my wonderful editor, Hilary Bell; and to Patsy Horton and all at Blackstaff Press.

First published in 2005 by
Blackstaff Press
4c Heron Wharf, Sydenham Business Park
Belfast BT3 9LE
with the assistance of
The Arts Council of Northern Ireland

ARTS
COUNCIL
of Northern Ireland

Typeset by CJWT Solutions, Newton-le-Willows, Merseyside

Printed in Ireland by ColourBooks Limited

A CIP catalogue record for this book is available from the British Library

ISBN 0-85640-767-4

www.blackstaffpress.com

*in memory
of my sister Maura,
with love*

1

It was the summer of the marble thing. The best summer ever. I still say it now, in spite of everything that happened. I always remember that first. Always the marble thing first.

And it was Pinhead's idea, he always had the good ideas. The gang was his too, the Rocket Gang P, and the P stood for Pinhead of course. He was fourteen then, a full year older than us, and the marble thing was the best laugh we ever had. We had done other stuff, like knocking off the Matterson's van outside the shop. Pinhead's ma kissed him when he brought home the rashers and sausages. My mam would have murdered me, so I just threw my share away when the lads were gone home. And we swam in the Forty Foot when the bigger fellas were chicken, even Pinhead's brother wouldn't swim there. Diet, we called him, because he was fat. But the marble thing was the best.

I knew on the last day of school, our very last day in that school before we all went to Secondary, that it was going to be a great summer. When I called for Pinhead that morning, the rain was flogging down. His house was only around the corner from mine, but when I got there, I was soaked to the skin. Pinhead answered the door the second I knocked and shouted 'Get lost!' to his mother as he came out. She wanted him to wear a Besco bag on his head to keep him dry. We both laughed at the idea of that. A plastic bag on your head.

We headed down St Patrick's Hill and out the Dublin Road, the two of us in great form, and Pinhead said it didn't matter about the rain, it didn't matter at all, because our holidays didn't really start till tomorrow, and that cheered us both up.

Pinhead was a year older than us but he was in our class over thinking he was Tarzan last summer. He tied a rope to a tree and swung into the quarry on it, except the knot gave and he broke his leg in five places and had to go to Croom for a few months. That's the bone hospital.

It brightened up after a while and we sat in the classroom with the hot sun streaming in the window, and Burke, our teacher, was doing Buntús Cainte at the blackboard. We were all wet from the rain and now, with the heat from the sun, steam started to rise from us, swirls of steam rising and climbing to the ceiling. Burke was so wrapped up in his Buntús Cainte, mouthing on in Irish and sticking the pictures onto the felt board, that we thought he didn't hear Pinhead say we were all a bunch of steamers. The whole class cracked up laughing and Burke roared at Pinhead.

'Kevin Duffy, we'll see where the laughs are when you go to the Tech in September. You won't be joking up there, mark my words.'

'Yes, sir,' said Pinhead, doing a Hitler salute. That got him sent outside the door, which Pinhead was used to and probably wanted in the first place.

We met up on the way home, the Rocket Gang P. Me and Pinhead, Dodge and Eyebrows. We stopped in Downes's shop and stood at the counter watching Mr Downes break off sixpence worth of Cleeves toffee for Eyebrows. Sometimes if he was in a good mood, he'd give you an extra bit, but not today. Pinhead said he was cranky because school was breaking up and he'd have no one to sell his sweets to.

Halfway home Pinhead had an idea. 'Let's go see if

Dodge's shit is still in the well,' he said, and we all laughed, even Dodge.

Two weeks earlier he had shat in St Patrick's Well, right in the middle of it, where St Patrick's holy footprints were, just for a laugh, like. But his cousin had heard about it and told his da and Dodge ended up being murdered. The hurley marks across his back were black and blue stripes even now. Fair play to Pinhead, though, he stood up to Dodge's da that day.

Pinhead hated O'Riordan, that's Dodge's da, way before the shit in the well. He hated him over the Knock-a-Dolly. We were playing it one night and it was Pinhead's turn to knock on a door. He knocked on Dodge's door and O'Riordan chased us and caught Pinhead. He tore him into the house and we hid in the bushes, waiting for Pinhead to come back out. We tried to make Dodge go in and get him, but no way would he go. Pinhead only came out when Dodge's ma arrived home from late Mass. We all asked, 'Did he kill you, Pin? What the fuck did he do all that time?' Pinhead shook us off and said, 'Nothing happened. Do ye hear me? Nothing fuckin' happened, nothing at all.' And he turned and went home. We never played Knock-a-Dolly again.

But I think that's why Pinhead tried to stand up for Dodge over shitting in the well. He back-answered O'Riordan and said that the marks couldn't be St Patrick's holy footprints because there was no cement back then and why would St Patrick be stupid enough to walk in wet cement anyway? But this made O'Riordan even madder and he made a swing for Pinhead, which was a bad idea because Pinhead was one tough bastard. He wasn't afraid of anybody or anything. He didn't lose his temper often but you knew when he was going to, because he became very quiet and his face went red and then he exploded. He did that with O'Riordan, who didn't know the warning signs, so he never ducked and got a head full force in the face. Pinhead was gone before the blood came.

O'Riordan went to Mrs Duffy to complain and she made a big deal of giving out to Pinhead in front of him. I was in the hall listening, and when O'Riordan was gone, she said, 'What happened, Kevin?' And Pinhead told her about the shit and the hurley marks on Dodge's back and she called O'Riordan a bad bastard and said he should hit men his own size, not women and children.

The shit was still there. Dark brown now, with a load of flies buzzing around it.

'Holy shit!' said Pinhead, and we all laughed.

'Who'll clean it out?' asked Eyebrows as he bent into the well for a better look.

They had Mass there sometimes and you couldn't have Mass with Dodge's big shit right in the middle of the well.

'I'll ask my da to clean it,' said Dodge, and we cracked up.

Noddy was my nickname but my mam always called me Seán. She was sick because she was having another baby, two really, twins, so that made her twice as sick. That's why I had to help her in the house on the first evening of my holidays. I didn't mind, but I'd never tell the lads. Imagine the slagging I'd get if they knew I washed up the dishes and put the small brothers to bed. I'd be Pinhead's Steamer of the Week.

When my dad came home from work in the ESB, I was able to get out. I met the lads in Pinhead's shed. He looked up as I sat down on the coal sacks. They had a lit candle and I could see him grinning at me. I knew that grin and I didn't like it.

'Noddy, why are you always the last to come?' he said.

'Fuck it, I know why! Cos you're a slow wanker, right?'
And he doubled over laughing.

I was glad it was dark in the shed because I had a
reddener and the others were hysterical but that was no
surprise. If Pinhead slagged you, everyone thought it was
hilarious. They forgot their turn would come.

We played cards because the rain wouldn't stop.
Torrential, it was, beating down on the tin roof of the
shed all that first night of our holidays. We didn't care,
though, because the summer stretched out in front of us
like it would last forever and Pinhead had Big Plans. That
was the first time we heard about the marble thing.

Pinhead always had money. He was just one of those
fellas that's good with it. He kept it in a nail jar in his room
with the lid screwed down. Dodge said Pinhead still had
his Communion money, that's how good he was with it.
So because of his stash, Pinhead had the biggest marble
collection in Limerick. Probably in Ireland. He called
them marbles because he came from Cork – they were
dobbers to us. He kept them in his sister's old doll's pram
and it was some sight. Full to the brim with dobbers, every
colour under the sun, right up to the brim. It took the
four of us to lift it.

We were in the dark about Pinhead's marble plan and
he liked keeping us that way. All he said was that
'conditions weren't right' because his da was on the dry.
That just made us more curious and when I went home
and up to bed, I kept thinking about the marble thing and
Pinhead's da on the dry and what they had to do with
each other.

The next day the rain was heavier than before and my
mam was sicker, and I had to help mind the brothers till
my aunt came at lunch-time. When I got to Pinhead's, his
Uncle Pat answered the door. I don't think he was his
uncle because he was too old and he was American, so we

never knew what to say to him. He made me come in and sit down with him in Pinhead's sitting room.

'Well, young man, I guess you're looking for Master Duffy, correct?' he said in his American twang.

'Yes,' I said to the flowery carpet on the floor.

I couldn't ever look at him after all the stuff Pinhead had told us. Like when Uncle Pat had too much whiskey one night and Pinhead and Diet caught him running around the Green, balls naked, and they had to catch him and put him to bed and he kept saying to them that he just needed to make a motion. And Pinhead made up a song about that night.

> Uncle Pat the nudey brat
> Got up one night to make a shite.

Every time I met him now, I could hear that in my head and I was afraid that one day I'd just start singing it out loud, like Pinhead did all the time, even to his face.

Pinhead's ma told me once how Uncle Pat came to live with them. He was born here but moved to America. When he was very old, say eighty or eighty-five, he went into hospital, and when he was better, there was no place for him to go. Pinhead's ma said he could live with them, even though there was a lot of people living in their house already and there wasn't room really. Mam said that was a kind thing to do, to take in an old man in his last years. They may have been his last years but he was as fit as a fiddle and could walk the legs off you.

So I was stuck with Uncle Pat and the time dragged. He was talking on and on, and I just kept nodding my head. Then Pinhead came into the room and gave me the nod to leave and we went up the stairs with him singing, 'Uncle Pat the nudey brat, got up one night to make a shite.'

We stayed in Pinhead's room that day, just me and him. It was great when it was just the two of us because you could relax and there'd be no danger of a slagging. All the others were gone out, even his sister Deirdre. She was thirteen and I liked her, but every time I saw her I got a reddener and this wasn't good if the lads noticed, so I just pretended she peeved me and tried to avoid her. When the father came home from work, he showed me and Pinhead how to cheat at cards. Lives, we were playing, and he joked about school and stuff and asked me about the hurling cup final in the Gaelic grounds and would our lads win. Pinhead never said a word.

I had my tea in Pinhead's house that evening with the rain still pelting down and all of us squashed around the table in the small kitchen. Me and Pinhead, Diet and the four sisters, the da and ma and Uncle Pat and Jesse the dog. All of us talking and laughing, but Pinhead was quiet. I knew that this had to do with me, with me staying for my tea or something. Pinhead didn't like you hanging around too long in his house. Like he didn't want you to know too much about him. But I stayed anyway and ate the boiled egg and tried not to look at Deirdre, even when she spoke to me, even when she asked me to pass the butter.

That night Dodge said the Garryoweners were coming, so we gathered at Mac's shop along with other lads from the estate, even the bigger fellas. The Garryoweners were trouble and we all had to stick together. We stood in the rain, a big crowd of us, and Pinhead was shouting at his sister Deirdre to go home. She liked hanging around with the lads. And she could fight better than some of the boys, so I thought she should be let stay.

We were just going home, all heading off in the dark, when the Garryoweners came. Not many of them, but Mossy Sheehan was with them and he was worth twenty of us. He was carrying a bottle, letting it swing from his hand, casual like, and I whispered to Pinhead that maybe it was drink and he was mad enough without drinking.

I wanted to go home then, it was late and I was afraid something was going to happen. You could feel it in the air, that something bad would happen. Eyebrows stood behind Diet. I think he thought the fat would hide him. Me and Dodge stood next to Pinhead, one on either side, a kind of show of strength. I needed to piss.

'Duffy,' said Mossy Sheehan as he came near, still swinging the bottle. I could see yellow liquid in it.

'Mossy, how's it going? What's up?' said Pinhead. His voice was steady and I knew he was smiling, even though I couldn't see his face.

'What the fuck is up, Duffy? You tell me what the fuck is up. Tell me who wrecked our hut and we'll all know what the fuck is up,' Mossy said. You could hear the anger bubbling in his voice.

The dogs started to growl, Pinhead's dog, Jesse, and Eyebrows' dog, Victor. Even they knew about Mossy Sheehan.

'I know fuck all about your hut, Mossy. Sweet fuck all. First I heard of it,' said Pinhead.

That wasn't true. The young lads from our estate had come across the hut and messed it up, but Pinhead wasn't going to grass them, they were just kids. Small guys.

Mossy laughed and stood there with his chest out, swinging the bottle from side to side.

The lads standing behind us were shuffling now, getting restless, as if they knew that this was a kind of stand-off but that someone would make a move soon.

And it happened in a kind of blur, a rush of relief when the Garryoweners turned to go, us relaxing and turning away too. Then one of the Garryoweners made a dive for Victor, a dopey, friendly kind of dog that copied other dogs but never really got the hang of being vicious. By the time we copped what was happening, it was too late. Mossy Sheehan had emptied the bottle over the dog and lit a match to him. There was a smell of petrol and then the stink of burning hair and the dog was squealing and running around in circles.

I stood rooted to the ground and Pinhead was up and gone, running after Mossy. Eyebrows had thrown his coat over the dog and was screaming and crying, the tears and snot running down his face. Pinhead jumped Mossy from behind and I could see his face in the streetlight, that look of rage. He started kicking Mossy like he was a bag of shit, howling as he kicked him in the balls and then in the face, and then he turned him over and danced on his back. Mossy's friends had run, because Pinhead had gone mad.

I still stood there like a fuckin' eejit, watching Pinhead kill Mossy, and I was aware of the others behind me, all in a circle around Eyebrows and Victor. People had come out to their gates to see what was going on and then my dad was there. He pulled Pinhead off Mossy – he had to put his arms around his waist from behind and drag him away.

Pinhead was screaming at my dad, 'Get off me, get away from me, I'll kill the bollocks, I swear I will.'

'Come on now, come on, that's enough, that's enough,' my dad said.

Mossy was up and limping away, holding his balls and trying to run at the same time.

We brought the dog to Eyebrows' house. My dad carried him in his arms and we followed, not saying anything to each other. Eyebrows sniffled and wiped his eyes with his coat sleeve. Eyebrows' da came out and talked to my father, the dog lying between them on an old blanket in the garden. We were told to go into the house, but we stood at the window looking out at them. We could hear the low rumble of their voices and my dad was shaking his head. Eyebrows' da went into the shed and came back with a shotgun he used for hunting rabbits and stuff.

The shot was deafening, everybody must have heard it, even the Garryoweners. I couldn't look at Eyebrows. Pinhead just got up and walked out and said over his shoulder to me, 'Victor wasn't a good name for that dog', and he grinned. But he wasn't trying to be funny.

In bed that night I cried. Quiet crying because I didn't want anyone to know. I was mad with Mossy Sheehan. But I was madder at myself for just standing there. Just standing there like a fuckin' statue.

Later I heard my dad come into my room and I shut my eyes, pretending I was asleep. 'It's OK, Seánie, it's OK,' he whispered, and left the room.

The sun came out from behind the clouds for Victor's funeral. You could feel the heat on your head and shoulders, and the whole place was a different colour. It felt like summer.

We were going to give Victor a great send-off. The whole works, Pinhead said to Eyebrows, even prayers, if we could remember them. We dug a deep hole in Eyebrows' back garden. We had to be careful in case we dug up the old cats and dogs, so every time the spade hit something hard we would all search the hole, wanting and not wanting the bones to be there. But it was only ever stones or chaney.

'I've an idea,' said Pinhead as he sat down watching Dodge dig. 'We have to make a sacrifice or something, so it's special. I mean, anyone can say an old prayer and dig a hole.'

We all looked at Pinhead. Dodge stopped digging and leaned on the spade, waiting. Sometimes I hated the thought of Pinhead's ideas and you could never talk him out of them, he thought they were always good. Sacrifices, though, was not good.

'We'll bury him tonight at seven. The very minute *The Man from Uncle* starts, the exact second. We'll time it on Dodge's watch,' said Pinhead.

That was a relief. I'd thought for a minute that Pinhead had the notion of capturing Mossy Sheehan and burying him alive with Victor or something, but I could manage missing one episode, for Victor, like. Dodge, though, was nearly in tears. He loved *The Man from Uncle* more than anything – he'd have preferred to bury Mossy Sheehan than miss even five minutes of it.

So Victor got buried just as *The Man from Uncle* started. Right on the dot of seven. We wrapped him in an old baby blanket and Eyebrows laid him in the hole, gentle like, and said, 'You were a good dog, Victor, and a loyal friend.' He had read the loyal friend bit in a comic that morning, I knew, because he asked me how to pronounce 'loyal'.

Pinhead filled in the hole and we all watched in silence. Then we tried to say the Our Father but every time we started we cracked up laughing, so we gave up and headed for the Green.

2

And then the summer came, no question about it. A heat wave. Clear blue skies, boiling by lunch-time. We wore T-shirts and short pants and Eyebrows got burnt the first day.

Eyebrows was called Eyebrows because he had none. Well, he had really but they were so white you couldn't see them, just like his hair, cropped close to his head. It was his head that burnt and his nose, so we called him Rudolph that first week. And all his freckles were starting to join up together.

'Don't be washing your face with shit, Eyebrows, use carbolic,' Pinhead said.

'Carbolic shit,' Eyebrows answered, and we all laughed. It was good when someone was smart back at Pinhead.

We wanted to go to the Forty Foot but there was one problem – the older lads had to bring us. We weren't allowed go without the big fellas. This was all right because we would always lose them on the long walk out to Plassey, but getting them to go in the first place wasn't always easy. So Pinhead was nice to Diet. If I had've been Diet, I would have known that Pinhead wanted something off me, but Diet hadn't a clue. He didn't like swimming, but he loved sweets, so Pinhead gave him some money.

The sun was roasting now and we were dreaming of jumping into the Forty Foot, ice cold water on hot skin, and we had collected lemonade bottles and brought them back to Mac's shop, so we had money for stuff on the way home. My mam was sick again but Dad said, 'Go, Seánie, go for your swim and I'll come home early.'

We set off with our swimming togs wrapped in towels under our arms. Eyebrows had no towel because there was thirteen children in his family, so towels were scarce. He had no togs either, just his underpants. Dodge's older brother Enda was supposed to come too, but when we got to his house, we could hear him in his room playing a Beatles' song on his guitar. He had just started to grow his hair and his da called him a sissy, but he didn't care. And he would never be Steamer of the Week, long hair or not, because of the hurling. He was the best hurler Claughaun ever had, that's what Pinhead's da said and he knew hurling. He said Enda played the game like the hurley was part of his body. I knew what he meant because he was great to watch and everybody said he would make the minors next season. But he didn't want to go swimming, so the four of us were left with Diet.

The sun pelted down on us and I could feel my skin tingling and warm. Out the line we went, as a shortcut, and the tar on the track was sticky. You could smell it in the air and Pinhead said that was the smell of summer, the smell of tar melting. Dodge touched the rails and they were red hot from the sun. If you put your ear down, you could hear a train coming, that's what people said anyway. I could never hear anything and I always thought that crouching down with your ear on the track was a dumb place to be if a train was coming. You were better off just looking.

And there was a new game – Pinhead's idea of course. I hated it. You had to cross the track when a train was coming, as near as possible to the train. If somebody tripped or even stumbled, they'd be dead. My dad would have gone mad if he knew about this. Once he tried to talk to me about friends and not having to do everything they do and I just put my head down and nodded. But

we weren't doing any of that stuff today. We were full of
the swim and the long day ahead and the crack on the
way home.

You knew you were getting near the Forty Foot when
you reached the woods. It was cool under the trees and as
you came nearer you could hear the noise of people
swimming and jumping in and diving off the bridge, and
we ran the last bit, with Diet sweating and panting, trying
to keep up with us. We all stripped off and didn't care
who saw us, there was no girls about anyway, and we
stood on the bridge and jumped in, one after another,
shouting and screaming as we sank into the cold water.
And then we all popped up again, like floats or swimming
tubes, unsinkable.

Diet sat on the bank, chubby legs crossed, smiling at us
and waving. He'd stripped into his togs and he sat there
with the rolls of fat hanging off him. Hours we stayed in
the water and when we came out, all our fingers were
wrinkled like Uncle Pat's. We let the sun dry us on the
bank, and just lay on the grass, using our towels as pillows.
I must have dozed off because Pinhead's low voice talking
to his brother woke me.

'Just dive in once. Just once and then you'll always be
able to do it. I swear it's a cinch, you'll just go down and
pop back up again,' he was saying, picking away at a scab
on his knee. His voice was kind, as if he believed Diet
would be able to jump into the Forty Foot, as if he wanted
him to do it.

'And what if I don't, like, pop up?' said Diet, laughing
and trying to avoid what was coming.

'You will. I promise you. It's easy. You don't want to
be a fat fuck forever, do you?' said Pinhead in that low,
steady voice, like it all made sense and you couldn't argue
with it.

Dodge and Eyebrows had gathered round and groups of

other lads were listening. Diet was smiling now, trying to make it go away.

'He doesn't have to. Don't, Diet, if you don't want to. We'll go to Sandy in a while and you can swim there,' I said without thinking.

'Swim in Sandy with the babies, is it? Shut the fuck up, Noddy, you prick. Diet can do this, can't you?' Pinhead said, without ever taking his eyes off his brother.

'I'll do it,' said Diet, knowing he had no choice. There was a whole audience now, gangs of fellas watching and waiting.

He got up and walked to the bridge and he reminded me of a film I saw once on telly where the guy was walking to the electric chair. I whispered to Pinhead to stop him, stop Diet jumping. Pinhead just looked at me and smiled. The smile that meant there was no going back.

Diet stood on the bridge, belly hanging out over his togs, looking into the river. Pinhead said to the crowd, 'Moby fuckin' Dick, tidal wave coming', and everybody laughed. Diet looked at us and the laughing kind of pushed him over the edge and he jumped, a big awkward jump, arms, legs and fat going everywhere. The splash was almighty and I held my breath, waiting for him to pop up.

'See, Nod, he could do it,' said Pinhead as he searched the water with his eyes for his brother.

And then Diet surfaced, exactly like a whale, spouting water and flailing with his arms, and then he was sucked under again. One of the older lads said, 'He's drowning, he's fuckin' drowning, I'll go in after him', and Pinhead shouted, 'No, he's fine, fuck off, let him alone', and then Diet surfaced again, sucking in air like he was starving and it was food. He swam towards us in spurts, stopping to suck in more air. When he reached the bank, I could see blood and I moved to go and help him but Pinhead caught my arm and stopped me. Diet dragged himself onto the bank and only then did we go to him.

He had a huge gash on his arm, blood poured out of it like a tap. He didn't know about the rocks, see, and had hurt his arm when he hit the water full force. But he didn't even notice the cut and searched the faces crowding around him, looking for Pinhead.

'I did it, Pin, I did it!' he shouted, a big stupid smile on his fat face.

Pinhead just nodded, never said well done or anything, just nodded, and got his T-shirt and tied it around Diet's arm.

'Take off the T-shirt a sec, Diet, go on. Let me look at the cut,' I said.

Diet looked at me and then at his brother.

'Take it off for a minute, will you?' I said, and reached out to do it for him.

The cut was long and deep. Diet smiled a big dumb smile at me as I tied the T-shirt tight around his arm again to stop the blood pouring out.

'He'll need stitches,' I said, and looked at Pinhead hard.

Even though Diet was happy, I was mad at Pinhead. Like the train game. I knew Diet would never jump into the Forty Foot again and so did Pinhead.

I hardly talked on the way home. We came to the lodge where last year me and Pinhead had put a piece of mirror inside a hole in the boarded-up window, so that when you looked in, you saw an eye looking back at you, even though it was just your own. We had tricked Eyebrows and he had been frightened of it. Pinhead now egged him on to look again but this year he kind of knew, him being a year older and all. So he looked and just laughed.

Diet's arm was hurting him, I could tell, but he never complained the whole way home. We stopped at the shop on the Dublin Road and we all had Patsi ice pops. They were our favourite but they were hard to get, not all the shops had them. Diet's favourite was the Wibbly Wobbly Wonder and I bought him one, even though he had his own money.

I went to Pinhead's house with him, but I knew he didn't want me to. Pinhead's ma was in the kitchen with Deirdre and the three small sisters having their tea. Boiled eggs it was again.

'I'll feed ye in a minute, when this lot are done. How did ye get on? Had ye a good swim?' she asked as she buttered thick cuts of bread.

'Mam. I dived, I did, I dived off the Forty Foot!' said Diet. He never said a word about his arm.

'Good for you. Do ye want sausages or boiled eggs? Ye can have eggs, there's only enough sausages for Uncle Pat,' said Mrs Duffy. She hadn't looked up once from buttering the bread.

'Diet ... I mean Joe ... hurt his arm, Mrs Duffy, I think he needs stitches,' I said, and avoided looking at the brothers.

She looked up then and saw Diet's arm, wrapped in the bloody T-shirt. 'Mother of Divine Jesus Christ, what happened you, you big gombeen? Show it to me, will you come here, you bloody half eejit, till I see it,' she said as she unwrapped the sodden T-shirt from Diet's arm.

Pinhead took a cut of bread from the table and started chewing.

'Jesus Christ Almighty! Get the Macuricom, Deirdre, and a clean rag from the dresser, hurry on. You feckin' eejit, Joe,' she said as she examined the deep gash. The blood was dripping onto the floor.

'Macuricom won't do, Mrs Duffy. He'll have to go to Barrington's,' I said, and walked to the door. I knew that's what Pinhead wanted me to do. Leave.

'Jesus Christ, God give me patience. And there isn't a sign of your father. The bloody pub, always the pub when he's needed. I'm sick to death of the lot of ye, so I am,' she said.

The young sisters started crying.

I had my hand on the door to leave but I felt I should do something. 'I'll go with him to Barrington's,' I said.

Pinhead sniggered and reached for another cut of bread.

'Stop that skitting, Kevin. No, I'll go down with him but you're a good lad for offering,' said Mrs Duffy and she glared at Pinhead.

She rushed around getting her bag and her scarf. She always wore a scarf, summer and winter, because her hair was snow white, even though she had no wrinkles or anything. She told us once that her hair went white the day Pinhead was born. We didn't know if she was joking or not. I left at the same time as them and never said goodbye to Pinhead, never even looked at him.

I didn't call for anyone for the next few days. The heat wave was still on but I stayed inside with my two little brothers. My mam had to lie on the couch nearly all the time now, she was so big. When they told me she was having another baby, I didn't believe them. I said, 'You can't, Mam, sure we have a baby, look at Brian, he's only a baby just learning to walk.' They laughed then, my mam and dad, and my dad said, 'It's true, Seánie, won't it be great!'

I was mortified when she started getting big. Once, I forgot my lunch and she walked all the way down to the school with the two brothers in the big pram and she came right into the classroom and gave me the lunch in a brown paper bag. The lads were sniggering and Pinhead was whispering something. I looked at my mam, not her face, but her belly sticking out in front of her like the opposite to a hunchback. I could feel the colour rising, up my body and my neck, flooding my face until it felt hot and burned my ears. See, they all knew that my mother and father had done it, like Jesse or Victor when it was the season. Sometimes I looked at Mam and Dad and I wondered when they did it. I never heard them in bed but they must have been doing it somewhere because of the belly. It was a bit disgusting to think about it.

So after Diet and the Forty Foot, I stayed in and helped my mam. I made her tea and I played with Colm and Brian. I locked the garden gate, so that they could play outside in the back. They loved that but they didn't get the chance often over Mam being sick. She wanted girls this time.

After I was born, when I was Brian's age, her baby girl died while she was asleep. Hannah, her name was. I don't remember it happening, I was too young, but my father told me about it a few times. He said that was why they were glad about the new babies, because they might be girls and our mam would love that. I nodded at this but I just thought it was stupid and what if they were two more boys, wouldn't she be in a right fix then? What made girls so good anyway? It wasn't fair, she had a baby already.

My dad came home a lot now during the day. He was given the easy jobs in the ESB because they all knew about the twins. I wondered at this, whether he was embarrassed at work, knowing they all knew what he did to his wife.

On the third day of me being inside, Dad called me into the sitting room at lunch-time after he had made soup for the others. 'Seán, is there anything wrong? You know … between you and your friends … well, I mean, nobody's calling for you. I haven't seen Kevin Duffy for a while, and that's unusual,' he said, examining my face for clues or answers.

'Hmm,' I said, trying to avoid his eyes. I couldn't put what happened into words, so even if I had wanted to, I couldn't tell him.

'Seán … look, did something happen? It's not like you

to be hanging around the house and it scorching outside. If something happened, you can tell me, you know that,' he said.

I shrugged and kicked the fireplace with my shoes.

'All right. When I come home this evening, you go over and call for the lads. Ye can play rounders or something ... or go up to Claughaun with your hurleys,' he said, and put his hand on my shoulder.

I left the room fast – I was afraid he might hug me or something.

So I called for Dodge. We never called for Dodge if we could help it. Pinhead was barred over giving O'Riordan a head in the face, and me and Eyebrows avoided the house if we could. If you called for Dodge, it was like a special visit. You were brought into the lock-away parlour, a dark room filled with furniture and ornaments and a huge picture of the Sacred Heart. And then the father would come in and ask loads of questions.

And there was another problem. O'Riordan liked me. Liked me way more than the others and was always asking me to come for my tea or go places with him and Dodge. I went a few times and that was enough to put me off for life. It was hard to explain him. He didn't do anything horrible to me. It was just the way he was, all of him. Mean.

The first time I went for my tea to Dodge's house I found out just how mean O'Riordan was. We all sat around the table, Dodge's ma and da, me and Dodge and Enda. The father said Grace before we ate. He asked me first did I want to say it. I shrugged and shook my head. We never said Grace or prayers at our house. I stole a look at Dodge and smothered a laugh. Dodge wouldn't look at me but his father made up for it with all his staring.

Through the prayer and the whole meal he never took his eyes off me and it was way worse than being given out to. His eyes followed my every move, my every bite of sausage or bread, my every sip of tea. The food stuck in my throat. I wanted to get out of that house and couldn't wait for everybody to finish, so I could make my escape. And nobody talked. It wasn't like my house or Pinhead's, where everybody chattered at the same time.

And then when O'Riordan did talk, it was to me and I wanted to melt away under the table.

'What do you think of Enda's hair?' he asked, and looked at me with those icy eyes.

I nearly choked on a piece of sausage and I looked at Enda and Dodge for help. They kept their heads down, as if they hadn't heard what he'd said. I looked across the table then at the mother but she smiled at me and buttered more bread. His eyes were like magnets, they kept drawing you back to them.

'Mmmn,' I mumbled and picked up another piece of sausage with my fork.

'Seán Hickey, I never took you for a mumbler. This house is full of mumblers already. So, what do you think of Enda's hair?' He'd put down his knife and fork and steepled his hands together in front of him.

I was suddenly very scared. Right there in Dodge's kitchen, with the whole family around the table, my legs began to shake and I needed a piss.

'Nice,' I said. 'His hair is nice.' I looked straight at him and he smiled at me.

'Do you hear that, Enda? Nice? We'll have to get you a hair band or some hair slides for it, what do you think?' he said, but he kept looking at me.

Enda shoved away his plate and stood up. 'I'm finished,' he said, and he walked out of the kitchen, leaving his half-eaten fry-up behind.

O'Riordan chuckled softly and nodded his head, as if

somebody had finally given him the right answer to a question.

When the meal was over, O'Riordan smiled at me as I made excuses to Dodge about having to go straight home after tea. A mean smile. I couldn't meet his eyes and knew then why Pinhead had stuck a head in him. Maybe that's what he did to Pinhead the night of the Knock-a-Dolly.

I avoided going anywhere with Dodge and his da after that. They wanted me to join the Confraternity but I wriggled out of it. And another time, Dodge wanted me to go to the Lyric one night, but I said I was going to the matinée with Pinhead. I knew Dodge wasn't allowed to the pictures without a grown-up, see.

When I called for Dodge this time, I was brought into the parlour as usual – they called it a parlour, not a sitting room – and I sat there eyeballing the Sacred Heart. It was the quietest house ever, not a sound, only the ticking of the clock in the room and no Dodge.

Pinhead's house was full of noise, there was always a scramble of people, Uncle Pat and the small sisters and the boys. And my house was the same, even noisier before my mam got sick. Eyebrows' house was the worst over there being so many of them.

I could stare down the Sacred Heart though. There he was thinking he was great, with his lit-up heart in his hand, and I tried out all my dirty looks on him.

O'Riordan came in and sat down across from me. 'Well now, who have we here? Young Hickey, is it? Have you anything to say for yourself?' he asked, trying to get me to look at him.

Fuck all to say to you, I said to myself, and stared at the diamonds in the carpet.

'It's good manners to look at a person when he speaks to you,' he said.

I raised my eyes as far as his hands. Big man's hands.

Hands that had put zebra stripes on Dodge's back. I stopped myself from thinking about that, and I thought instead of those big hands cleaning out Dodge's shit from St Patrick's Well.

Then Dodge came into the room and we left the house. O'Riordan called him back and I could hear him telling him what time he was to be home at. Dodge was always looking at his watch because of his da, he couldn't be a minute late. His da hated tardiness. That's what he called being late. Tardiness. It took me ages to find out what that word meant.

When we reached the Green, we saw crowds of fellas but Pinhead wasn't there. I was glad about that. Deirdre was sitting on the grass with some of her friends. They were chatting together and didn't notice us sitting down near them. The grass had just been cut and you could smell it in the air but it was turning brown now because of the heat wave.

Deirdre should be dead really, because she nearly drowned when she was three. Pinhead's ma told me about it once and I looked at Deirdre in a different way afterwards. I mean she should be dead but she wasn't and that was something. They were living in Cork and Deirdre had followed the boys down to the river, the Blackwater, it was called. They had been playing near the edge and Deirdre slipped in. She was sucked down with the current, right under the bridge, and Pinhead started screaming for help. A man jumped in off the bridge and saved her life. Just jumped in with all his clothes on and got her out and gave her the kiss of life. I saw a man do that on telly once, give the kiss of life, and it looked like a very hard thing to do. The man who saved Deirdre had his picture on the front page of the newspaper and Pinhead's ma said he was a hero.

Deirdre was funny and had the blackest eyes I ever saw.

They were a funny shape too, like thin slits, and my mam said that she looked Chinese. I had never seen a Chinese girl, so I didn't know if this was true. But she hated her hair. It was thick and wiry and once she had tried to iron it straight and her ma killed her. Pinhead sometimes called her Brillo Pad, but I liked her hair.

'Which girl do you like?' asked Dodge, grinning at me over his scabby knees.

'Angela Walsh,' I answered straight away, and we both cracked up at that.

Angela Walsh was seventeen and had the biggest chest ever and all the fellas loved her. Even the fathers, because sometimes when she walked up the road, you could see the fathers standing at the gates talking and the minute she came along with her platform shoes and perfume the talking stopped and they all looked. Pinhead thought he was in with a chance because she said once, 'Pinhead, you're going to be a fine-looking man in a few years.' It was the only time I ever saw him get a reddener.

'Enda likes her too and I saw them kissing,' said Dodge.

'Fuck off, Dodge, are you serious?'

'Yeah. A few weeks ago, out my bedroom window. I saw them kissing and rubbing up against each other. I swear, Nod, I swear on Blackie's life.'

'Great,' I said. 'Swearing on a scabby cat's life.'

'My da came out and caught them and called her a hoor. Seriously, Noddy, it happened, I swear it.'

'Jesus,' I said. 'Lucky Enda. Good hurlers always get the women.' And we laughed again.

'That fucks us so, we'll have to put up with the Pissy Murphys.' Dodge laughed.

'Stop, Dodge, or I'll vomit all over you!'

The Murphys lived in the next estate. Five girls, all with buck teeth and freckles, every single one of them. They got the name Pissy from the smell of piss off them. How could five of them all have the habit of pissing their knickers? I asked Dodge this.

'Dunno, Nod, maybe pissing your knickers is like having blue eyes or red hair. You're just born with it. What a gifted family!' We cracked up again.

And then Pinhead was coming towards us. Walking slow and looking straight at me with that steady gaze that made it hard for you to turn away. There was a crowd of fellas around him. Like he was fuckin' royal or something.

'Noddy,' he said, ignoring Dodge.

'How's it going,' I said, trying to keep my voice casual.

He sat down beside me, looking at me and half smiling. 'Hey Nod, remember the marble thing, the plan I had? Tomorrow at lunch-time, meet you here, on the Green. You too, Dodge,' he said.

The marble thing! At last, the marble thing. My heart sang with the thought of it and I loved Pinhead that second. I loved him for the excitement and the plans and the not knowing what would happen next.

And then he got up and walked away and looked over his shoulder with that smile. It was his way of saying goodbye.

3

I couldn't sleep that night. I stayed awake for ages thinking about the marble thing. But all I knew about it was what I knew at the very start – that Pinhead's da must be on the drink for the marble thing to work. I could hear my two brothers breathing in the other bed. Brian would sometimes cry out in his sleep, like he was having a bad dream or something. Then he'd suck his thumb and that kept me awake even more.

But I must have slept, because then it was morning and Colm was in on top of me in bed, jumping on me and running his hands over the back of the headboard to see if there was any old chewing gum stuck there. Then he sat on my face with his big, soggy, smelly nappy, so I got up.

The time dragged until I had to meet the lads. I went early and stretched out on the Green with my hands behind my head as a pillow. The sun was beating down, right down on my face, and everything was still, even though it was almost lunch-time.

Eyebrows was the first to come.

'Noddy, you here already?' he asked.

'You know what, Eyebrows? You're a fuckin' genius!' I answered, and we both laughed.

Then the others came, Pinhead and Dodge, and we all lay on the grass, not asking Pinhead anything, not rushing it, like. It felt good to be there with them, like the Rocket Gang P were back with a bang, and everybody should watch out.

We compared scabs while we waited. It was a scab competition and Eyebrows had a beaut on his elbow but it didn't count, see, it had to be the knees. Then Pinhead got up, nice and slow, as if nothing was going on, and stretched his body, with his back to the three of us. I was bursting to ask him what we were going to do but I didn't say anything, just acted casual. And then he glanced over his shoulder, that slow, lazy smile on his face, and gave us the nod and we knew it was time and followed him to his house.

Pinhead's ma was sitting in the back garden on a kitchen chair and the three little girls were playing with the cat. They had him in a basket with a blanket around him. We said hello to Mrs Duffy and followed Pinhead into the house.

'Be very quiet, OK? My da is in bed still, and we don't want to wake him, not yet anyway!' whispered Pinhead, and then laughed and headed for the stairs.

But it was hard to keep quiet because we could feel the danger and excitement and the stairs had no carpet, just bare timber. Pinhead whispered the plan to us on the landing and I copped it then, the marble thing. He was going to tip the pram-load of marbles down the stairs, but there was a rule, nobody could run till the pram was empty. This was the dangerous part, that you had to wait till the marbles were emptied and the da would have a fair chance of getting you before you hit the bottom of the stairs.

It was brilliant, only Pinhead could have thought of it, and we stood there on the dark landing watching him wheel the pram to the top step. I thought I was going to piss myself with the excitement, and Pinhead seemed to take hours lining up the pram. Eyebrows made a false start and Pinhead stopped him in his tracks with just a look. Then he bent down real slow and whispered, 'Ready steady go', and tipped out the marbles all at once and there was an almighty crash as they tumbled down the stairs.

His da came running out of the bedroom in stained long johns, spluttering and swearing as the four of us elbowed our way down the steps, slipping on marbles as we tried to escape. The stairway was a blur of marbles and us all trying to get to the bottom and the da looming at the top and just missing grabbing Pinhead by the hair. We ran for our lives, with the father screaming, 'Come back here, ye scut ye, with yer pinhead arse', and we raced through the kitchen and out the back door, and there was Pinhead's ma laughing, holding her sides laughing, and we ran and ran to Danahers' back shed and safety.

We all pissed up against the shed wall, all pissed together before we even said anything, a kind of celebration piss, because we were the Rocket Gang P and we were the greatest. We sat down with our backs up against the wall. Eyebrows was still trying to get his breath and the rest of us were laughing and talking about it all at the same time.

'Did you see the fucking head on my da?'

'No, did you see him standing there like a prick in his long johns? And the noise of the fuckin' marbles – '

'No, the funniest was us trying to get down the stairs together, the four of us pushing each other. I never laughed so much.'

'He'll fuckin' lacerate you, Pinhead, he'll kill you.'

'My father would murder me if I did that, I'd get – '

'It was the best laugh ever. Jesus, Pinhead, can we do it again? When? When?'

Pinhead laughed and shook his head. 'Nope, we'll save it now, we won't use it up all in one go. It's too good.'

'He must have some fuckin' sore head now!' I said, and we all cracked up again.

Pinhead got up and started walking away.

'Where are you going?' said Dodge.

'Home, where else?' said Pinhead, and laughed as he walked away.

We looked at each other in shock. Only Pinhead would have the nerve to do that. To go home.

That night we met up on the Green and went over it all again. We laughed and laughed and all the younger fellas and the girls kept coming over wanting to know what was so funny and Eyebrows said, 'You'd have to be there to know.' He was right about that.

Then Libby Bourke came over and asked if we would play a game of Jailer, all of us and the next estate too. We let Pinhead answer her because there was a thing about him and her a few weeks ago, so he would know if we could join in. Libby had asked me to ask Pinhead if there was any chance and he said there was and he went off with her. Next thing, her older brother came after him in school and said, 'Duffy, you perv, don't ever touch my fuckin' sister again.'

Pinhead told me what happened when I asked, but not the others. See, I had brought them together, so he told me. He'd kissed her the first time he went away with her and then he put his hand under her T-shirt and felt her chest. Tits, Pinhead said, her tits. He thought she liked it, so he dropped the hand lower and into her knickers and then she started screaming and running away and saying, 'You bollocks, I hate you, you bollocks.' Pinhead shrugged after he told me this. A kind of I-don't-know-what-her-problem-is shrug, and I thought, thank God I don't have sisters with Pinhead around. But I admired him too. I would have loved to feel a girl's chest but I probably would never do it in my whole life.

So we had a game of Jailer that night, loads of us, split into two crowds, the jailers and the robbers, and we could use the whole back road to hide in. Nowhere was out of bounds, people's sheds, dog kennels, trees, they were all allowed, but if you were caught, the game got boring – you had to stand in the jail all night listening to the others have fun chasing each other.

I thought of a great hide-out though. I got Listons' shed door and opened it back against their wall and hid behind this. The jailers would come and look in the shed and never check behind the open door. And then Deirdre came. I could see her coming through a tiny crack on the door, her fuzzy hair moving up and down as she came towards me. She wasn't a jailer.

'Deirdre, in here,' I whispered, feeling brave.

'Noddy, is that you? Brilliant!' she whispered back as she edged her way into the small space beside me, both of us flattened to the wall by the door.

This was not a good idea. I was mortified already. I could feel the heat of her body next to mine and I wanted her to go away that second. Instead, she pinched my arm and leaned closer, right into me, as someone came towards us. I could see them through the crack and it was Dodge, a jailer.

We stood still and she pressed herself against me when Dodge stuck his head into the shed. I could smell her hair and it didn't smell like Brillo Pads, more like apples. Dodge ran off, but she kept her body pressed close and looked straight at me. I could have kissed her then, I knew that afterwards, but I turned my head away and cocked my ear as if someone was coming again.

Going home that night, I knew that if Pinhead was behind the door with a girl he liked – fuck it, he wouldn't even have to like her – he would have kissed her. Maybe the marble thing had been enough action for one day. But I knew deep inside that kissing Deirdre would have beat the marble thing, beat it hands down.

The rain came back. We had just made great plans, the Rocket Gang P, we were going to catch birds in traps we had made ages ago and keep them in cages in Pinhead's yard. We wanted singing birds but Pinhead said chaffinches and bullfinches were lovely and maybe they could sing as well. But the rain ruined all that. Sheets of rain even worse than the start of the holidays. I could hear it belting off the window when I woke up.

My mam was sitting in the kitchen with the brothers, all of them eating boiled eggs and toast. She smiled at me when I came in but I just looked at her big belly and turned away to get some cornflakes.

'Seán, will you give me a hand until Aunty Mary comes at lunch-time? I need you to look after these two while I lie down. My back is killing me again,' she said as she buttered toast for Brian.

I was in a bad mood over the rain and her always asking me to help, so I said nothing, just ate my cornflakes standing up, and then I left, sneaking out the door quiet like, so she wouldn't hear me. It was her belly and her problem.

Everybody was up in Pinhead's house, all of them falling over each other half-dressed and talking to me all at once, telling me that the postman was bringing a Parcel from America. I always wished that we would get one of these parcels. I asked my dad once why Pinhead's family got them and we didn't and he said laughing that you would need relations in America to send you one and the Duffys had loads of relations.

Me and Pinhead waited at the window for the postman and tried to guess what would be in the parcel. Dresses for the girls and frilly ankle socks and denim jeans. We knew this from the last Parcel from America, but the surprises were the best. You never knew what the surprises would be, toys or books and comics that were special because they came from the States and nobody else had them but everybody wanted them. Pinhead loved that.

The parcel was huge, the biggest ever, and we all

crowded around when the postman handed it over to Mrs Duffy. She could barely lift it into the sitting room and Pinhead and me had to carry the other end. Uncle Pat sat in his chair watching us all trying to get the string off. In the end, Pinhead's ma got the big bread knife and cut the string and tore at the layers of brown paper. Pinhead and Diet fought over the American stamps and the girls helped tear off the paper, jumping up and down with excitement. I sat a bit away from it all, because it wasn't my parcel or my house, see.

All the paper was off at last and Mrs Duffy lifted the lid of the big cardboard box and everyone tried to look in at the same time. She pulled out stuff – dresses for the girls that you'd never see in Limerick and little socks, bobby socks, Uncle Pat called them, and a boy's sweatshirt that said UCLA across the front. I'd have loved one of those. Uncle Pat said that was a university, UCLA. And there was a Batman suit that would fit one of the small girls and everybody oohed and aahed at it, and then there was something magic.

We didn't know what it was at first and Pinhead said it was an American hurley but Uncle Pat called it a baseball bat and he showed us how to swing it and told us the rules and all, but we were too excited to listen and we went back to the box. The whole floor was now covered in stuff. Diet and Pinhead were fighting over a pair of denim jeans called Levi's. Diet said they were his because Pinhead got the bat and the sweatshirt and Pinhead said, 'Go ahead so, Fatty, you can wear them on your arm.' This was true because Diet would never squash himself into them.

Deirdre got a pair of Levi's as well – she would never wear the frilly dresses – and all the Duffys put on their new American clothes and paraded around the house. It changed them completely and I wondered at that, how different clothes can change you and make you look foreign. I looked down at my own gear, shorts and T-shirt, even though it was raining, and they looked dull. I wanted to look American like Pinhead, standing there with his UCLA sweatshirt and swinging the baseball bat.

'A houseful of Yanks, that's what ye look like,' said Pinhead's ma, looking at all the Duffys, and then she scooped up the rest of the clothes from the floor.

We were dying to try out the baseball bat but the rain was flogging down, so when Dodge and Eyebrows called we decided we would build headquarters in Pinhead's attic instead. You had to climb on the banisters and then into the attic, careful to walk only on the timber, because if you walked on the plaster you'd drop into one of the bedrooms unexpected like.

It was a great headquarters because nobody could get in. Diet wasn't able to get up there because of the fat and the stitches in his arm from the Forty Foot. But we let Deirdre come up, even though she wasn't a member of the Rocket Gang P. She was a girl and there was no girls allowed, but we let her come on account of the rain. We sat around in the dark with flashlights and told ghost stories, which scared the shit out of Eyebrows. He hated ghost stories and believed them all, so when Pinhead got to the scary bit, Eyebrows said he had to go home. He stood up in a rush and ruined it when he walked on the plaster and smashed through the ceiling and it had to be Pinhead's da's bedroom and he had to be in bed when it happened. The rest of us made a dash down through the trapdoor and we left Eyebrows there, stuck, with one leg dangling over the father and bits of pink plaster everywhere.

When I came home at dinner-time, my aunt was on her hands and knees scrubbing a dark stain on the carpet. 'Your mother is in the hospital, thanks to you,' she said.

She never looked around when she spoke to me, just kept scrubbing away.

Colm and Brian were sitting on the couch, sucking their thumbs, terrified looking. I wanted to ask her what happened my mam and would she be all right but I went and sat with the boys instead. I watched her scrub and scrub and she looked over at me as if I was shit on a shoe. Pinhead was right when he called her Hatchet Face.

'Gone all day, without a thought or care for anyone,' she said, and turned back to her scrubbing. 'Your poor mother ... lying on this very floor by herself for I don't know how long!' she said and sighed.

I blinked back tears but never spoke to her.

I watched her scrub the stain and lift the brush and dip it into a basin of clean water beside her. The water went red. And then I knew what the stain was. Blood. My mam's blood. My heart thumped and I started sweating and tears were coming to my eyes but I blinked them away again. Colm started to cry, a soft baby-cry, and he caught a piece of my T-shirt in his hand and rubbed it over and over.

My aunt got up and looked at me. 'You were to stay with her until I came. Selfish, that's what I call you. Plain selfish, slinking off with your friends. She could have bled to death on this very carpet, you know.'

'I didn't mean to be gone long, I – '

'Shut up with your excuses, Mr Selfish.'

Brian was bawling now and I wanted my dad to be there. More than anything I wanted my dad to walk into the room, his big shoulders almost the width of the door, I wanted him to walk in and pick up the brothers and tell me that it would be fine, that it wasn't my fault.

'She could lose her babies now, Mr Selfish. Go on, get out of my sight.'

I got up and ran out of the room, up the stairs and into

the bedroom. I flung myself on the bed and let the tears come, but quiet, so she wouldn't hear me.

I killed my mother because of the Parcel from America. She had asked me to stay and I had run off to Pinhead's. I begged God then and there to let everything be all right and if it was, I would never leave the house again, I would never look at a girl's chest again, I would do anything to make it all right, anything God wanted me to do.

My aunt came up to put the brothers to bed. I pretended to be asleep and I could feel her hate for me even with my eyes shut. My stomach growled at me with hunger, but no way was I going downstairs. Anyway, how could I be thinking of my belly when I just killed my mam and her babies? That was another thing I would never do if by some miracle they were all right. I'd never eat again. That was a good punishment – starvation.

Hours later I heard my dad's key in the door. I could hear him talking to Aunty Mary and then her saying goodbye as she went out the door. I got out of bed and went downstairs, dreading what he'd say but anything was better than not knowing.

He was in the kitchen, sitting at the table, his head in his hands. I knew she was dead, I knew it, and it was my fault. I bawled out loud, not caring who heard.

'Seán, Jesus, you took the heart out of me. Calm down, for God's sake, calm down,' he said, and he got up and pulled me into his chest. A warm comfortable chest, with big arms wrapped around me. The weight of the arms always made me feel better but not this time.

'I killed her, Dad … I'm sorry, I'm sorry, I should have stayed, she asked and all, you know. I killed her, Dad, I killed her on you.'

'Seánie, what are you talking about?'

'Mam. I killed her, Dad, but I'll never eat again … I'm sorry. Aunty Mary said – '

'Your mother is fine. She was sitting up eating toast when I left the Maternity. Seánie, wait till I tell you! You've two little sisters, beauties they are, little beauties!'

'What?'

'Two little girls, twenty fingers, twenty toes. Identical twins. They're gorgeous, so they are. I'll bring you over there tomorrow to see them.'

'But the blood, Dad, and Aunty Mary said I – '

'Don't mind your aunt, aren't I telling ye it's grand? It's better than grand, it's bloody brilliant!' And he lifted me up off the floor and whooped like an Indian.

I felt new the next morning and promised God even before I got out of bed that I would never want to feel a girl's chest, I wouldn't even look at a girl's chest, not even Angela Walsh's, because God had made everything all right. But I was dying for my breakfast, so I decided to put off the starvation thing till lunch-time.

Colm and Brian were already downstairs, dressed and all, but they had their T-shirts on inside out and there was piss on the floor. Dad had forgotten Brian's nappy. That's what happens when you have too many babies all together, you forget about the old babies. I got a nappy from the sideboard and called my dad to put it on him.

He sang while he fixed Brian up, he sang baby songs, like 'On the baby's knuckle, on the baby's knee, where will the baby's dimple be?' I felt so happy that I joined in too and my father said, 'I knew it, Seánie, I knew you would be happy about the babies.' But that wasn't the reason at all, I was happy because I hadn't killed my mam, but I said nothing, just kept singing.

We walked to the Maternity, me and my dad. Aunty Mary came to mind the boys and she stared at me for ages but I stared back at her, like I did to the Sacred Heart in Dodge's house. But I hadn't the guts to try out a dirty look on her, that would have been pushing my luck.

We walked down Mulgrave Street, past the jail and through the town. It was quiet because it was early and my dad bought a big bunch of flowers in a shop near the bridge. He told the woman there about the twin girls and she said, 'Well done, you must be so proud.' He carried the flowers over the bridge, smiling at everyone.

At the Maternity I had to wait downstairs, because they wouldn't let children up to the ward. I sat in a plastic seat waiting for my dad. And then my mam was there in front of me. She was wearing a pink dressing gown and her belly was still there, but not so big now. She pulled me to her and hugged me.

'Mam ... I'm sorry ... I am, I swear ... I'll ...' I said into her chest, but she shushed me.

'Stop that, you eejit. Haven't you two lovely sisters? You're a real big brother now!' she said, stroking my hair.

I was glad nobody could see me. Well, anybody I knew anyway. She kissed me then, right in front of everyone. And she gave me some chocolates that she took from her pocket. Quality Street they were, the same ones she gave me when Brian was born and I wondered if all the mothers were given Quality Street after they had babies.

Then my dad brought me outside and we looked up at the first-floor window of the hospital. My mam stood there with a baby in each arm. Fuzzy, dark, half-bald heads and crinkled up faces like Uncle Pat's, exactly the same faces, like you were seeing double or something. They were ugly, uglier even than Brian when he was just born and that was ugly, and there was my dad saying, 'Aren't they two beauties, son?' I didn't like to tell him how ugly they were, so I asked him their names instead. 'Hansel and Gretel,' he said laughing. I laughed too. I would have laughed at anything that day.

On the way home we stopped off in Kelly's bar. I sat

on the step outside and my dad brought me out a bottle
of Coca-Cola with a straw in it. The sun was warm now
and I could smell the tar melting. I could see the counter
through the open door and my dad was standing there
drinking a pint of stout, and everyone was clapping him
on the back and someone was telling him he was a quare
hawk, twins if you don't mind, double-barrelled shotgun.
They all laughed at this and I could hear Pinhead's da
shouting over to my father, 'Are you trying to catch up
with me, doing the double like that?' And they all
laughed again.

I drank my Coke, warm now from the sun, and
Pinhead's da came out to me. I could tell he'd had a
few when he sat down on the step. He took four bars of
chocolate from his pocket and gave them to me. I never
had four bars of chocolate to myself before, all different
ones, Tiffin and Wholenut and two Turkish Delight. He
ruffled my hair and said, 'We can't forget the big brother,
the big man, now can we?' and he left me there
unwrapping the chocolate before the sun got at it.

I told the lads about the babies when I met them on the
Green that night. Pinhead was all decked out in his
American clothes, his UCLA sweatshirt and denim jeans.
When I saw him, I wanted the clothes badly but I never
let on. Nobody was interested in the babies except
Deirdre and Libby Bourke and I didn't blame the lads for
the lack of interest because they were our babies and I had
no interest in them either. But the girls loved the idea of
identical twins and couldn't wait to see them.

Pinhead had his baseball bat with him and all the lads
had gathered around to admire it, and Pinhead standing
there like a Yank, smiling at the girls. We were going to
have a game of baseball. Pinhead said he knew the rules
from Uncle Pat and Dodge had a sliotar we could use as a
ball. We picked teams – Pinhead always got to be a picker

and I was always his first choice, like it was an unspoken rule or something. He tried to explain the game to us but it was hard to understand when we had never seen it played and didn't have a proper pitch or anything. Eyebrows was lost before we even started and stood there scratching his head, trying to make sense of Pinhead's talk of home runs and first base. So when Pinhead said, 'Fuck it, let's play rounders instead', everybody cheered and we played good old Limerick rounders, using the baseball bat and not a hurley.

Our team was winning and we were having a great run when Pinhead called half-time. I said, 'Wait until this run is over, you eejit', but he wasn't listening to me. I followed his gaze up the road and saw his reason for stopping the game. Angela Walsh in a miniskirt. Jesus she was gorgeous. We watched her as she walked towards us, long legs and platform shoes and a white miniskirt that just barely covered the tops of her legs. Her chest stuck out in front of her, never wobbling or anything, solid, like muscle. Pinhead was whistling softly and then almost to himself he said, 'I can't wait for the back view.' Men working in their gardens had stopped and were leaning on their spades, watching her.

As she came closer I watched Pinhead do his look on her, the one where it's impossible to turn away, and she looked at him and smiled and gave him a huge wink. Pinhead laughed softly to himself as she passed right by, her chest out, proud and standing to attention. He turned right around to look at her from the back and didn't even try to hide it from the rest of us.

It was Pinhead's night, with his American clothes, his baseball bat and a wink from Angela Walsh. And after we finished the game of rounders, all the girls gathered around him, like he was God or something, and I said to myself then, it must be the UCLA sweatshirt.

Libby Bourke was sitting down next to Pinhead on the grass, her brown legs crossed and her bra straps showing through her white T-shirt. She was whispering something to him and her blond hair fell across his face. He reached up his hand and put her hair behind her ear for her, like a boyfriend would. And then the two of them got up together and walked away, not holding hands or anything, but close, like they were a pair, and we sat there like eejits just looking after them, Pinhead raising an arm in a goodbye or a victory salute, I didn't know which, but never turning around. I wanted to be Pinhead that night.

I went to Dodge's house with him for a while, as a kind of last resort with Pinhead gone. It was still early and O'Riordan was gone to the Confraternity. We could hear Enda playing the guitar upstairs and singing a song in a soft voice. 'Norwegian Wood', I knew it from the radio and liked it. We played cards in the parlour with the Sacred Heart looking on, stern and staring and unhappy.

'Hi lads, what are ye playing?' Enda said as he came in and sat on the green velvet sofa.

'Lives, is it? Deal me in, Dodge,' he said and smiled over at me.

I smiled back but I was shy when Enda was around. I mean, he was the best hurler in Limerick and then there was the Angela Walsh thing.

'We just saw Angela Walsh,' I blurted out, just to have something to say, like.

He looked at me and then at Dodge and he laughed, so I knew it was all right.

We played a few hands, not talking or anything.

'Wouldn't you think he'd be happy?' said Enda after a while, nodding at the wall.

'Who?' I asked.

Dodge was busy dealing the cards.

'Him up there on the wall with a big dirty scowl on his face,' said Enda as he picked up his hand. 'I mean, he's God, you can't get a better job than that. He should be smiling, he rules the universe!' He laughed and slapped his leg with his hand of cards.

I thought of something but I didn't know whether I should say it or not. I mean, this was Enda and I didn't want him to think I was a smart aleck. But I couldn't keep quiet. 'There's one problem, Enda, about the scowl,' I said.

'What is it?'

'I'd be scowling too if I knew I was going to be crucified. He's God, he knows.'

Enda and Dodge looked at me and then Enda started shaking his head and laughing. 'He knows he's going to be crucified. Brilliant, Noddy, brilliant, you're quick off the mark, you are,' he said.

I glowed at the praise. I was so happy I could have kissed the Sacred Heart, scowl and all.

'What time did ye see Angela?' Enda asked then, casual, like he didn't really care and it was just something to talk about.

'About half an hour ago,' said Dodge as he dealt a new hand of cards.

Enda stayed for the next game but I knew he was edgy, that he had somewhere to go. He looked at his watch and got up to leave. 'I'm out, Dodge, play away the two of ye,' he said and threw sixpence at us.

They caught the birds without me. My mam was still in the Maternity and I had to mind the brothers in the mornings until Aunty Mary came. I didn't mind because I was still relieved that I hadn't killed my mother, but they could have waited till I was there to catch the birds.

The first morning my dad went back to work, Pinhead called, walked right in on top of me while I was wiping shit off Brian's arse. I wouldn't have been wiping the shit at all, I would have left it for my aunt, but he got the nappy off himself and was sitting on the floor playing with it. He had shit everywhere, even on his face, and Colm was saying, 'He ate it, Seánie, he ate it.' I washed his face and had him on the floor cleaning his arse when Pinhead walked into the room. Colm had opened the door for him, the little bastard. I didn't turn around when he said hi but I could feel my ears burning as I scrubbed away at Brian. I was going to be Steamer of the Week and I'd have to live down a terrible slagging.

'Jesus Christ, Noddy, the smell in here would knock you over,' he said and sat down right across from me.

I got a clean nappy from the sideboard and shoved it on Brian any old way. I took the dirty nappy off the floor and left the room and stood in the kitchen for a minute just to get away from him, like. When I went back in, Pinhead was putting a pair of shorts on Brian and pulling faces to make Colm laugh. I thought then that I might ask him to say nothing to the lads but I couldn't do it, couldn't ask him straight out. If we caught Dodge or Eyebrows cleaning a shitty arse, we'd have slagged them for weeks. So I said nothing.

'We're going out to set the bird traps, Nod,' Pinhead said, just like that, and left.

I sat on the Green in the afternoon waiting for them to come back. I knew I was in for a slagging but I didn't want to miss anything either. Deirdre was there with Libby Bourke and they sat down with me in the hot sun. There was no air at all, and the heat rose up from the road.

Mr Whippy came round and the van pulled up near us. We watched all the small children get their ice creams, huge dollops on cones, some with flakes stuck in the side and others with raspberry sauce dripping down.

'Libby's in love, Noddy,' Deirdre said and collapsed in a fit of giggles.

Libby was laughing too and nudging Deirdre to shut up.

'Libby's in love with Pinhead, she's meeting him again later, aren't you Libby, aren't you?' Deirdre said, all in a rush before Libby could stop her.

'Shut up, Dee, you fool,' said Libby, still laughing.

'He's too old for you, Libby, he's fourteen, you know, a full year older than you,' I said, dead serious.

They both looked at me as if I was mad. I don't know what made me say it, I sounded like her father or something. They stared at me, the two of them, and nobody was laughing now.

'So, he's fourteen, a year older, so what's the big deal, Nod, what's your problem?' Libby asked, looking straight at me, taking me on.

I played with a blade of brown grass trying to think of a way out.

'Maybe you're in love yourself, Nod,' said Libby, narrowing her eyes.

I could feel a reddener creeping up my neck. All the time she kept her eyes narrowed at me. Sly.

'Nope, but Pinhead's in love ... with Angela Walsh!' I said and they both laughed.

I had escaped something. I didn't know what it was, just that I had escaped.

'Guess what's coming next week, Noddy, go on guess, guess!' Deirdre said then.

'I don't know, The Beatles, your mad uncle from Cork, rain ...'

'No, you eejit. The carnival is coming to the Fairgreen. Great isn't it?' she said, smiling at me.

It was after tea when they came back. They were in Pinhead's yard with the birds, lovely ones, chaffinches and bullfinches. By the time I got there they had a couple of cages made and Pinhead was feeding the birds goody he had mixed from bread and milk, but they didn't like it.

'You'll have to get birdseed from the pet shop for them, Pinhead, they won't eat that,' I said, coming up behind them. I waited for the slagging.

'Nod, you missed it, we had a job catching the first one but the rest were a cinch!' said Dodge as he sawed a piece of wood into strips for the cage bars.

No slagging. But I knew why. They were so excited about the birds that they had forgotten it for now.

'So, what did you do all day?' Pinhead asked.

He stopped trying to feed the birds and looked at me. He was smiling a bit, teasing me maybe. I was sorry I'd called down. I should have waited a day or two until they'd forgotten it.

I shrugged and played with a piece of wood that was sitting on top of one of the cages. 'This and that. Nothing much.'

'Hmm. You should have come with us. Catching birds is a laugh, and you never caught a bird in your life. You need the bloody practice!' he said, and we all laughed at this. Birds were girls too.

He was beaming at me now. A big smile, a Pinhead special. And then he winked at me, and I knew I was all right, that he wouldn't tell and that he knew what I was waiting for all along. That minute I thought he could read my mind and it wasn't the first time it had happened. It would give you the shivers.

But there was one thing I knew for sure now. This proved it, even though I half-believed it before. Pinhead and me were best friends, it was really me and him, and the rest, Dodge and Eyebrows and even Libby, were outside of it. Outside of us. That minute I would have done anything for him, anything at all. And not because he hadn't told the lads about me changing shitty arses. No, it wasn't that at all. It was because he chose me.

4

'We'll beat the shit out of them, I bet you anything, we'll beat the fuckers,' Pinhead said as he stood at the kitchen table buttering a thick slice of bread.

It was cup final night, Claughaun against Na Piarsaigh, and a whole gang of us, even the fathers and the girls, were going out to the Gaelic grounds to watch the match.

'We've the best team ever this year, and Enda, I mean, *Enda*, is like ten forwards,' Pinhead went on, stuffing the bread into his mouth.

'The County Board are going to be there looking for players for the minors. I heard your da saying it yesterday,' I said.

'Come on, let's go,' he said, and grabbed the green and white flags that would do for Claughaun and Limerick. That was handy.

We walked the whole way out to the Gaelic grounds, a big crowd of us, a moving sea of green. We walked ahead of the adults but Dodge had to stay with his da. Deirdre and Libby came too, but Libby wasn't talking to us over Pinhead not showing up on the Green the night before. The birds made him forget about his date. But Pinhead just shrugged when she wouldn't talk to him or answer him and he ran up behind me then and jumped on my back, whooping and shouting 'Come on the champions'. I looked back at Libby and she gave me a real Sacred Heart stare, like it was my fault or something that he forgot to meet her. I just grinned at her and ran after Pinhead.

The grounds were half-empty but we crowded together in the stand, the lot of us, the Garryoweners and all. We sang and clapped, and after the anthem, we let out an almighty roar as the teams took up positions and I wondered what it must be like at a Munster final or, better still, an All-Ireland. Pinhead was at the Munster final a few weeks before, when Limerick beat the shit out of Cork, and he said it was the best day of his life and he would be going to the All-Ireland semi-finals if his da got the tickets. I'd have cut off my arm to go.

But we were thirteen points down at half-time and the noise at our end went lower and lower until all you could hear was the sound of the hurleys clashing together – the clash of the ash, my dad called it – and the men giving out when a Claughaun lad took a bad free or lost a tackle.

The Na Piarsaigh fans were at the other end and dived on their team at half-time, as if the match was over already. And Pinhead's da said it was over, unless they got off their arses and fed the sliotar up the pitch to the forwards. Dodge and his da were right in front of us. I could see the shiny top of O'Riordan's bald head and Dodge beside him having to stay with him for the whole match. Jesus, I'd have hated that. Having to stay with Dodge's da for a whole match.

Pinhead's da was still talking about what they should do, when O'Riordan snapped his head around to see who was talking. His eyes gave me the creeps and I looked away, over the heads of the crowd.

'They just aren't good enough, simple as that,' he said to Mr Duffy. 'They weren't good enough last year and they certainly aren't good enough this year.'

I looked at him out of the corner of my eye. He had a know-it-all smile on his face.

'And what they don't need now are the armchair

hurlers,' said Mr Duffy, with a look on his face exactly like Pinhead's.

Dodge had his head down and Pinhead and me sat there, not saying anything, waiting.

'Hurling is for fools and drunks. My lad would be better off concentrating on the books. A doctor in the family is what we want, not a hurler,' said O'Riordan, turning his back to us as the teams came back out on the pitch.

'Then ye'll have a doctor and a wanker in the house,' whispered Pinhead's da to us and smiled.

'And a steamer too,' added Pinhead, and nudged me in the side.

We laughed, but Dodge's father had heard. I saw his shoulders tighten and knew he heard.

And then Claughaun tore into the game. They went onto the pitch and played their hearts out and we roared them on till we were hoarse, and Enda was there and he moved so quick that it was hard to keep sight of him scoring point after point, like he was possessed or something. It was nearly full-time and Na Piarsaigh were two points ahead. We were screaming at our team now, even Dodge's da was screaming, 'Come on, Claughaun, ye can do it, ye can, ye can', and then Enda got a great pass from the backs and set off running, ducking and diving through the other team, the ball out in front of him on his hurley, and then a beautiful shot and into the back of the net.

We went crazy then and didn't even hear the final whistle. We invaded the pitch and there was Enda being carried by the team, up on top of their shoulders. And O'Riordan was there, with his chest stuck out as proud as punch, saying to the manager, 'I knew ye would do it', and Pinhead said to me, 'Look at that wanker now', and then we found Diet and the girls and we all jumped around hugging and kissing each other.

We headed for Kirby's bar – the team were bringing the
cup there – and all of us sat outside on the barrels, drinking
Nash's lemonade and eating Taytos on the house. Deirdre
was sitting next to me and then it hit me that I had kissed
her in the Gaelic grounds. I had kissed her in the middle
of all the excitement and couldn't even remember what it
was like.

Mossy Sheehan was there talking to Pinhead, like they
were friends, and then the lorry came with the team and
the cup and we all went mad again, chanting 'Enda is the
greatest'. Enda jumped down off the lorry and walked
straight over to us, chatting about the match and what
great supporters we were all season. I liked Enda for that,
for not having a big head and talking to us and all. Dodge
was beaming at him. Enda just nodded at the da and
walked over to Angela Walsh and kissed her on the neck
in front of everyone. Even Pinhead was staring at that,
shaking his head, not believing, like. We sat on the barrels
again not wanting the night to be over, and Mossy sat with
us too, next to Pinhead.

'Any chance of getting a drink here?' said Mossy,
laughing and winking at Pinhead.

'Wait here,' said Pinhead, and he left me sitting on the
barrel looking at Mossy.

Pinhead came back empty-handed, no more Nash's for
free. And then Pinhead's da came out with two glasses
in his hands. Pinhead reached for the glasses and put
them down beside him, casual like, and then I copped
that it was beer. The father had given him beer. Pinhead
was trying to give me the eye but I got up then and
went to the jacks and stopped on the way back to talk
to Dodge, looking over all the time at Pinhead and
Mossy, drinking out of the half-pint glasses and laughing
together.

I went home with Dodge and his da, even though I

didn't want to, and waved goodbye at Pinhead, knowing he was calling me back, not saying good luck.

Everybody wanted to see the twin babies when they came home from the hospital. There was nearly a queue forming outside our house. They were mostly girls and Pinhead said, 'This is great, Noddy, all the girls outside your house', and he wanted to charge them for a look at the twins but I said, 'Come on, Pinhead, my dad would kill me.'

The sun was shining and I thought that it might be all right having more babies in the house, except we might run out of room for them. The small brothers sat very quiet in the sitting room on the sofa, Brian sucking his thumb, and the room was full of neighbours and Moses baskets. These were wicker baskets on stands that we had borrowed and my dad said that's what they were called, Moses baskets.

'Seánie, give Aunty Mary a hand with the sandwiches,' he said, with a twin in each arm and half the estate gooing and gaaing around him.

My mam was having a rest and I thought she was pure lazy, getting out of her bed in the Maternity and going straight to bed when she got home, even though the house was full of neighbours and babies.

Pinhead helped with the sandwiches. 'And how are you, Mrs Hogan? You look great, did you get a new hairstyle? It's lovely,' he said, using his little half smile on her. See, even on old women the smile worked. He took over handing out the cake, chatting to everyone and joking, and the women loved it.

'He's a lovely lad. Is that the young Duffy boy? He looks just like the Duffys with those dark eyes.'

'Sure his father was very handsome in his day. And he was a great hurler too. I heard there was Spanish blood somewhere along the line, that's where they get the colouring.'

'Spanish, with a name like Duffy? I doubt it, but he's a lovely polite lad ...'

'Are they anything to the Duffys at the top of Garryowen? Sure they're very dark too.'

Pinhead looked over at me and winked and the two of us started skitting but we didn't let them see us. When they all had their tea and cake and sandwiches, we sneaked out to the kitchen with a plate of stuff we had stashed earlier and the two of us sat there eating swiss roll and sandwiches and chatting about the match. I said nothing about the beer or Mossy Sheehan, because you didn't with Pinhead, you just didn't do that.

'Dodge's da is a prick,' I said through a mouthful of cake.

'No, he's a wanker,' Pinhead said, and we laughed at that. 'Hey Nod, I never told you, I built a swing,' he said, helping himself to another slice of swiss roll.

'A swing? What do you want a swing for? Your sisters, is it?'

Pinhead smiled that half smile and I knew this swing was no ordinary swing for his little sisters. I grinned at him. 'Come on, tell me so, tell me!'

'I'll show you if you like,' he said, laughing.

I went looking for my dad to tell him I was going out but all I could see in the sitting room was the neighbours and Brian asleep on the sofa. I went upstairs and stood outside my mam's bedroom and I was thinking of knocking because of the babies but didn't and just opened the door like I always did, and boy was I sorry about that.

There was my mam sitting up in the bed, a twin in each arm. She was looking at me and I was looking at my mother's chest, tits, Pinhead called them, my mother's tits. The babies were sucking on them. Big slabs of white marble, with the babies noisily sucking. Blue veins like rivers running down. Disgusting. My first sight of tits and they had to be my mother's and they were ugly. Angela Walsh's tits stood to attention, they weren't these big droopy yokes with a baby's mouth at the end of them.

But I couldn't look away. It was disgusting but you had to keep looking, like watching a horror film. You put your hands over your face but you look through your fingers anyway. I could feel my face turning bright red.

'Seánie, it's all right, here, sit down on the bed, and give me over that blanket ...' she said, trying to cover herself up. The babies sucked away, they didn't care that I had to look at my mam's disgusting chest.

I dragged my eyes away and looked at her face. Tears were starting to come but I blinked them away and then my feet took over and I ran downstairs shouting, 'Come on, Pinhead', and we left.

The swing looked like a swing, like an ordinary swing that you make yourself with planks of wood and a wooden seat with ropes through it. I said this to Pinhead and he laughed. 'Let's feed the birds first and clean out the cages and then I'll show you,' he said.

The birds were lovely. I liked the chaffinches the best and Pinhead said the Rocket Gang P owned them, even though they were all kept in his yard. And Pinhead loved the birds, more than the rest of us really, and would remember to feed them and fill the drinking spouts with fresh water every day. If they were in my back yard, I would love them for a few days and then start forgetting them.

And the birds were different for Pinhead too. Like, if me or Eyebrows or Dodge tried to grab them so we could take them out and clean the cages, they went mad and tried to peck us. But they were quiet for Pinhead, they never even flapped their wings for him.

We cleaned the three cages, taking turns to hold the birds while the other scraped off the bird shit. Pinhead said, 'How can something that small shit so much?' and I said, 'You should see our twins shitting', and we cracked up. But that reminded me of my mam's huge ugly chest again, but I stopped the picture coming in my mind. Just like that, like turning off the telly.

'What are their names?' Pinhead said, putting fresh seed into the trays.

'Chaffinches, bullfinches, we didn't give them names,' I said, dead serious.

'Ghoul, the twins, you ghoul,' he said, and thumped my arm.

I didn't know their names and we got a fit of laughing at that, I didn't know my sisters' names.

'Fuck it, just call them the twins, that's grand,' said Pinhead.

Dodge and Eyebrows just arrived when we had the cages cleaned and the birds fed and watered. They timed it well, the bastards.

Eyebrows had ringworm. When we heard this first, we all cracked up and we made Eyebrows lift up his T-shirt to show us the circles on his belly. Pinhead said worms got into you and formed a circle under your skin, but Pinhead's ma took a look and said it was only called ringworm but it had nothing to do with worms, which made it a stupid name.

Eyebrows was always getting weird things. Last year the whole family had scabies, bugs that really did crawl under your skin. O'Riordan went mad over the scabies and he wouldn't let Dodge hang around with Eyebrows for weeks. That was lousy for Eyebrows and Pinhead called him the leper but he just laughed. O'Riordan caught

Dodge walking down the street with Eyebrows and dragged him home by the ear, shouting, 'Didn't I tell you to stay away from him till he learns how to wash himself?'

We stuck with Eyebrows, though, because it wasn't his fault that bugs liked his family. They had boodies too another time. Head lice, my dad said was the proper name for them, and all the children, all thirteen of them, girls and all, had to have their heads shaved. Even me and Pinhead's lot had to have Defesto put on our heads. The smell would knock a horse and you had to go to school with it on, but Pinhead stole some Brylcreem from his da so the smell wouldn't be as bad.

Now Eyebrows had ringworm on his face. It had cleared up on his belly but had moved onto his face. He looked funny and Pinhead made a laugh of it, which was all right because Eyebrows preferred you to laugh and joke about it.

We went straight to the swing.

'I'll go first and show ye what to do,' said Pinhead and climbed onto the swing. He started off swinging, slow and steady, then gathering speed, higher and higher. He had built the swing facing right in front of the Duffys' sitting-room window, positioned so that if you were sitting in the room, you would think the person was going to fly off the swing right in on top of you. Pinhead went as high as he could go and swung and swung, looking straight in through the window.

And there was poor Uncle Pat inside, sitting on his armchair, his eyes bulging out of his head and his mouth shaped in a big O and us cracking up, holding our sides laughing, and Pinhead dead serious, staring at Uncle Pat and swinging harder and harder.

'Jesus wept,' said Pinhead's ma as she came running out the back door, with a trail of small girls behind her. 'You little scut, I'll toe the arse off you, are you trying to kill

Uncle Pat, give him a heart attack, is it?' she shouted at Pinhead.

As she got near the swing she looked in the window and then she started laughing too at the sight of Uncle Pat thinking Pinhead was going to fly through the glass and land right on top of his skinny old man's lap at any second. She laughed until tears were streaming down her face and Uncle Pat was at the back door shouting for his heart tablets and Pinhead still swinging right up in the air, higher than the ash tree he planted when he was eight. He was going to make hurleys out of it and sell them but he hadn't known how long it took for a tree to grow.

Pinhead's ma brought us all into her kitchen and gave us slices of rhubarb tart that she'd made herself and when she put the young ones to bed, she took out the good deck of cards and tried to teach us a game called Forty-five. It was a hard game to learn and Eyebrows scratched his head every time it was his turn. I had the hang of it because Pinhead had shown me ages ago how to play, but Pinhead and his ma were sharks at it. So Eyebrows and Dodge went home and I stayed in the kitchen, just me, Pinhead and his ma, and Pinhead didn't even mind, it was like he wanted me to stay.

That night I never slept a wink. The new babies cried all night and Brian joined in too. I'd just be dozing off and a baby would start up and then the other one would begin to wail. Brian woke up screaming and for the first time ever nobody came in to get him, so I stumbled out of my bed and felt my way across the room to him and lifted him into my bed with me. He sobbed for ages, quiet sobs though, and sucked his thumb until he fell asleep. Aunty Mary woke me up the next day, her hatchet face with the mouth in a straight line was the first thing I saw. I thought I was still asleep, dreaming or having a nightmare or something.

'Get up out of it, Mr Lazy Bones, still lolling in bed at a quarter to ten, if you don't mind! And your poor mother up all night with the babies. Come on, up out of it,' she said as she yanked the covers off me.

I got up and dressed myself in yesterday's clothes, ate my cornflakes standing up, and headed straight out the door to Pinhead's before anyone had time to think.

Pinhead had fixed up an old bike and we were going to go out the Bloodmill Road for a spin. We could take turns carrying each other on the bar. We were going to cycle out to Groody and come back in the Ballysimon Road. Just the two of us. Except Jesse had different ideas. We started off with me on the bar and Pinhead trying to balance us and just as we got to Singland there was Jesse, tongue hanging out, flying towards us like the cavalry.

'Go home, you ghoul,' shouted Pinhead back at the dog, nearly tipping the two of us over the handlebars. 'Fuck off, Jesse, you'll get yourself killed, go home, you eejit.'

But Jesse could smell an adventure and refused to budge. We stopped the bike and pelted him with stones and he stood there, mouth hanging open as if he was smiling at us. No way was he going home. So we set off up the Bloodmill, with Jesse panting beside us. Down the hill we went, the two of us skitting as the bike gathered speed. The sun was shining and I could feel my face starting to burn. Pinhead never got burned over being so dark. When we got to Groody, Jesse jumped straight into the stream and we lay on the grassy bank eating fig rolls that Pinhead had brought in his pocket.

'Hey Nod, I've something to ask you … about a girl,' said Pinhead, just as I was dozing off. I was jaded from the night before.

I sat bolt upright and caught Pinhead's eye looking at

me, so I tried to be casual then. 'About a girl? So what is it so?'

'How badly do you want to know?' he asked, grinning at me.

'Fuck off, Pinhead.' I lay back down on the grass and pretended to fall asleep.

'Something about a girl that likes you,' he said, playing with the wrapping from the biscuits.

Bastard. He was a bastard when he knew something that you wanted to hear. I said nothing because I knew that was the best way when Pinhead was doing this.

'Something about a girl that likes you and wants to know if there's any chance.'

Deirdre liked me! I knew it that time we were playing Jailer, I knew it, I knew it! I was dying to hear the rest but I couldn't let him see my face. I turned over on my belly. 'So spit it out, you're taking all day,' I said to the grass in front of me.

Pinhead laughed and sat up to take off his shoes. He walked down the bank of the stream and waded right in, the dog following him. I went too, leaving my sandals on the bank, and we spent ages there trying to catch thorny-backs with our hands. Then I splashed Pinhead, kind of on purpose, and we drenched each other in the shallow water, Jesse barking at us and egging us on like an audience.

For once I took the legs from under him and got him down in the water, throwing my whole weight on top of him when he fell. I caught both sides of his head and tried to shove it under the water. He was spluttering and shouting, 'Stop, Nod, you madman, I'll tell you so, I'll tell you.' But I liked it. Liked the feel of his head in my hands and him struggling, fighting me back. He pushed me hard then and I fell beside him in the stream and we looked at each other, surprised, and then we both cracked up laughing.

'I was talking to Deirdre last night,' he said when we got back to the bank.

My heart flipped over in my chest but I said nothing. Steam was rising already from our wet clothes. He was sitting very close to me, inches away only, his legs crossed like an Indian. I knew he was looking at me. I stared at my bare feet, like they were the most interesting thing in the whole world.

'She asked me to ask you something.'

I still said nothing. Didn't even move. I wished he would just get the fuck on with it.

'She wanted to know if there was any chance ...'

My heart flipped again and I looked at him, smiling.

'Any chance for her friend Karen, you know Karen, she's Libby Bourke's cousin,' he said looking straight into my eyes, holding me with his stare.

I couldn't believe it. That Deirdre could give me away just like that to some friend of hers. I kept my face blank though. Fucking bastard Pinhead.

'That right?' I said and grinned at him.

He smiled back at me. 'She's a good-looking bird, I wouldn't mind her myself, except she's Libby's cousin. So come on, Noddy, what do you say? We'll take the two of them out the track tomorrow night.'

Me out the track with a girl I didn't know. She'd probably want me to kiss her because that's what you did out the track, you kissed and tried to drop the hand.

'Come on, Nod, you, me and the two blondie cousins, it's perfect,' he said in that low, how-can-you-argue-with-me voice.

Fuck Deirdre. She knew I liked her, so fuck her. She gave me away to her friend.

'OK, it'll be a laugh, we'll do it,' I said as I put on my sandals.

'It'll be more than a laugh, Nod, it'll be more than that.'

He said that without smiling.

The road back was harder because some of it was uphill and it was busy with lorries flying past all the time. Jesse was struggling to keep up with us and when we heard the screech of brakes, we knew what it was before we looked. We tore back down the hill and there was poor Jesse at the side of the road, lifeless but not dead yet because I could see his eyes following Pinhead. Pinhead was leaning down beside him, saying 'Come on, Jess, good dog, you'll be all right.'

I didn't know about that, the all right bit, and I knelt down and started looking for blood. Pinhead was lying down on the road now, his head right next to the dog, whispering to him. And then Jesse just sat up, like he had been fooling us all along or something, and licked Pinhead's face. But his leg was busted. I could see where it was broken, the bones sticking out as plain as day. Pinhead was saying, 'Ah Jesse, your leg, your leg.'

I pushed the bike and Pinhead carried the dog in his arms, not complaining, even though he was heavy.

'We'll have to take him to Croom, Nod, they're good with broken bones there.'

'But Croom is only for people and it's miles away. We can't walk to Croom carrying him,' I said, and Pinhead looked at me as if I was mad.

'We'll get the bus to Croom, you eejit, I know where it is, I know the bus stop. They fixed my leg and it was way worse than Jesse's. It'll only take them a few minutes to fix it, that's all.'

There was no way Croom would fix a dog's leg, but Pinhead had decided already what to do.

'I know what, there's a vet near St John's Cathedral, we'll take him there. The vet is better with dogs than doctors are.' I looked at Pinhead, weighed down to a crawl by the heavy dog in his arms and the sweat pouring out of him. St John's was nearer.

'All right, but I still think Croom would be better. I mean, bones is their thing out there.'

'Yeah, but not dogs. The vet will fix him up, you'll see, Pin, you'll see.'

At Duignam's shop we dumped the bike over the wall and got the bus into John's Square, Jesse sitting up on a seat with his gammy leg just hanging there. The conductor was nice to us on account of the dog and him knowing Pinhead's da. He didn't even charge us and said, 'Good luck with the dog, lads', when we got off the bus carrying Jesse.

We waited in a small room to see the vet and Jesse was definitely getting better because he made a go for a little terrier that came in with green stuff in his eye. The vet called us just as things were getting rough.

'Dog's name, lads?' he said as he hoisted Jesse onto a table.

Jesse growled and showed the vet his teeth. That wasn't like him.

'Jes −' I was just about to say his name when Pinhead butted in.

'Jasper. Jasper O'Riordan, 22 Lilac Terrace, St Patrick's Road, Limerick,' said Pinhead, glaring at me.

The cute fucker. He had given Dodge's name and address.

'Who will I send the bill to now, lads? This fella needs plaster of Paris on the leg,' said the vet as he bent over the dog, examining him. Jesse was still growling.

'Send it to Martin O'Riordan, Esquire, my dad. He'll pay, he will. He works in the Corporation. Do you know him?' asked Pinhead.

I had to swallow a big laugh that started in my belly.

'No, but that's fine, I'll just send him the bill.'

'Right,' said Pinhead as he stroked Jesse's head. 'It was

a lorry that knocked him down. He must be a strong dog to survive a belt of a lorry.'

'He's a grand dog. Look at him already, his tail is wagging and all. I bet he left a grand dent in the lorry,' the vet said.

Jesse was a howl with the cast on his leg. We carried him onto the bus and everyone laughed when they saw him sitting up on the seat with the one leg straight out in front of him, stiff as a poker in new white plaster. He was trying to tear it off and Pinhead slapped him on the snout every time he went near it.

When we got him home, we paraded him out on the Green. Jesse was famous and they all wanted to sign his cast, so we let them for threepence a go. The cast was full of names in no time and we had money. Just Pinhead and me, because we'd carried him to the vet. We were going to keep it for the carnival next week. We'd be able to have a go on everything.

Dodge was sour with us because we went to Groody without him and Pinhead said, 'Fuck yourself, Dodge', and walked away with Jesse limping after him. He lay down on the Green a bit away from us, and left me sitting there with Eyebrows and Dodge, nobody talking. I played with a threepenny piece, flicking it up and down in the air with the lads watching me. I wanted to walk away too, to say fuck yourselves, the two of you, but I hadn't the guts. And when I looked over at Pinhead, he was surrounded by girls. All around him, laughing and messing with him, and Deirdre was there, waving at me as if nothing had happened.

I got up then and walked over, not realising till I got there that Karen was sitting down next to Deirdre. I was mortified and I knew Pinhead had said something because the girls were giggling. But the giggling made me brave and I tried out a Pinhead stare on Karen. Well, she did like me, after all, and she had asked for a chance, not me. She was lovely, though, pretty and girly, with blond hair the colour of our bathroom walls.

'Hi Seán, how's it going?' she said in a soft voice.

And then the others cracked up laughing. She didn't know why they were laughing but I did – it was me being called Seán instead of Noddy. I laughed too and thumped Pinhead in the arm, messing. We all talked together after that, about the carnival coming and Jesse's leg, lots of stuff. Karen was nice, easy to talk to in the crowd, and I never once looked at Deirdre. If she asked me something, I answered, but looked over her head, never at her.

Dodge and Eyebrows came over after a while and Pinhead nudged me as they came towards us and said 'Look at them, Noddy, they can't piss without us', and laughed. And when they sat down, Dodge was all over Pinhead like a rash, laughing too loud at his jokes. I wanted to catch Dodge by the throat and say, don't do that Dodge, that's what he wants you to do. See, if I was them, I'd have gone home ages ago and said, go fuck yourself, Pinhead, not to his face, just in my head, but Pinhead would still have known.

There was murder in my house the next day. It was Saturday and my dad was off work. They were all crying together, the babies and the two brothers and my mam was crying too. I did my usual – grabbed my clothes and ate toast standing up and was just sneaking out the door when my dad caught me.

'Seán, where are you off to so early? You're like a lodger here lately. Come back a minute, I want to talk to you.'

This was bad. He was in his talking mood and I couldn't even hear myself think over all the bawling.

'Look, I know it's hard for you,' he said. 'I mean, will you listen to the bloody racket right now, but things will settle in a week or two.'

I was nodding and edging out the door at the same time. It didn't work.

'No, come back and sit down for a minute. You'd swear you had a war to win the way you're running out that door!' he said.

I was trapped. I sat on the sofa, opposite him. The babies raised the racket a couple of notches.

'So what have you been up to? You're back with young Kevin Duffy anyway. I saw ye all on the Green last night when I was coming home from work. So ... what are ye up to?' He smiled at me when he stopped talking.

I smiled back at him but I knew that wasn't enough. He wanted more. How could I answer that question and not tell but keep him happy?

'This and that, nothing really.' A bad answer. I knew the minute I said it that it was bad.

'Come on, Seán, ye must be doing stuff, playing games and stuff, right?'

Yeah, right, like the games Pinhead was planning for tonight with the two blond cousins. I reddened at the thought of that. Then I had a brilliant idea.

'We caught birds, Dad. And we made cages in Pinhead's back. We feed them every day and we even bought real birdseed for them.'

He loved this. I knew he would.

'Isn't that a great thing to be doing, Seánie. What kind of birds are they?'

'Chaffinches and bullfinches.'

And two blond cousins, I thought, almost laughing out loud.

'So that's why you're running off to Pinhead's all the time. We were saying last night that we'll have to give Mrs Duffy your children's allowance.'

He meant this as a joke because he was laughing, so I

laughed too. I thought it was a good time to escape and I stood up and backed out of the room. He called me back again.

'One thing, Seán, your neck is filthy, will you go up and wash yourself or you'll be the talk of the place. Oh and Nana is coming for her tea, so you'll have to be here later. Now off you go.'

Great. My first date and I'd have to sit through Nana for an hour first. She could never remember my name and always thought I was a neighbour's child, someone she knew from when she was a girl who was probably dead now. She thought I was a dead person.

I stood in front of the mirror in the bathroom and scrubbed my face and neck. They were beginning to turn brown from the sun, so it was hard to tell what was dirt and what was burn. I made faces in the mirror and practised looks for tonight. I wasn't nervous, not a bit. See, I didn't care. I didn't even know the girl. I had decided I would kiss her because I'd never kissed a girl before and I needed to get in training. I tried it now on the mirror, kissing my reflection in the glass, but I just felt stupid.

We went to Claughaun for a while that day. The seniors were training and we took our hurleys with us because sometimes the older lads would give you a game and we all wanted to hurl like Enda now. We played at the side of the pitch, just the Rocket Gang P and another lad, Pisspot, who was a good hurler. All the girls were there swooning over Enda and when training finished, Enda called us over and showed us how to rise the sliotar and fend off the backs at the same time. And he made us practise taking frees, sailing them over the bar or into the back of the net if we could manage it.

Deirdre was there too, because she loved camogie, and I watched her as Enda put his arms around her and lifted her hurley the proper way. She was smiling over at her friends when he did this and then I realised who my competition was. Enda O'Riordan. And Pinhead watched me, stood leaning on his hurley half smiling and watching me. And his look gave me the creeps again and a shiver went down my spine. I mean, it's not normal to know what someone else is thinking, to be able to read another fella's mind. Pinhead could do that. I couldn't prove it or anything, but I knew he could. And he knew I knew he could.

But now I looked straight back at him and rose the sliotar, never taking my eyes off Pinhead, and whacked it right at him full force. The ball caught him on the side of the head and he just laughed and said, 'Noddy, you mad bastard.' Then I laughed too.

I brought Pinhead home with me for our tea and Nana was there already, on the couch in the sitting room, talking away to the telly. She did this all the time, she thought they could all hear her in there and sometimes she got upset if she missed the end of the news and didn't get saying goodnight to Charles Mitchell. This peeved me though, that she could always remember Charles Mitchell's name but not mine. I was her bloody grandson.

'Hi Seán, who's that with you, love? Oh Kevin, how are you? How's your mother keeping?' said my mam when we came into the kitchen to eat.

Her chest looked huge, bigger than yesterday even. But at least it was covered.

'Hi Mrs Hickey,' Pinhead said. 'Mam is grand.'

'Is that Small Jim?' said Nana, who was now at the table pouring salt into her tea. 'Small Jim,' she said to Pinhead, 'I haven't seen you for years, not since we were in Matterson's together. Did you milk the cows today?'

Pinhead looked at me and I looked at him. We hadn't

a fucking clue who Small Jim was but Nana thought Pinhead was him. My dad was buttering bread at the table for the small brothers and I could hear him laughing softly to himself.

So we ate the ham sandwiches and the hard–boiled eggs and tomatoes, and every time we needed Pinhead to pass us something like the salt or the salad cream, we called him Small Jim, even my mam, and we'd all laugh, Nana and all, her saying, 'You haven't changed a bit Small Jim, you were never any good with women or cows.' Pinhead nearly choked on his apple tart when she said that.

I got nervous all of a sudden about my date with Karen. It hit me out of the blue, like a slap in the face, when I went upstairs after tea to have a piss. I mean, a date with a real girl with real tits and stuff. A real girl that liked me. I didn't want to go.

Pinhead had gone home to change his clothes. I knew he'd wear the UCLA sweatshirt and the Levi's and his best know–it–all face, always sure of himself. I sat waiting for him to call for me, and listened to my dad chatting to Nana, telling her she could stay to watch *The Fugitive* and Aunty Mary would drive her home. That's what I wanted to do. Sit down and watch *The Fugitive* with my dad and forget about the track and Karen and even Pinhead. I went to the bathroom again and brushed my teeth. We were meeting them at eight o'clock at the railway gates. There was no way I could change things now. I would just play hard to get and not kiss her or anything.

My mam's bedroom door was open and as I passed I heard noises in there but I knocked anyway, just to be on the safe side. The babies were lying in their baskets, one asleep and the other one staring up at me, kind of curious, examining me. I put out my hand and she grabbed my little finger with a grip like a vice. I stood there like that for a few minutes. I could hear birds singing outside and it felt quiet and safe in my mam's room, like it was another world, far away from the one I lived in.

I heard Pinhead knocking downstairs and I touched the baby's head, and stroked her soft dark hair. Then I ran downstairs.

Pinhead stood at the door in his American sweatshirt and said, 'Are you right so, Nod?'

I wasn't, but I went anyway.

5

Silence. Dead silence except for the birds singing and Pinhead's low voice in the ditch behind us. I knew I should try to make conversation but the longer the silence went on, the harder it was to talk. We were sitting under a tree next to the track. I could smell the tar from the sun that day, so I took a stick from the ground beside me and poked it, just as it was beginning to harden. It gave me something to do.

I hadn't looked at her since we met at the railway gates. I hadn't looked at her face at all and when she spoke to me, I just said yes or no, and then I said nothing and she stopped trying. I didn't know what to do and it was easier to do nothing. To let the silence happen until we could go home. I wished the crowd was around us and we could chat away, and if we stopped, then you wouldn't even notice. Now you could almost hear the seconds tick by, as if there was a clock timing the silence. One minute with nothing to say, five minutes, ten minutes, twenty.

'I heard ye have twins, is that right?' she said when she couldn't bear it any longer.

'Yeah,' I said.

'What are they like, are they lovely?'

'Yeah.' I poked the warm tar with the stick after this brilliant answer.

'What age are they, how many weeks?'

'Don't know. A few, I think.' I was getting better at the bad answers. I was also mortified and wanted badly to go home. I could hear giggling coming from behind the ditch. I knew she could hear it too but both of us pretended we didn't.

The clock in my head ticked louder as silence took over again. She was getting fed up with me and I didn't blame her. I was a ghoul with girls.

'Are you friends with Pinhead for a long time? I mean, is he, like, your best friend?' She had stopped the clock. But it was a girl's question, a cross-my-heart-and-hope-to-die question.

'Kind of,' I said. Another ace answer.

'He's fun though, isn't he?'

Familiar territory at last. And when I started talking, you couldn't shut me up. Anything was better than that awful silence. So I told her stories of stuff Pinhead and me had done together. I told her about hogging Togher's orchard last year and how Dodge stepped on a beehive just as we were running off with our T-shirts stuffed with apples and how we had to drag him home with the swarm of bees not giving up until we reached Pinhead's house. And how Dodge was covered in bee stings, all over his body, even his mickey, but I left that bit out for her.

I told her about the Forty Foot and swimming and how we were going fishing next week and the Parcels from America. And as I talked about me and Pinhead she leaned closer until I could feel her soft hair on my bare arm, her head a dead weight against me. I told her about Pinhead's house and the swing and Uncle Pat. About the time Pinhead threw the used battery from Uncle Pat's hearing aid into the fire and we ducked behind the sofa and waited for it to explode and watched Uncle Pat leap from his armchair. She laughed out loud at that and looked up at me with blue eyes, and without thinking about it, I reached up and put my hand through her hair and leaned towards her and kissed her on the mouth. Barely touching her lips with mine, but still a kiss.

And then she talked about herself and how she read all the time and she didn't believe me when I told her I read too but not in the summer, not this summer with the Rocket Gang P and the new babies and all. None of the other lads read. Eyebrows couldn't even read a comic, so I never told them about books. About my favourite book ever, *Lord of the Rings*, and how you could lose yourself in another world, and she knew this. She was the first person ever that knew this. We held hands and there was no silences. We filled every second like we were making up for lost time and we never even noticed Pinhead and Libby until they stood right in front of us. It was getting dark.

'Well look at the love birds. Are we interrupting?' Pinhead said, with his arm draped casually over Libby's shoulder, his hand touching her chest. Libby's hair was messed and there was grass stains on her white T-shirt.

'Come on, let's go,' I said to Karen and gave her my hand to pull herself up. But I took my hand away then and me and Pinhead walked the two cousins home, down the bottom of the Well Hill, and when they went into Libby's house, Pinhead started.

'How far, Nod, how far did you get?'

I looked at him and smiled and just shook my head, like he was a fool or something.

'You, Nod, are a dark horse and a mad bastard,' he said, dead serious. 'So what did ye do?'

I didn't answer.

He tried again. 'Did she like it? Come on, Nod, spill the beans, that's part of the fun of it.'

I wanted to belt him, standing there looking at me in his UCLA sweatshirt, like he owned the night. Like he owned me.

'Did you like it?' he asked, his eyes smirking at me.

I laughed then and said, 'Go fuck yourself, Pinhead', and he laughed too.

The carnival came one morning just as Pinhead and me were planning to take the bike and head right out by Clonlara, where there was good fishing. We met early and went to the fishing tackle shop first for a tin of maggots. It was a bit of a walk but Pinhead said it was well worth it because they had the best maggots in town.

We didn't get back to Pinhead's till lunch and we were just clearing out the birdcages when Diet came running up the back road, his big belly wobbling with the effort.

Pinhead laughed when he saw him coming. 'Look Nod, did you ever see Moby Dick trying to run?' he said as he put the tin of maggots into the shed with the fishing rods.

'It's here, lads. They're setting it up now in the Fairgreen. I saw it from the bus and I got off and went up and they talked to me and all!' Diet was panting while he told us this and sweat was making his hair stick to his head. You could still see the scar from the Forty Foot on his arm. A deep, red, angry line with marks where the stitches had been.

'Come on, Nod, let's go and have a look,' said Pinhead as he examined the birdcages to make sure the birds had enough water.

'I'll come with ye and show ye,' said Diet, smiling at the two of us.

'Fuck off, Fatso,' said Pinhead, and we walked out the gate.

I looked back and there was Diet still smiling. He looked just like Jesse the day he followed us to Groody.

We let Jesse come, with his banjaxed leg sticking out.

He could run now, even with the cast on, and I thought dogs were great the way they could get used to anything. I said this to Pinhead as we headed down St Patrick's Road.

'I always knew that about dogs. And it's not just dogs, most animals get used to anything. There's a three-legged dog in Mulgrave Street and he's a flier,' said Pinhead, as we passed Dodge's house.

'You mean, he can run and jump over walls and stuff?' I asked.

'Yep. And there's a cat on the Dublin Road with only two legs and he's a terror altogether.'

'Can he jump walls and climb with just the two legs?'

Pinhead fell about the place laughing and I thumped the arm off him. But I was annoyed with myself for falling for the joke.

'Fuck, run! Dive in behind Duignam's wall, hurry, Jesus, he'll see us, he'll see Jesse,' shouted Pinhead and took off across the road.

I stood frozen for a second and then I saw O'Riordan coming up St Patrick's Road in his shiny car. He was staring at Jesse running after Pinhead with his gammy leg. I ran then, ran for my life, and made a brilliant dive over Duignam's wall, and there was Pinhead, hiding in the jungle of a garden with Jesse beside him. The two of us burst out laughing when we saw each other and then we tried to shush each other as we heard a car stop and a door open.

We heard him before we saw him. He didn't walk, he kind of marched, and his breathing was loud and it marched too in a sort of rhythm. I was scared and I think Pinhead was as well. Then O'Riordan leapt over the wall in one clear jump, just using his hand on the wall for a second. We held our breath. Jesse's tail thumped off the ground and Pinhead made a grab for it to stop the noise.

We could see O'Riordan through the thorny tangle of shrubs. He was examining everything exactly like a soldier I saw in a war film at Easter. The soldier was after Japs in a jungle, but the Japs got him in the end. I liked that bit.

I nearly pissed myself when O'Riordan spoke.

'Come on out, boys, come on out, I just want to have a little chat with ye,' he whispered, but loud enough for us to hear.

Jesse, the ghoul, thumped the ground again with his stupid fucking tail. I was really scared now. O'Riordan was heading straight towards us and he was smiling, but not a big smile that showed his teeth. A mean smile that made his face look tight, like it was too small for him. I grabbed Pinhead's arm. Jesse started growling.

'Don't be frightened, I just want to talk to ye, I think someone played a trick on me. I want to talk to ye, that's all,' said O' Riordan as he tried to make his way into our bushy hide-out.

'Play with yourself, you fuckin' oul steamer,' shouted Pinhead and ran backwards through the jungle of thorns towards Buckleys' wall.

I followed and we both scrambled up and over the wall, never looking back once. We got out onto St Patrick's Road and passed Duignam's. There was O'Riordan all tangled up in the thorny bush. There was no sign of Jesse. We ran down towards the Ballysimon Road and didn't stop till we reached the wall of the Fairgreen. We collapsed once we jumped the wall, laughing now with relief.

'Jesus Christ!'

'Fucking Jesse and his tail!'

'Do you think he recognised us? I don't think he saw our faces. He saw Jesse and his gammy leg though!' And we fell around laughing again.

'Hi, lads, what's the joke?' a voice said. Then two hands appeared over the wall, followed by long legs dressed in blue denim jeans. It was Enda, I knew it by his Adidas sneakers. We all wanted a pair of those sneakers but you could only get them in Dublin.

'So, what's so funny?' he asked as he sat down beside us on the grass.

We could hear the noise of the carnival behind us. Enda's hair was getting longer and it shone in the sun.

'A joke, that's all, a private joke,' said Pinhead, looking straight at Enda.

'A joke about a dog called Jasper O'Riordan maybe? With a name like that, you'd think I'd know him. And the funny thing is, I don't. Now there's a joke for you!' Enda said and laughed.

But I didn't know if it was a good laugh or not. We said nothing. I kept my head down but I knew Pinhead was still looking at him.

'Jasper O'Riordan. It does ring a bell. Would he be Rover O'Riordan's son?' asked Pinhead, his face serious.

Enda laughed and shook his head. 'Just be careful around my father. I'm just warning ye. I saw what happened a while ago from my bedroom window and ye got away and all, but one day ye might get caught,' he said.

I nodded my head furiously. Pinhead stared at Enda.

'Dodge got a tough time over the vet's bill, did ye think of that?'

'But it had nothing to do with Dodge, he wasn't even there — '

Pinhead punched me to shut up.

'I know that, but my father thinks he might know who was there. That's the problem,' said Enda quietly.

'I'm sorry, tell Dodge I'm sorry. Pinhead, you're sorry

too, we'll own up, won't we, Pin, we'll own up,' I said, my voice unsteady.

'It's fine. Dodge was killed already but he might be killed some more if my father sees that dog with ye and puts two and two together. Just be careful, that's all,' Enda said and stood up. 'And keep the bloody dog away from our place for now. Or better still, lock him up in your back garden until the cast is gone, that's a real giveaway, the cast!' He laughed as he headed towards the carnival, his long legs taking big strides as he walked.

'We should own up. Dodge will get killed,' I said as I got up off the dry brown grass. 'And what will we do if he tells? Then we'll be murdered.'

'You heard Enda. Dodge was killed already, so there's no point now. And Dodge won't grass us. We'll only make it way worse for him if we do anything. Hey look Nod, they have some of the amusements up.' And Pinhead walked away, his mind already on something else.

The carnival was nearly ready. The Fairgreeen looked different, full of caravans and people milling around working at the amusements. The waltzer was set up and Pinhead said it was the best in Ireland, that Pisspot was on it in Salthill last week and it nearly broke his neck. Chairoplanes were half up and a ghost tunnel and stalls with dart games and soft toys for prizes.

We ran from one place to another and tried to decide how we would spend the money from Jesse's broken leg. Then we sat on the grass and watched the carnival people working away in the hot sun. The men wore nothing on top and wiped the sweat off their faces with bandanas. Their skin was dark from being outdoors all the time and they looked foreign, but I knew they were Irish because I heard them talking. The women worked too and the children ran around with no shoes on their feet, shouting and calling out to each other. A crowd had gathered by now to watch the carnival spring up like magic in the Fairgreen.

By tea-time it was all finished and ready for the first night. We saw them testing the amusements and the music and the lights before we left to get money and food. You could hear our stomachs rumbling even when the carnival music was blaring away.

We saw Pinhead's da ahead of us, on his way home from work. I called out to him, although Pinhead was saying that we should stay behind him and find a way to annoy him. But I'd had enough of that for one day.

'Are ye all excited with the carnival? It looks bigger than last year,' said Mr Duffy as we caught up with him. 'I'll take the girls down tonight. I can't wait to see their faces.' He wore his heavy CIE jacket, even though the sun would have melted you.

Pinhead slouched behind and left me do all the talking.

'We're going tonight too. The first night is always the best, isn't it, Pin?' I said, looking back at him.

'Answer when you're spoken to, Kevin,' said Mr Duffy evenly, and Pinhead mouthed fuck off to his back and gave him the fingers. I smothered a laugh.

'I've great news!' Mr Duffy said as we turned the corner towards our road.

'What is it, Mr Duffy, what, what?' I asked because Pinhead just walked behind with his hands in his pockets, head down.

'Wait till we get home. I want ye all to hear it together.' He winked at me then and that made me curious.

So I went into Pinhead's for a minute on my way home. The father called everybody, even the small girls, into the kitchen. Mrs Duffy was at the cooker, stirring something that smelled great in a pot.

'The CIE Mystery Tour,' he said to the lot of us with a big smile and a nod of the head, like we knew what he meant. 'Next weekend, this Sunday coming.'

And then we understood. Diet and Deirdre clapped and the small girls copied them. Pinhead stood there looking like he didn't care, watching his mother working at the cooker. The CIE Mystery Tour was a bus that ran every summer and you never knew where you were going till you got there. That was the mystery bit.

'Where is it going?' said Diet, and everybody laughed. Everybody, that is, except Pinhead.

I laughed too but I knew I wouldn't be going. Not with all the babies in our house. Last year we tried to go but Brian was sick that morning and my dad had to get the doctor out. We were packed and all, buckets and spades and a picnic and our raincoats. I could nearly smell the sea already and then Brian, the little bollocks, came out in spots, measles, I think, and that was that. It was too late for my dad to bring just me and Colm by the time the doctor came. The Duffys never missed the Mystery Tour, no matter what.

'It'll be great, lads, I promise, it'll be the best ever. Now, who wants to go to the carnival tonight?' he said and all the little ones started screaming, 'Me, me, me', and I went home.

'Dad, the CIE Mystery Tour is on next Sunday, can we go?' I said when we were having our tea.

Mam was in bed again. You could hear the soft wail of one of the babies upstairs. Colm and Brian were eating thick slices of bread. My dad wasn't very good at cutting loaves.

'More egg, more egg, more egg,' Colm chanted. Then Brian joined in too.

'Wait a minute, for God's sake,' said my dad to the boys, 'wait and have patience, will ye?'

I buttered my own bread and put cold sausages between the slices and some ketchup.

'Drink now, a drink, a drink, a stinky drink,' sang Colm as he banged his fork on the table.

'Jesus, give me a break, will ye! What was that, Seán? What did you ask me? Christ I can't hear myself think in this house lately.'

'Nothing.'

I got up with my sandwich in my hand and went upstairs, tiptoeing past my mam's room. There was silence in there now. All asleep. I went to the jacks and then ran noisily down the stairs, pounding my feet on the steps. I banged the front door behind me and nobody even noticed I was gone.

Pinhead's house was full of noise and excitement. The small girls were dressed up in their American clothes and the youngest one was crying because she wanted to wear the Batman suit to the carnival. Pinhead's da was all spruced up and had shaved himself. I could tell, because he had a piece of newspaper stuck on a cut on his face. Deirdre came with Pinhead and me and we ran down the road to the Fairgreen, Jesse's money jangling in our pockets.

We could hear the noise as we took the shortcut over the stone wall, and there it was in front of us, like magic, filling the night with music and laughter and screams.

'Bumpers first,' said Pinhead, and we raced over, ignoring the queue, and grabbed a car each.

We tore around the place, banging into each other head on, like two madmen, and the carnival worker shouted at us to stop. But we pretended we couldn't hear. We stayed in the bumpers for a second go and Eyebrows arrived and hopped in with Deirdre. We staged crashes and chased each other and I was nearly sick from laughing and crashing and Pinhead wanted a third go but I said, 'No, let's try something else.' We saw Diet trying to squeeze himself onto a chairoplane and Pinhead shouted, 'Breathe in, Diet, breathe in', and we cracked up again.

'The ghost tunnel,' shouted Pinhead over his shoulder and we all ran after him and jumped into the carriages that would take us into the tunnel on a little track.

'This will be as scary as Daithi Lacha,' said Pinhead as the carriages moved off through a beaded curtain and gathered speed.

It was pitch dark in the tunnel and every so often a cardboard ghost or vampire would appear in front of us and Pinhead would jump up in mock fright. Eyebrows, sitting behind with Deirdre, would jump too, but for real. Almost at the end of the tunnel they had one scary thing. A real person dressed in black stuck out his hand and rubbed the person in the carriage nearest, which happened to be Pinhead and then Eyebrows. Pinhead got a fright, I knew because he grabbed my leg, and then he laughed, realising. Eyebrows nearly pissed himself. He screamed just like a girl and even the man pretending to be a ghost got a fright.

'We'll go in again,' said Pinhead when we got out of the tunnel. 'I want to show ye something.'

So off we went again through the beaded curtain and I wondered what Pinhead was up to. Just as we got to the place where the real ghost was standing in the dark Pinhead reached out and grabbed him and I knew by the scream he had grabbed him by the balls. He tried to chase us but the little train was too fast for him, especially with his sore balls and all. We jumped out when the train stopped and ran behind the waltzer and threw ourselves on the grass. Deirdre sat down beside me and we held on to each other and couldn't even talk we were laughing so much. She had her head buried in my chest and I could smell her hair. Apples. And then I looked up and there was Karen and Libby, two halos of blond hair looking down at us.

'Hi,' I said and jumped to my feet.

Pinhead never moved a muscle, he just lay there with his arms behind his head. I looked at my feet and Eyebrows scratched his head. And then the girls walked off, they didn't say good luck or anything. Deirdre got up then and stood there looking after the two cousins.

'Come on, let's get something to eat,' I said.

'That was good, Nod, playing hard to get. You're catching on to this girl thing fast, you mad bastard,' Pinhead whispered to me as we queued for candy floss.

I didn't answer.

Deirdre was quiet for the rest of the night. We went on everything, the chairoplanes and the bumpers again and I nearly broke my neck on the waltzer. You had to let your body go with it as it got faster and faster but I didn't. I stiffened and was nearly sick when I got off and the others laughed. We met Pinhead's da at the carousel, the three little sisters were having a go on it, the youngest one dressed up in her Batman suit. He thought Pinhead had no money, so he gave us a whole pound between the lot of us. We took it and said nothing about Jesse's money.

It was dark when we left. Pinhead was carrying a pink teddy bear that he won at the hoopla stall and we slagged him about it but half-hearted, bored. The carnival seemed smaller now and kind of dumb.

She was waiting on the wall when we turned into St Patrick's Road. By herself in the dark. First I thought it was Karen, the same blond hair, but she called Pinhead's name and he went over and gave her the teddy, like he won it specially for her and knew she would be waiting for him.

We walked on, just me and Deirdre. Eyebrows walking ahead. I wanted to say something to her, to make it all right, to fix it, but I couldn't because I didn't know myself what was wrong. So I just said good luck when we got to her house and kept walking home.

I hated the fucking babies that night. I hated them all, Colm and Brian too. My dad was wrong, it was getting worse, not better. They cried without letting up, Brian sniffling and sobbing in the bed beside me. And then Hatchet Face came first thing the next morning, ordering us all around and taking down the net curtains, saying they were filthy. My mam was in bed again. She was always in fuckin' bed and I wanted to run up the stairs and tell her she should get up, that she had other children, and she should get the fuck up and stop Aunty Mary scrubbing and cleaning and tut-tutting at us, like we shouldn't be in the house at all.

'You can mind the boys today. The christening is next Sunday and I want to get the house straightened out, your poor mother is ...'

I didn't hear the rest of what my aunt was saying. All I heard was that the christening was on the same day as the CIE Mystery Tour. I gave her a Sacred Heart stare, so she'd shut up, and when she left the kitchen, I ate my breakfast, Colm and Brian watching me. I gave them a dirty look too and I walked out the front door, and went straight to Pinhead's.

Balls of Flour was coming. We sat in the kitchen and when he knocked on the door, Mrs Duffy winked at us and went to open it. We followed her and stood under the stairs, so we could hear.

'Well how are you, Mrs Duffy? I haven't seen himself in Kelly's for ages. How is he?'

'He's fine, working hard. Now what have you for me?' She looked back at us and winked again. We were skitting already.

'I've lovely carrots, fresh, just dug up, sure the earth is

still on them. And I've lettuces and toms. What'll you have?'

'And how about your spuds? Are they nice?'

'They're balls of flour, Mrs Duffy, balls of flour.'

'I love balls of flour,' said Pinhead's ma.

We were nearly on the floor laughing.

'Wait, I'll show you them,' said Balls of Flour.

We were hysterical now and trying to stay quiet at the same time and I didn't know how Mrs Duffy was managing to keep a straight face.

'See, balls of flour, aren't they grand? Listen, I wanted to ask you something now that I remember it. Is your young lad there, Kevin, that's his name, isn't it? I need a hand for a while, my own lads are gone camping,' he said as he went back to the van to get Mrs Duffy's vegetables.

So we ended up working for Balls of Flour that day. We filled the boxes with orders and brought them up to the doors, while Balls of Flour chatted to all the women. When we came to Walshes', we fought over who would knock, in the hope that Angela Walsh would answer. And she did and I nearly died of shock. She had the tightest pink sweater on, so tight I had to look away, but not Pinhead, he stood there brazen, asking her chest did it want any vegetables. I swear, he never took his eyes off her chest even when he carried in the box of turnips and cabbage and bananas.

'Enda must be some fucker to have her,' he said when she closed the door.

'Enda's sound though,' I said as we walked back to the van.

'Sound doesn't come into it. He has the looks, you ghoul, that's the thing with girls like her,' said Pinhead.

He was wrong. Just because she had a big chest didn't make her a ride or anything.

'She's sound too, Pin.'

'She's dying for it. Would you like it if your girlfriend was dying for it all the time? Just think about it, every bloke eyeing her up and down.'

'But I like her. She's always nice and she says hello and stuff. And Enda, he's always nice, even if he's the star of the hurling team. He's not a bighead at all.'

Pinhead looked at me and laughed. I felt stupid. As if he knew everything there was to know about girls and how to treat them and I was just an oul eejit. But I knew I was right about Angela. And Enda too.

'Bullshit, Pinhead. That's bull. She's good-looking, that's not her fault.'

'She wants sex, Nod. I know. See, there's a type of girl like that. That loves it more than the others and you can feel it from her. You can't, Nod, you're too young yet,' he said laughing.

I wanted to change the subject. 'Hey Pin, will we go fishing tomorrow in Clonlara?' I said and helped myself to an apple.

'Oh fuck, fuck fuck.'

'What is it, what's wrong? Jesus, I just asked will we go fishing – '

'Fuck me pink, Nod, let's go.'

And he raced off down the road with me after him, flying past Balls of Flour and him shouting at us, 'Come back, will ye, I need ye.' We ran all the way to Pinhead's back yard and he went to the shed door and cocked his ear up against it.

'What's up? What are you doing?' I asked, but he just waved at me to shut up.

He opened the door of the shed slowly, like he was afraid of something jumping out. And then I heard it, a low buzzing noise, getting louder as he opened the door wider. And out they came in a huge black swarm, thousands of them. Bluebottles. We had forgotten about the maggots and they had turned into bluebottles. They were everywhere. The kitchen window was open and they headed straight for it.

Mrs Duffy came running out. 'Pinhead, you little scut, what are you up to?'

We could barely see her for bluebottles. They were going in the open kitchen door now, like they had an invitation or something. And then Pinhead started laughing, leaned up against the shed wall and held his stomach laughing, and I joined in. His ma had a tea towel and was trying to shoo the bluebottles out. Then she laughed too. We helped her then to get them out of the kitchen with rolled up newspapers until the last one was gone.

'Are ye hungry, lads? I'll make ye something, scrambled eggs and toast. Ye had no lunch.'

So we sat at the table, with the little girls wandering in and out and Uncle Pat calling out from the sitting room for his coffee. The Duffys never had coffee until Uncle Pat came from America. Now all of them drank it except the da. He called it coffee fuck. He would get up in the morning and feel the teapot and if it was cold, he would say coffee fuck. One morning before we went to school Pinhead filled the teapot with hot water and we watched as the father put his hands around the pot and smiled when he found it was warm. We ran just as he poured himself a nice hot cup of water.

'How's your mother coping with the babies?' asked Mrs Duffy, buttering a big plate of toast. Pinhead was gone to the jacks.

'Fine,' I said. I couldn't tell her the truth.

She looked at me. 'It's a big change, isn't it? You must be worn out yourself from it,' she said, but it was a question.

'The christening is next Sunday,' I said and ate my

scrambled egg, not looking at her.

'Next Sunday, is it?' She finished buttering the toast and went to call the children for their tea.

I thought for a minute she might ask me to go with them. To go with them on the CIE Mystery Tour, but maybe she couldn't over having so many of her own to bring. She was never in bed like my mam, even though she had more children. She was always there and always had time to talk to you.

'I'll miss the CIE Mystery Tour,' I said when she came back into the kitchen.

'You will that, son, but sure there'll be others.'

My heart sank but I just said, 'Yeah, there will', and ate my eggs.

6

The birds were dead. All six of them, dead in their cages, with the little doors left open. They couldn't fly away now. It was early in the morning and we were going fishing, just three of us. I was first to arrive at Pinhead's and saw the shed door open and the little birds on the floor of the cages, silent and dead. I knocked hard on Pinhead's door and could tell by his face that he knew already. He had that look, like someone had given him a hiding, and he was very quiet, not talking about it or anything.

'Mossy Sheehan, I bet you anything it was him, the bastard,' I said.

Pinhead was standing with his back to me and just shrugged his shoulders.

'It must have been him, the fuckin' lousy coward, nobody else would do it to you, Pin, nobody else.'

Another shrug of the shoulders.

Eyebrows came and we stood outside looking at the cages. We didn't know what to do.

'Who would do a lousy thing like that?' asked Eyebrows as he picked up one of the dead birds. He rubbed the bird's chest like he could bring it back to life.

Pinhead stared at him with the poor dead bird in his hand and I could see that mad look in his eyes. I thought he was going to lash out at Eyebrows.

'Put the bird back, Eyebrows. Who do you think you are, Doctor fucking Kildare?' I said and snatched the bird out of Eyebrows' hand and put it back in its cage.

'We'll have a funeral, a big one,' said Eyebrows.

Pinhead just stared at him again. Then he took the birds out one by one and dumped them in the dustbin. Just like that, one after another till all six were gone.

'I know, we'll catch some more today and ... and ...' Eyebrows again, trying to make it all right.

Pinhead said nothing but got one of the cages and smashed it up until it was a pile of busted sticks. He did the same with the others and then went to the shed and got the traps.

'Ah Pinhead, not our traps, they took us ages to make ...' said Eyebrows.

Pinhead didn't even hear, just kept smashing away. Then he climbed on the swing and started swinging and swinging, like a maniac, until the frame of the swing looked like it would take off into the air by itself. He went higher and higher and poor Uncle Pat was at the window shaking his fist and shouting at him.

Eyebrows went away. I think he was a bit scared of Pinhead, he thought he would do something mad. I stood there watching, never telling him to stop or anything, just watching and waiting for him to stop himself. And he did. The swing slowed down and he just sat on it with his head down.

I went to the shed and got the fishing rods and the bike. We had no maggots but we could go to the fishing tackle shop on our way.

'Come on, Pinhead, let's go. There's fish in Clonlara with our names on them,' I said.

I thought for a minute he wouldn't come. That he would sit on the swing like that forever. But he got up and locked Jesse in the shed and followed me out the path.

We got some good maggots at the shop, then we stopped at Downes's and stocked up with sweets, penny biscuits, fizzle sticks and Cleeves toffee. I cycled and Pinhead sat on the bar, balancing the rods and the tin of maggots, and off we went over the bridge and out the Corbally Road. The sun was scorching and I thought we might still have a good day, that we'd catch a pile of fish, maybe even a salmon. We got to Clonlara and dumped the bike behind a wall and set off across the fields towards the Shannon. Pinhead still hadn't said a word, not one word all that time.

We fished for hours. Not talking at all, silent, but a comfortable, easy silence. I didn't try to make Pinhead talk or cheer him up or anything. We took a break in the afternoon and ate our goodies and lay down on the grassy bank with our arms behind our heads.

'Nod, where are all the fish with our names on them?' he said at last.

'Gone on a fuckin' CIE Mystery Tour up the river,' I said, and we both laughed then.

We caught a few perch and pike after that but they were too small, so we threw them back in. Then the two of us stripped right off and dived into the water, even though you weren't allowed to swim there because of the electricity station. And we swam like mad, with long deep strokes that took us over to the other bank and we turned back straight away, without taking a rest. We dried off in the sun, balls naked, and we didn't care.

'Hey, I know where to get some great fish,' I said as we dressed.

'Where?'

'Come on, I'll show you.'

And we cycled back towards town with Pinhead saying, 'Where the fuck are the fish, Nod? Not Sarsfield Bridge, they won't be there this late.' And he kept asking and asking until we stopped outside Donkey Ford's chip shop. He laughed then and punched me in the arm.

We were starving and the smell in Donkey's was lovely. We got a takeaway with the last of Jesse's money and sat on the wall next door and ate the fish wrapped in batter and the big fat chips that stuck together with grease.

There was a big gang on the Green when we got back. I didn't bother going home – fuck it, they'd have to do a head count to miss me – and we dumped the bike and the rods and headed over. I could see Karen and Libby sitting on the grass and went in their direction.

'Come back, you ghoul, walk the other way,' said Pinhead through his teeth, smiling at the girls the whole time. 'Treat them mean, you eejit, let them do the running.'

We walked a good bit away and sat down with our backs to the girls. Dodge and Eyebrows came over and sat down with us. Eyebrows was looking at Pinhead, trying to read his mood, and relaxed when Pinhead smiled at him.

'My da got the vet's bill for Jasper,' said Dodge. It was our first time talking to Dodge since that day. 'He was sitting there having his breakfast with the letters piled up beside him and he nearly exploded when he opened it. He screamed at me, "What dog? What dog?", and sure I knew straight away what ye did. It was very hard keeping a straight face.'

'So what did he do? Did he hit you, Dodge?' I asked.

Dodge shrugged and smiled at us. 'Just a couple of belts in the head, but Enda was there and he's bigger than him now. I swear, when I'm as tall as Enda, I'll fuckin' kill the bastard, I will, I swear it.'

'I'll do it. I'll kill the fucker, I'll do it, Dodge,' said Pinhead. He wasn't smiling.

Dodge laughed. 'How?'

'I'll think of a plan, that's the fuckin' easy part. I'll do it if you want, I'm dead serious.'

Dodge didn't answer. Nobody spoke at all.

I laughed and tried to make a joke. 'Cop on, Pin, do

the marble thing to him, and he might die with the fright,'
I said, and we all laughed then.

'That's what we'll do! We'll do the marble thing to
him! Jesus, that'd be some laugh. Your da and the marble
thing. Will we do it, Dodge?' asked Pinhead.

Dodge looked down at his hands and didn't answer.

'Come on, don't be a fuckin' chicken! He knows
you're afraid of him. He knows, so teach him a lesson.
We'll do it, Dodge. I'll bring the marbles over and we'll
do it early on a Sunday morning or something. Come on,
for the laugh,' said Pinhead in his low sensible voice.

Dodge would never do the marble thing to his da,
never in a million years, and if I knew that, then Pinhead
must have known it too. I glared at Pinhead to shut up and
he looked me straight in the eye.

'Come on, Dodge, just say the word and – '

'Hi, how's it going?' I said in a loud happy voice as
Karen and Libby came towards us.

They sat down and we talked for a while and the other
lads moved off until it was just Pinhead and me and the
two girls. And when Pinhead and Libby got up, he
nodded at me to follow and we did, down the back lane
where it was private.

I kissed her as soon as we were alone, just kissed her, on
the mouth, hard. I thought she liked it because she pressed
her body against me and it felt good. Then we talked for
a while and I draped my arm around her shoulder and let
my hand rest on her chest. I kissed her again while she was
in the middle of saying something and I felt her chest,
small and hard, not like my mam's at all. She pulled back
then and slapped me across the face. She started crying and
looked at me like she was the one that got the slap in the
face and then she ran up the dark lane. I could hear the
clatter of her footsteps running, sounding further and
further away.

I stood there, leaning against a shed door. It was night now, late and dark, but the birds were still singing in the trees. They do that sometimes in the summer, like they don't want the warm day to be over. I wanted to run after her, to say I was sorry. I wanted to tell her that I didn't know what came over me and to say something about what she thought happened with Deirdre and me. But I just stood there instead. And then I walked home and started whistling. I felt happy. Even after the slap in the face, I was happy. I had dropped the hand and I liked it. It was no big deal. Girls were strange and Pinhead was dead right. Treat them mean.

My dad was waiting in the kitchen when I got home.

'Seán, what hour is this to be coming in? Your mam was worried sick about you.'

'Where is she?'

'She's gone to bed. Do you know what time it is?'

'Gone to bed. That makes a change,' I said and smirked at him. I was pleased with my little joke.

He got mad. I think it was the smirk that did it. 'Listen here you. I'm getting tired of you dropping in here whenever you feel like it. Gone all day and all night and laughing about it. What's up with you these days, Seán? I want an answer. What's going on?'

'Nothing, Dad.' I thought the Dad bit would soften him.

'Don't nothing me, you little shit. Your poor mother has enough on her plate without you acting up as well. You never give her a hand with the boys or anything. I don't know what the hell has got into you lately. You're like a different child.'

I didn't answer. But questions were flashing in my head like ads on the telly – the CIE Mystery Tour, a room of my own that they had promised me, peace and quiet, no fucking crying babies, a mother that wasn't always in bed.

I decided to try out the Mystery Tour on him.

'Can we go on the CIE Mystery Tour?' I shouted at him. Tears were coming to my eyes and I bit them back, squeezed them back in.

'Is that what all the sulking and skulking is about? A bloody day at the seaside? You're a selfish little shit, that's what you are.'

I stood there in front of him and enjoyed making him angry. I smirked then, knowing it would really torment him. Boy was I right about that one.

'I'm not putting up with this attitude of yours any longer and neither is your mother ... as if we don't have enough to worry about. And take that bloody face off you, that bloody smirk, stop it or I'll wipe it off myself this minute ... '

'Go on then, I don't care.' I stood there looking at him, smiling at him, watching him get madder and madder.

'Stop it now, you little shit ... '

And then he hit me. I could see his hand rising, palm out coming towards me, and he hit me hard across the face. He had never hit me, never hit any of us before. I stood there rubbing my face and staring at him. The tears came and I couldn't stop them but I smiled at him to show him I didn't care.

'Seán ... Jesus, Seán ... I'm sorry ... Jesus ... ' He was looking at his hand when he said this, as if his hand had done it off its own bat and now he was giving out to it.

I walked out of the kitchen then and shouldered his hand out of the way when he tried to stop me. I ran up the stairs and pushed past my mam, who was just coming out of their bedroom.

'Seán, where were you? We were so worried ... '

I ran into my room and went straight to bed with all my clothes on. I stopped myself from crying, closing my eyes tight, so that no tears would get out, and kept swallowing and swallowing till the big lump in my throat was gone. I could hear their voices downstairs and I wondered would he tell her what he did, and would she care at all.

I woke early the next morning. Brian was asleep beside me. He didn't cry any more during the night, he just came into my bed by himself now. I looked at the ceiling for a while and then I remembered. Two slaps in the face in one night. I laughed then and I swore I would never talk to my father again for as long as I lived. No matter what he said, I would never talk to him again. I heard one of the babies crying in the other room and I thought of the night they were born and my father whooping around the kitchen like an Indian. It seemed like years ago.

I left the house before any of them were up and sat on the Green by myself waiting for movement in Duffys' house.

'Let's go into town, we can look at the new records in Woolworths,' I said to Pinhead and Dodge. We were lying on the Green, the sun pelting down on us.

'I thought you weren't allowed into town without Mammy,' said Pinhead, smiling at me but trying to rise me too.

'Fuck that! There's so many in my house now they wouldn't even notice. Come on, we'll go in for the laugh. Are you on, Dodge?' I looked at Dodge, sitting there with his head down, like I'd asked him to murder his mother or something. 'Are you coming to town or what? We'll hold your hand crossing the roads, won't we Pinhead?'

Pinhead laughed and Dodge said nothing, still sitting there with his head bent, looking at the grass.

'Come on, Dodge! Fuck them all at home, let's just go,' I said, getting up.

Pinhead got up too and both of us stood there looking down at Dodge.

'How long will we be?' Dodge asked. He was still looking at the ground.

'Not long, an hour maybe. Let's go,' I said, and walked down the road with Pinhead.

I glanced back over my shoulder, and Dodge was still sitting there, examining his hands.

'You're a chicken, Dodge, a yellowbelly, fuck off for yourself,' I shouted back at him.

But I knew he'd follow us. The meaner you were to Dodge, the more he liked you. So the three of us headed off into town, along St Patrick's Road, ducking down as we ran past Dodge's house. The sun beat down on our heads and we found an old can in Mulgrave Street and kicked it between us the whole way, right as far as O'Connell Street. We stopped outside the Wimpy for a while watching the hippies go in. That's what Pinhead said they were, hippies, with long hair and weird, colourful clothes. He said they were from America but that wasn't true because I knew one of them played hurling for Na Piarsaigh. We walked up the street, the three of us, laughing and pushing each other.

Woolworths was crowded because it was Friday and we wandered around looking at all the new stuff that had come in. Sweets and sherbets and dolly mixtures. Drinks in little bottles that were funny colours and biscuits and jellies. We were starving just looking at it all but we hadn't a bob between us. Pinhead was picking up some of the stuff and then he smiled at me and dropped some of it into his pocket, real casual. I smiled then and did the same, trying to pick stuff that was different to Pinhead's.

I walked over to Dodge and whispered to him to knock off some stuff too, that we'd share it out afterwards. I said, 'Come on, Dodge, for the laugh, it's a cinch. We'll split up and do it.' He kept his head down and never answered me and I wanted to thump him again, to catch him and shake the shit out of him and tell him fuck his father that none of it matters. But I just caught his arm in a tight pinch and said, 'Fuck off out of the Rocket Gang so', and I walked away over to the pencils and rubbers and picked up two *Man from Uncle* pens and slipped them down inside my shorts, nothing to it at all. Pinhead was way over in the other aisle and he looked up as if he knew I was searching him out and winked and walked off, looking at stuff as he made his way down the aisle. I took two rubbers shaped like tropical fish and a lovely penknife with a bone handle.

It was great fun, and I was getting better at it every time. It gave you a kind of thrill in your stomach, like kissing a girl, even better than that because you had something at the end of it, your pockets heavy and bulky with all the knocked-off stuff. I scanned the shop for Dodge and saw him a bit away from me looking at a Viewmaster. He held it up to the light and looked through the lens, clicking the lever to change the pictures. And then I knew what he was going to do. I wanted to call out to him, to stop him, but I stood rooted to the ground and watched him look around with a big guilty head on him before pushing the Viewmaster under his jumper. The fuckin' big ghoul. My breath was going funny, like the time we did the marble thing to Pinhead's da. It was getting faster and faster and I couldn't get enough air into my lungs. A man was coming up behind Dodge and Dodge, the old eejit, standing there with a grin on his face, proud of himself. I mean, fuck it, you could see the Viewmaster sticking out under his jumper from where I was standing and that was a mile away. The man put his hand on Dodge's shoulder and poor Dodge looked up at him, still smiling and then realising what was going on. My legs were shaking and I was talking out loud, 'No, no, please let this not be happening.'

Next thing Pinhead was behind me talking to me in a low, steady voice, 'Walk out the door, Nod, slow, like you don't know anyone, do you hear me, Nod? Walk in front of me, slow and casual.' I made my legs move slow and fought back the urge to run like hell towards the door. I kept my eyes on the door and I could hear Dodge crying behind me, 'I'm sorry, I'm sorry, don't tell my father, please don't tell my father.' I never looked back, I wanted to but I knew I couldn't. I got to the door and pushed it out and then I ran like hell down O'Connell Street and, without thinking, I ran up the steps into the Augustinians.

My breath was loud in the quiet church and my heart was thumping. There was a few people kneeling in the pews but nobody looked up. I sat in a pew at the back of the church and tried to steady myself. I put my head down between my knees and when I looked up again, Pinhead was sitting next to me.

'Nod, what did you knock off? Come on, put it out on the seat, give us a look,' he whispered.

I looked at him then and he was smiling. Dodge was in trouble and Pinhead was smiling. Wanting to see what I knocked off and smiling. I shoved my hands into my pockets and pulled out the stuff, banging it down on the seat next to Pinhead. The fish rubbers, the fancy pens, parers like the leaning tower of Pisa, and then the penknife with the bone handle.

'Jesus, it's lovely. Some fuckin' penknife, that's a fuckin' beaut so it is,' he whispered, picking up the knife and examining it.

'Keep it,' I said out loud and the people praying all looked up together. 'Keep the fuckin' knife, Pinhead, keep it, shove it up your arse!' I said and pushed past, leaving Pinhead there surrounded by all the stuff.

I walked out of the church and up the town towards

Woolworths. I saw the squad car almost immediately. It was just pulling off like it had waited for me to come back to see it before it took Dodge away. I followed it with my eyes as it moved slowly up the street. I could see Dodge's head through the back window with a guard sitting beside him. His head was bent down but I knew he'd turn around and look back and then he did and our eyes locked for a second. In my head I was saying, sorry, Dodge, it's my fault, blame me, but I did fuck all. Just stood there like a statue, watching the car disappear into the traffic.

I was nearly home before I noticed the rain. Heavy sheets of rain pelting down from a black sky. This morning it was summer, T-shirts and sunburn and sweat, and now my clothes stuck to me, not with sweat but rain. It dripped down my face and down the back of my neck and I ran the rest of the way home not realising because of the rain that I was crying. I wiped my eyes with my wet T-shirt before I went in.

They had the house shining. You could smell polish and Ajax mixed together and something roasting in the oven. My aunt had made apple tarts and they sat in rows on the kitchen table, steam still rising from them. Someone had iced a cake, white with pink writing, that said Máire and Bríd. The names of my sisters. Máire and Bríd.

'Seánie, are you hungry?' my dad asked from the doorway.

I hadn't heard him come in. I wanted to run to him then, to bury my head in him and cry. I wanted to tell him what I did to Dodge, about his eyes looking at me from the back of the squad car. I looked up at him and then shook my head. I wasn't hungry.

'I'm really sorry about … you know … about last night … I … ' He stopped talking and hung his head the way Dodge did.

I ran then, out the door and up the stairs, pushing past Aunty Mary on the landing with the hoover in her hand.

My mam called me just as I got to my bedroom door. 'Seán, is that you? Come in a minute,' she said. She was sitting up in bed with her dressing gown buttoned right up to her neck. I was glad about that. 'Sit down on the bed there. You're getting so tall, like your dad.'

There was a kind of silence after she mentioned Dad, as if she had said the wrong thing and didn't know what to say next. I went over to the babies, both of them were asleep in the same Moses basket. They were lovely, all cuddled up together. One looked like she had her arm around the other.

'Which is which?' I asked and rubbed one of the little faces. They were exactly the same.

My mam laughed softly from the bed behind me.

'I mean, how do you tell them apart? Which one is Máire and which one is Bríd?'

'I can tell nearly all the time. You'll learn to when you get to know them better. Your dad still can't tell either.'

His name again, followed by silence. I stayed rubbing the tiny little face, Máire or Bríd, I didn't know which, with my back to my mam.

'Come over here and sit down beside me, I didn't get a proper look at you for ages!' She laughed and patted the bed beside her.

I went over and sat on the bed, a bit away from her. She moved close then and pulled me into her in a hug that only mothers can do right. I was mortified because I wasn't Colm or Brian, I was too old for this, but I liked it as well. For that minute I forgot about the knocking off and poor Dodge and my dad. Just for that minute, though, because then a baby started roaring her head off and my mam was up like a shot, running to the crib before the other one woke. But she was too late and they both yelled. She turned back to me with a roaring baby in each arm and then we both laughed. I left before she started feeding them. Didn't ever want to see that sight again.

Tea-time was hard. We all sat around the kitchen table and Aunty Mary served up the scrambled eggs and sausages. She kept staring at me and I thought she knew about the knocking off for a while, but she couldn't know. Brian and Colm were funny though. They kept spitting out her scrambled eggs, saying they were yucky and could they have cornflakes instead. My dad ate his tea without saying a word, except thanks and pass the salt please. There was a knock on our front door just as we were finished and I answered, thinking it was Pinhead.

'Hi Seán, is your dad home?'

It was Mrs Duffy. My legs went weak and my heart started a mad thumping thing in my chest. She knew about the robbing and she was here to tell on me.

'I'll get him for you, Mrs Duffy,' I said, surprised that my voice sounded so ordinary.

But my dad was already standing behind me in the hall and I walked back into the kitchen. I sat there watching Aunty Mary clearing off the table. Brian and Colm were fighting over a chocolate biscuit, so I couldn't make out what was being said in the hall. I couldn't believe Pinhead had squealed on us. He never told, no matter what. My dad would kill me over knocking off. He'd never let me out again. He would be glad he hit me now. Like he knew last night what I would do today. He hit me in advance and I deserved it.

I heard the door closing and my dad running up the stairs to my mam's bedroom. I could hear the low murmur of voices upstairs, and even when I went out to the hall, I couldn't make out what they were saying.

So I sat with the little brothers watching a cartoon on

telly, laughing at the funny bits, although I really felt like crying. He came into the room after a while, my dad, just sat on the armchair a bit away from us and never said a thing. I knew he'd wait until the lads were in bed, so I tried to keep them up for as long as I could. I played games with them, and when Aunty Mary went home, I whispered to Colm to get the cards and I got another half-hour out of playing Snap with them. But he put them to bed in the end and I could hear his footsteps coming back down the stairs and along the hall and into the room until he was standing behind me. I kept watching the telly, it was Charles Mitchell saying the news, and Dad walked over and turned the telly off. He was standing right in front of me now. I looked down at his shoes.

'Seán, Mrs Duffy wanted to talk to us about something.'

Here it was, coming at last. It would be good in a way to have it over.

'She asked us if she could bring you on the CIE Mystery Tour on Sunday. It'll mean you won't be here for the christening, but Mam and I think you might enjoy a day out, so would you like to go?'

Would I like to go? If Pinhead was in the room then, I'd have kissed him, I'd have jumped on his back and hugged and kissed the oul bastard. Would I like to go? Jesus, I'd love to go. I just shrugged though, a kind of yes shrug and kept my eyes on his shoes.

'She wants you to sleep in Duffys' tomorrow night because ye'll have to get up so early on Sunday to catch the bus.'

This was getting better and better. Sleeping in Pinhead's, going on the bus with the Duffys to the seaside.

He bent down then and rubbed the top of my head and said, 'Come on, son, let's go to bed.'

I still didn't look at him. At his face.

7

It took me all night to go to sleep. My head was full of the Mystery Tour and sleeping in Pinhead's and beaches and sun. Then I started worrying about the sun and if it would shine for us on Sunday, like it had been shining for weeks and weeks, and I tried to listen for rain against the window and I must have slept then because the morning came quickly and I must have remembered about the weather because I ran to the window and pulled back the curtains and saw the sky the colour of lead. Kind of dirty-looking with no blue at all.

I ran to Pinhead's after my cornflakes and got him out of bed.

'I'm going with ye! Did you hear already?' I said to him as he opened the door for me.

We went into the kitchen and he started to butter some bread for himself.

'Yeah, my ma told us last night. We'll have a right laugh. I hope it's going somewhere good though. One year we went to a stupid place with just a beach and a few houses. Quilty it was called, a right dive. I hope we're going to Youghal, there's a big carnival there,' he said and then stuffed the bread into his mouth.

'I want to go to Salthill, Pisspot said Salthill was brilliant. There's a diving board and amusements arcades and everything.'

'It never went there, though, the Mystery Tour. We went to Lahinch last year and my da knew the bus driver and got him to take us to the Cliffs of Moher before we went home. Jesus they were brilliant, they were.'

He took another bite of his bread and I was jealous that he saw the Cliffs of Moher. I only saw them on a postcard.

'What were they like? Did ye go near the edge?'

'They're huge, bigger than mountains even, and we crawled to the edge on our bellies, me and my da. Diet was too scared and Deirdre was too young. Jesus, when you look over the edge and the sea is miles below you, it's scary.'

'I'd love if we went there tomorrow. That would be the best,' I said.

'Naw, they never bring you to the same place two years in a row. We'll be grand as long as it isn't Quilty. Come on, let's tell the others and see if any of them are going.'

Only Eyebrows was on the Green, sitting there with his legs crossed watching Pinhead's small sisters playing. They had a rope tied to a lamppost and were taking turns swinging around on it. It looked like fun but boys couldn't do it. They'd be sissies if they did.

'I'm going! I'm going on the Mystery Tour with the Duffys tomorrow. Jesus, we can't wait, we'll have such a laugh. Are ye going at all?' I said to Eyebrows as we sat on the grass next to him. It felt wet.

'We'd need a bus to ourselves if we went,' he said laughing.

And then I thought of him. Dodge. I had forgotten about poor Dodge in all the excitement of the Mystery Tour. He sneaked into my head, his eyes looking at me from the back of the squad car, seeing me for a split second and then turning away and hanging his head, a big guard by his side. I tried to push the picture of him away, and I saw sea and sand and sun, but then Dodge's eyes were back again. Blaming me.

'Let's call for Dodge, see if he's going tomorrow,' I said and started to get up. My arse was damp from the grass.

Pinhead was looking at me like I was mad.

'I called already. He's not allowed out. His ma told me that. I'm off anyway, I'm collecting scrap iron with the brother,' said Eyebrows and he walked away home.

'I'm not going anywhere near that fuckin' house,' Pinhead said.

'Who's a chicken now?'

'I'm not a chicken, I'm just not a thick fucker like you,' he answered.

'I'm calling for him.' I got up and walked down the road towards Dodge's house.

Pinhead followed. I knew he would.

O'Riordan's car was there in the drive. He minded it like a pet or a child, always polishing it. We decided to hang about till the car was gone before we knocked. We knew O'Riordan would blame us over the robbing and the squad car. We split some of the stuff from Woolworths while we were waiting. I didn't really want any of it now, because it'd always make me think of yesterday, but I took it anyway. The rubbers and parers were nice. I let Pinhead keep the knife.

Dodge's da finally came out and we hid behind a pillar watching him, his bald head as shiny as his car. He walked around the car twice, circling it like he couldn't believe it was his, and then he wiped something off the bonnet with his shirtsleeve, a spot of dirt or a birdshit maybe. Pinhead was starting to laugh and he made me laugh too, and we watched him get into the car, trying to hold our laughs in. He reversed out of the driveway like he was reversing a juggernaut truck, eyes darting everywhere so that he wouldn't scratch his precious car, and this only made us laugh more. We waited till he was well out of sight before we knocked on Dodge's door. Enda answered.

'Is Dodge there please?' I asked, not looking at Enda's eyes. He'd on his lovely Adidas sneakers with red stripes down the sides.

I waited for him to say something about yesterday, to blame us or give out to us or something. I liked Enda and I didn't want him to hate me. I didn't mind if the father hated me, or even the mother. But not Enda.

But he said nothing. He stood there at the door for a minute, looking at us. I kept my eyes on his sneakers. Then he just called Dodge softly, like he didn't want anyone else to hear. I could hear Dodge coming down the hall towards us. Enda moved away from the door to let Dodge through.

'Hi, how's it going?' I asked.

Pinhead stayed behind me, letting me do the talking. Dodge was half-hidden behind the door. I put my foot on the door jamb, so he'd open the door wider. I wanted to see his face. I wanted the look in the squad car to be gone before I went on the Mystery Tour.

'I'm all right. I was in loads of trouble last night but it's grand now. It's over now,' he said, giving me a watery smile.

And when he looked straight at me, I saw them. His eyes. Swollen and bruised and battered. And his neck. Marks on his neck. He saw me looking and put his hands up to his neck, like he was trying to rub the marks away. He wouldn't look at me now.

'Are you all right?' said Pinhead.

Sometimes Pinhead was very dumb. I punched him in the arm to shut him up.

'How bad was it?' I asked, my foot still in the doorway, like I was afraid he would close the door on me. He just shrugged his shoulders.

'I'm sorry ... about ... you got killed, I'm sorry,' I said.

Another shrug as he examined the jamb of the door.

'We kept you a share of the stuff,' I blurted and knew right away it was the wrong thing to say.

He looked at me with his swollen eyes, his hand still on his neck and nodded and closed the door. I stood looking at the green door until Pinhead pulled me by the arm down the path with the perfect flower borders on each side. I didn't talk for a long time then.

Pinhead broke the silence as we headed towards my house to get my stuff for the trip. 'I have a plan,' he said, with the lazy smile on his face. The dangerous smile that frightened me but thrilled me all at the same time.

'For what?'

'To fix him. To fix him good.'

'You're not going to kill him, you'll be caught and you'll have to go to jail and anyway he'd probably kill you first, he's one mean bastard.'

Pinhead laughed. 'I'll have to think it out properly but I have a beaut of a plan. I'm going to fix him good, I swear I will.'

'What is it? Tell me what it is? Come on, tell, will you?'

He shook his head. 'Nope. I have to work it out first, but learn to spell "steamer", Nod, and maybe "wanker" too. Now, that's all I'm saying!'

'I can spell steamer, and wanker too, but what's the plan?'

''Course you can spell wanker, and you can do it as well, you bastard!' Pinhead said, but I told him to shut up as we came to our front door. Aunty Mary would die if she heard the word 'wanker'.

My mam had packed a bag for me. I rooted through it and saw all the goodies for tomorrow. A whole packet of fig rolls, a bottle of Nash's Cream Soda, a bag of pink-and-white clove rock, my favourite. There were sandwiches too, wrapped in the sliced bread paper. I could smell ham and eggs. And apples and a small orange that I'd eat when all the nice things were gone. Pinhead sat in the kitchen with my mam. She had cut him a big slice of apple tart and Aunty Mary was giving him dirty looks for eating the tarts meant for the christening. But Pinhead was all smiles and manners, like he knew this would annoy her even more.

'Would you like another slice? Ah have another, you're half-starved, a big strapping boy like you,' said my mam as she cut a chunk of apple tart for Pinhead.

She cut a slice for me too and made me sit down next to Pinhead to eat it.

'I've your bag packed. And I packed your bucket and spade too, just in case,' she said to me half smiling. We all laughed at that. Except Aunty Mary. Hatchet Face.

'It's wrong, you know, him not going to his sisters' christening. It's not right for him to be going off on their christening day,' she said over her shoulder to my mam. She was washing dishes at the sink. Washing them and banging them down on the drainer to dry. I was waiting for one to break.

'I want you to have a great time tomorrow and, Seán, you're to thank Mrs Duffy for bringing you. She's very good to do it with her own gang and all,' said my mam as she divided the last of the apple tart between myself and Pinhead.

'Did you hear what I said? It's wrong him going off and a christening in the house,' said Aunty Mary.

My mam never answered her.

I thought when we were heading off to Pinhead's that she'd try to kiss me in front of him, but she didn't. Instead, she slipped a whole ten shilling note into my hand and stood at the door with one of the babies in her arms and Colm and Brian waving at us from behind her skirt. My dad wasn't around and I was glad about that.

Pinhead's was a madhouse when we got there. We had to climb over all the bags in the hall, with buckets and spades and brollies peeking out of them and a big canvas shopping bag that had all the food in it. You could smell the ham and mustard and eggs. The Duffys loved eggs. Pinhead's da called us all in to watch the forecast after the news and we sat there, very quiet, even the little ones, and I thought Charles Mitchell would never shut up and get to the weather. It wasn't good. Rain coming from the West, wherever that was, and clearing towards the evening. That wasn't much good to us. But the father made a joke about how they always got it wrong and he said the sun always shone for the Duffys and we all laughed except Pinhead.

I loved staying with the Duffys that night. I wished that Mr Duffy was my father. That this was my house, no babies and full of fun and American uncles and boiled eggs all the time. Even when I went to the jacks and overheard Mrs Duffy warning the da to stay on the dry tomorrow and not to disgrace them, I still thought they were the greatest.

We were put in the sitting room, me and Pinhead, with two army sleeping bags. Diet wanted to sleep there too but Pinhead said, 'Fuck off, Fatty, you'd need two rooms', and I laughed but Deirdre didn't. She just looked at us with her eyes narrowed and walked away. Pinhead threw up his hands and shrugged and we cracked up laughing.

I was just falling asleep when he did it to me. Pinhead. He farted on my face, almost sat on me and let rip the loudest, longest fart I ever heard, right in my face. The smell came then, creeping up on you, up your nostrils and under your skin, like rotten eggs or old vegetables that Balls of Flour gave away for free. Pinhead was hysterical and I was laughing too, but I hung out the window to breathe in fresh air.

'That was a message from General Fart to say that Colonel Shit is on the way,' said Pinhead and I nearly fell out the window from laughing.

It was flogging down outside and poor Jesse was jumping up trying to get in. So we let him and as he shook his wet body all over the two of us I noticed that his cast was nearly gone.

'Jesus, he ate the fuckin' cast off,' I said.

Pinhead bent down and examined Jesse's leg. There was a small bit of cast left near his foot. It looked like a white bracelet.

'Will he have to go back to the vet?' I asked as I knelt down and had a look.

'If we put another one on, he'll only gnaw that off too,' said Pinhead. He got up and nudged Jesse so that the dog walked. 'Fuck it, he's grand, he's holding it out while he's walking,' he said and climbed back into his sleeping bag.

Then I let off a huge fart and we were cracking up again. Someone was banging the floor above, so we lay down in our sleeping bags and Pinhead fell asleep straight away, I could hear his soft snore and Jesse's breathing beside him.

I couldn't get to sleep. The house was strange and I missed Brian's body beside me. I never thought I'd miss that and the harder I tried to fall asleep, the wider awake I was. Someone was coughing upstairs and the rain beat hard against the window. Pinhead muttered something in sleep talk. No babies cried. I felt myself drifting off and I saw Dodge looking at me from the back of a squad car, his eyes black and swollen and this time I hung my head in the dream.

Mr Duffy woke us in the middle of the night. That's what it felt like anyway.

'Rise and shine, rise and shine, come on, up with ye now,' he said as he pulled back the curtains.

There was a lovely smell and when we went into the kitchen, Mrs Duffy had a big fry-up ready for us. Rashers and sausages, eggs and black pudding and fried bread.

We all sat around the table eating, it was like a big party in the middle of the night. Diet had six slices of fried bread.

Pinhead ran upstairs to get money, I followed but he told me to wait outside the door, like he thought I was going to rob him or something, and I could hear him rooting for the nail jar under the bed and then the rustle of notes and coins. He was a rich bastard, Pinhead.

Then it was all a mad rush and the da examining the sky every few minutes, saying, 'It'll clear up, I can feel it in the air', and Mrs Duffy handing us bags to carry and we set off down St Patrick's Road, a big procession in the early morning light heading towards Colbert Station.

The station was packed and a long queue had formed already. Jesus, these people mustn't have gone to bed at all. I started to get worried then that there would be no room on the bus for us. It was a double-decker but there was an awful lot of families waiting to get on and Pinhead and me tried to do a head count but every time we did it we ended up with a different number.

And then Pinhead's da went over to the driver, who was standing away from the bus, smoking a fag. They talked for a while and joked and next thing we were called up to the top of the queue. Some of the mothers who had been waiting way longer than us grumbled under their breath but we didn't care because Mr Duffy worked in CIE and we had our seats picked out, the front seats at the top of the bus.

They fitted everyone on the bus in the end. They managed it somehow, all those families with prams and bags and babies. Nobody was left behind. We had the good seats though, and when the engine revved up and the bus pulled out of the station, I thought my heart would burst with excitement.

'When will we know where the tour's going?' I asked

Pinhead. 'When will we know it's not the dive, what's it called, Quilty?'

'We're going out the Ennis Road, so it's not Youghal. Can we open the clove rock now?' he asked as he reached into my bag for the sweets.

Deirdre was sitting behind us with Diet and I passed the bag of sweets back to them. Deirdre took one and Diet took a handful.

'Never hand him the bag, you ghoul. At the turn off at Ennis. We'll know then,' said Pinhead.

I looked at the road racing by below us but I still didn't have a clue where we were headed. So I kept my eye on the road and looked for the names of the towns and villages as we passed them by. Newmarket-on-Fergus, Clarecastle, and then, at last, Ennis. We drove through the town and I thought Limerick was a massive city in comparison. Pinhead said if you blinked, you'd miss it. And then we came to the outskirts, to the turn-off. Not Quilty, not Quilty, I said to myself as we came up to the turn.

'It's coming up now ... now ... right now!' said Pinhead and everyone around him was listening. Pinhead had a fuckin' audience even on the Mystery Tour. 'Not Quilty! It's definitely not Quilty! We're going to Galway, I bet it's Galway,' he said, his voice carrying to the back of the bus.

Everyone started to clap and a father began singing 'Galway Bay' in a loud deep voice that made the babies cry. Someone said, 'Shut up, Dinny, you'll wake the dead with that oul song.' And then the whole top of the bus sang 'It's a Long Way to Tipperary' and it was great. I sang too and clapped my hands but still kept my eye on the road to watch the names of the villages and the towns. Barefield, that was a funny name. And Crusheen. They sounded foreign, these places, and I searched the houses and streets for boys my age, just to see if they were like me, the same clothes and stuff.

The sky had cleared now and there was way more blue than grey. It was going to be a brilliant day. The best day of my life.

We had to stop the bus once because somebody was sick, we could hear them vomiting outside on the road. My stomach felt funny, not sick, just jittery, and we ate the full packet of fig rolls, me and Pinhead, before we got to Gort. The last half-hour was the longest and I thought every village we could see in the distance was Galway. And then I saw it. It was a big town like Limerick, so it had to be Galway. As we drove through the narrow streets towards Salthill, Pinhead and me were leaning right up against the window for our first sight of the sea.

I thought it would be blue, the sea, but it wasn't, it was grey. There was a big, long beach with dull yellow sand and a diving board at the end of it and I loved Salthill from the first minute I saw it. We all spilled out of the bus and made our way down, loads of us from Limerick, with our bags and buckets and spades. There was a long prom and loads of shops and noise and arcades. Pinhead and me didn't know what to do first but the diving board was kind of calling us to it, so we changed into our togs before Mrs Duffy had a chance to sit down on the sand. I gave my ten shilling note to Mr Duffy to mind and we raced off to the diving board, with some of the other Limerick lads following us.

'Me first,' said Pinhead as he rushed up the ladder in front of me.

He dived and it was a beaut, even though he had never dived off a real diving board before, and I followed with a belly flop. We laughed and then he brought me up and showed me how to do it but it looked way easier than it was. The sun was hot now on our bodies and I thought of what Pinhead's da said about the sun always shining on them and I knew he was right, that if my father brought us here, it'd rain all day.

Deirdre came for us at lunch-time and we all sat on the sand in a circle and Mr Duffy handed out sandwiches, cut thick, with butter and pink ham, and plastic cups of lemonade. The grub tasted nicer than any I ever had before and I ate everything that came my way. Then I opened my food. There was only sandwiches and fruit left but we were all full by then. Mr and Mrs Duffy had a big flask of tea, not coffee fuck, and they drank that and the father smoked a fag. His fingers were brown where he held it.

We swam in the sea then, with Deirdre and Diet, and built a tunnel in the sand for the small sisters. We were dying to go into Salthill, just me and Pinhead on our own, and we went to ask Mr Duffy could we but he was gone. Mrs Duffy sat on a check rug with the youngest girl asleep on her lap.

'Where's Da?' Pinhead asked her.

A look passed between them, but I didn't know what it meant.

'He's gone for the racing results, will ye follow him and tell him come back straight away? I don't want to be looking for anyone when the bus is going,' she said, looking at Pinhead in that way again.

Pinhead didn't answer, just hunched his shoulders and turned his back to us.

'Come on. I have to find him for my ten bob. He's minding it for me,' I said.

'You go yourself, or ask Dee to go with you. I'm going for a swim.' And Pinhead walked away into the sea leaving me standing there mortified with Mrs Duffy.

'Deirdre will go, call her over here to me,' she said.

So I ended up walking down Salthill with Deirdre,

looking for her da. I didn't know where to start and neither did she, so I said we'd look for a betting shop, they put the results on the windows for people to check.

The sun was warm now and we walked along the busy street, full of tourists and shops and souvenirs. Deirdre kept grabbing my arm, saying, 'Look at this, Nod, isn't it lovely?'

I saw a black man through the glass of a souvenir shop, he was holding a small, hand-carved currach and I did a kind of double take.

'You won't believe this,' I whispered to Deirdre. 'I just saw a black man, I swear, a shiny black man, look at him, over there.'

She looked around her. 'Where?' she asked, and then she saw him too.

You couldn't miss him, he was a mile taller than anyone else in the shop. He was dressed in a suit, although it was roasting outside, but he wasn't sweating or anything. I went nearer for a closer look and then I saw a black woman, it must have been his wife, coming from behind a glass display case. She was nearly as tall as her husband and she wore a suit too. An ordinary suit that you wouldn't even notice on your mother or even Angela Walsh, but she made it look foreign and special. Her hair was beautiful, wiry, like Deirdre's, but jet black, the colour of coal. I wanted to reach out and touch it and stroke the shiny dark skin of her face. The husband walked over to the counter in long strides, like an athlete in the Olympics.

'Stop staring,' Deirdre whispered fiercely, grabbing my arm and pulling me away.

But I couldn't stop. I never saw a black person before and I wanted to hear his voice, to see if he talked like us. When he did speak to the shopkeeper, it was a shock. He talked like Uncle Pat! I couldn't believe that. He spoke

American. I watched him pay for the souvenirs, smiling and joking with the shopkeeper. When he took his change, the palms of his hands were white. Then he took his wife's hand and left, smiling a big grin our way, all lips and teeth and happiness. I watched them through the glass as they joined the stream of tourists on the street, taller than everyone.

'Come on, let's find Dad and get your money,' Deirdre said and we walked back out to the street, my eyes searching over the tops of heads for the tall black people, but they were gone.

I don't know what made me look in that pub. Deirdre had gone into a small shop that sold girls' things and I was waiting for her outside. The pub was across the street, its door flung open like it was telling me to go in, to look there. I could hear the clink of glasses as I reached the door and loud laughter and a hurling match on a radio somewhere. I knew he would be there. I just knew it before I even went in, before my eyes got used to the dark smoky light inside.

He was sitting at the bar with his back to me. There was a row of empty pint glasses on the counter near him and he held a small glass in his hand, full of yellow liquid. It reminded me of Mossy Sheehan and his bottle, the night they burned Eyebrows' dog. That's what I was thinking of when he turned around and saw me. He smiled.

'I ... my ... my money ...' I said in a whisper. Then louder, almost too loud, almost a shout. 'My money ... I came for my money.'

He said nothing. Just put his hand in his pocket and pulled out some notes and held up a green one, a pound note, not my ten shillings. I walked towards him and took the note like it was a dream and started to walk backwards away from him. He winked at me then and put one finger to his lips, a secret between us, and then I turned and stumbled out the door and ran across the road without even looking. I leaned against a shop window, the pound wet and clammy in my hand. I tried to remember which shop Deirdre had gone into but then I saw her coming towards me, smiling.

'Where did you disappear to? I came out of the shop and you were gone and I don't know the way back. Are you all right?' she said. She had a new necklace of tiny coloured beads around her neck.

I talked to her necklace, not looking at her eyes. 'I met your da outside the betting shop, he's just on his way back,' I lied, remembering then that I never told him to go back like Mrs Duffy said.

'That's grand so, we can have a good look around now,' she said and walked off down Salthill, her hair bouncing as she moved.

I followed her in a kind of daze, in and out of shops, her leading the way. We met Pinhead in the arcade near the beach, sitting at a one-armed bandit, a lot of coins in his hand. He grinned when he saw us and we played the machines for a while. I changed the pound note without them seeing it and I threw it into the machines any old way, not caring about winning. But I kept my ten bob of it, kept that for presents and sweets and stuff.

Pinhead had a whole pile of coins now and he stood at a money waterfall, coins dropping into the slot, like he was a magnet or something. Smaller children were following him around, hoping he'd leave some of his luck at a machine after he finished playing it.

Deirdre wanted to buy souvenirs, and when we left the arcade, we were blinded by the sudden white light of the sun. We followed her into the shops, Pinhead weighed down with his winnings. I bought some rock for Colm and Brian that said 'A Present from Salthill' inside it. And a Connemara marble brooch for my mam, that was a whole five bob, but I wouldn't buy my dad a thing, not even a rock, so she got the best present. Pinhead said it was plastic, not marble, and tried to bite the stone.

I wanted to buy Karen something, so she'd know I liked her still, even after the slap, but I didn't know what to get unless I asked Deirdre, but I liked Deirdre too, so I couldn't ask her. I got some rock for Karen in the end and a huge fat one for Dodge. Deirdre bought Uncle Pat a tiepin and Pinhead bought nothing. With all his money, he bought nothing.

We passed a small carnival, just down from the souvenir shop, and Deirdre and Pinhead had a go on the waltzer but I'd learned my lesson in the Fairgreen and I didn't want a broken neck. We got fish and chips on the way back to the beach and ate them as we walked along the prom. I told Pinhead about the black man and his wife but he said, 'So what? Sure isn't there a whole black family living in Garryowen and it's no big deal.' We had ice-cream then, big ninety-nines with a double flake. Deirdre couldn't finish hers, so I ate it for her.

We saw Mrs Duffy waving at us as we slouched along the prom. She had all the stuff packed up and the little sisters dressed and ready to go.

'Did ye meet him?' she asked as we got near.

Pinhead was whipping off his clothes for one last swim, saying, 'Come on, Nod, come on in.'

Mrs Duffy was looking right at me.

'Yeah, he's on his way, he'll be here in a minute,' I said straight to her face. I was getting good at lying.

'Where was … where did you meet him?' she asked. She stood between me and the sea, her arms folded, her face bright red from the sun.

'Outside the betting shop, like you said,' I answered as I stripped off my clothes.

She turned away then and I let out a sigh. Lying was

hard work. I ran into the waves and dived on Pinhead's back, both of us going under and spluttering as more waves knocked us over. Then we floated on our backs, and let the waves carry us up and down.

My stomach started to feel funny. I checked the prom to see if Pinhead's da was coming and I prayed to God to make him come this minute because it was all my fault, but I couldn't tell on him, not now. I saw Mrs Duffy searching for him too. She caught me then, with my hand over my eyes, looking down the prom, and the lie was between us. She knew. So I turned my back and swam some more, even though Pinhead was gone from the water and I had a small pain in my stomach that was spreading and spreading.

There was still no sign of him by the time Pinhead and me were dressed and we were all walking towards the bus. I kept looking up the prom, hoping to see him, so I could say, there he is now, Mrs Duffy, see I told you, just getting the racing results like you said. The pain in my stomach was worse.

And then he was there. Like magic, he was there leaning against the door of the bus, chatting away with the bus driver, a fag in his hand. The younger Duffys ran to him and he laughed and stubbed out the fag and swung the youngest one into the air. I could see the relief on Mrs Duffy's face. Everything was going to be all right. Except for the pain in my stomach. It was churning now and I could nearly see it inside, the fry-up, the ham sandwiches, boiled eggs and fig rolls, chips and icecream, all churning inside like my mam's twin tub on wash day.

And then I could really see it as I vomited up my whole day on the tarmac near the bus. My stomach emptied and I could smell the tar melting. Mrs Duffy was behind me holding my shoulder, saying, 'That's it now, lad, get it all up, you'll feel better now and sure aren't you glad it didn't happen you on the bus?' I could hear Pinhead sniggering in the background. Bastard Pinhead. They made me sit with them on the bus then. Mrs Duffy wouldn't let me sit at the front with Pinhead, she made me sit with the father instead. She sat behind with the three small girls and I sat next to Mr Duffy. I felt dizzy and my stomach still hurt and his smell made me feel sick all over again, fags and that pub. I could smell the pub.

I closed my eyes and must have dozed off because something woke me with a start just before Ennis. Mr Duffy was asleep beside me, snoring loudly, but I knew the snoring hadn't woken me. I felt like I was dreaming and I could hear a dripping noise. My leg felt warm and wet. I looked down and first I thought I'd done it. That I'd pissed myself in my sleep, but I saw the dark stain on his pants and knew then that it was him. My heart thumped in my chest and my stomach started doing the washing-machine thing again. I looked around but nobody else had noticed anything. I could hear Pinhead and Deirdre singing 'Roll her over in the Clover' but it sounded far away.

'Are you all right, Seán? Will I get them to stop the bus for you?' asked Mrs Duffy from behind me.

'No, I'm grand, I'm fine,' I said, without turning around.

My hand touched the wet patch on my shorts and I rubbed it against the seat to get his piss away from me. Tears were ready to come but I forced them back. The piss had stopped dripping onto the floor and I sat there like a poker, afraid to move. I thought we'd never get to Limerick. It was dark outside now and I couldn't see the names of the towns as we passed. I just wanted to get home. I wanted to wash the piss off myself, strip my clothes off me, and scrub my skin until the smell was gone. My stomach was heaving but I fought the pain and the urge to vomit, forced it back down. I was sweating and I wanted to die, to lie down somewhere and just die.

'There's the lights of Limerick, look, can you see them?' said Mrs Duffy.

I nodded my head and he stirred beside me. I didn't want him to wake.

The bus driver drove us all the way to the Ballysimon Road, and I was nearly first off, remembering to grab my bag of souvenirs from the floor under my seat. The bag was wet. I shouted, 'Good luck, Mrs Duffy, and thanks', and flew out the door, sucking the night air into my lungs as I headed up the road towards home.

'Wait for me. Ma said I was to walk you home.' It was Pinhead.

I didn't answer. I felt weak and found it hard to walk. I was afraid to open my mouth in case I vomited again.

'You big oul sissy! I have to walk little Noddy home. Will I hold your hand?' he said, but I didn't laugh and he got the message.

We walked home in silence and I groaned with the pain in my stomach and tried not to let Pinhead hear. I ran to the bathroom as soon as my dad opened the door, just pushed him out of the way while he was talking to me and ran up. I wanted to vomit badly but I needed to get the clothes off me first, with the smell of his piss on them. I was groaning as I stripped off and I hung over the toilet and vomited and vomited until there was nothing left to vomit except air. My mam was beside me then, holding my head and saying, 'You poor fella', and sponging my face when I finished.

She cleaned me up and put pyjamas on me and half-carried me into bed. Then she tucked me in like she did when I was younger, and as she stroked my hair I wanted to tell her what happened, all the stuff, the piss, the knocking off, the pound he made me take, but it all came out in a mumble, my mouth couldn't say the words, and then I started to drift off to sleep, with the smell of his piss still on me.

I didn't call for Pinhead the next day. I couldn't, because his da might be there and I wouldn't be able to look at him and then Pinhead might cop something and I didn't want that to happen. I was starving after being sick, so I ate all the leftover grub from the christening and for once my mam was up. She was even dressed in proper clothes and we talked for a while in the kitchen and no babies cried. But I told her nothing about what had happened, just that the Mystery Tour was brilliant and it was a pity I got sick at the end of it. I was just getting up to watch *The Man from Uncle* when she broke the news. Bad news.

'Your cousin is coming for a week or two to give us a hand here, isn't that great?' she said as she cleared dishes off the table.

I stopped in my tracks. 'Which cousin?' I asked, knowing in my heart which cousin, but hoping I was wrong.

'Marian, of course. Marian is coming down from Dublin to give me a hand.'

Time Tunnel. Time Tunnel was coming back. She was fourteen and she never stopped talking. Pinhead had christened her Time Tunnel when she came last summer. She had the biggest mouth we ever saw and boy did she know how to use it. Mrs Duffy called her Four More At Home because no matter what you had, she had four more at home, always better than yours. She was from Dublin and she said we were culchies. I hated her. We all hated her and I was mortified that she was my cousin.

'I hope ye'll be nice to her, not like last year,' said my mam.

A baby started screaming upstairs and Colm shouted

from the sitting room that Brian was eating his shit again. I banged the kitchen door when I left.

I called for Dodge. I checked first to make sure the car was gone from the drive and then I knocked hard on the door, the big stick of rock from Salthill in my hand. His mother let me in and I sat with the Sacred Heart in the parlour, waiting for Dodge to finish his tea. Enda was playing the guitar upstairs, softly, and he sounded really good. Next year he'd be so good that he'd probably be asked to join The Beatles. The song was 'Norwegian Wood' again. The Sacred Heart was eyeing me but I wasn't in the mood for a staring competition. Dodge came in then and sat next to me on the couch. I tried not to look at his eyes but it was hard talking to his shoulder or his knee all the time. But you had to look at his eyes, they were turning great colours. He looked like a boxer.

'I brought you this from Salthill,' I said, and handed him the rock.

'Do you want some?' he asked as he broke a big chunk off and gave it to me.

We ate the rock between us and I was glad my mouth was full because I didn't know what to say. I could hear the clock ticking in the background and Enda singing in a low, deep voice upstairs.

'He's really good, Enda, at the guitar. He's getting better and better every time I hear him,' I said.

'He's good at everything,' Dodge answered, and the silence fell again.

'I'm going out with Karen,' I said after a while. I wanted to tell him something important, like a secret or something, and that was the best I could do.

He just smiled.

'I really like her but I did something stupid the other night. I ... Dodge I dropped the hand on her, I didn't mean to, it just happened and she hit me and I still didn't say sorry … and what will I do?' I asked.

He was laughing now. 'You lucky bastard. I wish I had the guts to do it. Was it good? What was it like?'

'Worth the slap, I think. But what will I do?'

'Call down and say sorry, you eejit. Just call down and tell her. Ask her to go with you, I mean properly, official like.'

'I'd be mortified.'

'You'll get over it, if you like her enough. I wouldn't mind her myself, she's lovely looking.' He winked at me then with his mad black eye and the two of us laughed.

Mrs O'Riordan came in with two glasses of lemonade and a whole plate of chocolate biscuits and we ate the lot while I told him about the Mystery Tour, about the diving board and the black people and Pinhead winning all around him in the arcade. And then I suddenly remembered Time Tunnel. Jesus, how could I have forgotten that?

'Bad news, Dodge.'

'What?'

'Time Tunnel is coming back.'

He burst out laughing. 'Fuck off. She wouldn't have the nerve after last year. After the knickers and Pinhead and all. I don't believe you.' He was laughing and slapping his knee.

I didn't think it was that funny, I hated her fuckin' guts and it was easy to laugh if she wasn't your cousin. But at least I cheered Dodge up. I was glad about that. And we did catch her a beaut with the knickers, Pinhead's idea of course, and that shut her big mouth for a while and that was a very hard thing to do.

It started when I saw my mam putting Time Tunnel's knickers in the twin tub. Five pairs of polka dot knickers all the way from Dublin, and I told Pinhead and he said, 'Steal them, Nod and we'll hang the lot of them off the tree in the Green and we'll make a big sign and pin it to the tree, and I promise you, she'll shut up, I swear she will.' And boy she shut up all right. We got the knickers, all in bright colours and covered in spots and we climbed the big willow tree and hung them up on the branches. And the sign was great – SPOT THE DUBLIN ARSE. We spent ages doing that sign, getting it just right.

We all waited for her to come out and she took an age. She came with Brian in his pram, her mouth jabbering away at us, and then she saw the tree and screamed and let the pram go. Dodge had to run after it before it took off down the hill. We were cracking up laughing, Pinhead was bent over the wall hysterical.

I was killed and had to stay in my room for a whole day but it was worth every minute of sitting in my room alone. I could hear them slagging her every time she put her nose outside the door, Spotty Arse, Dotty Hole, Polka Pussy. That was Pinhead's slag, Polka Pussy, and he looked up at my window after he said it and gave me the thumbs up, even though he couldn't see me behind the net curtains. But that was last year. She would be older this time, bossier.

'What did Pinhead say when you told him? Did he laugh?' asked Dodge.

'I didn't see him today. My stomach was still hurting me until tea-time and then I wanted to give you the rock and stuff,' I said and stole a look at the Sacred Heart to see if he heard the lie.

'He'll die laughing when he hears she's coming. It'll be great crack. Tell Pinhead, he'll want time to plan.'

'Yeah, I'll tell him tomorrow. I better go, see you then,' I said. I wanted to be gone before O'Riordan got home.

Outside I could hear Enda as plain as day, the bedroom window was open. It was magic, his voice and the guitar

together, soft but strong at the same time. I sat on the wall
for a while, listening. 'I once had a girl, or should I say,
she once had me. She showed me her room, isn't it good,
Norwegian wood.' I saw O'Riordan's car then, coming
up the road, and I edged further down the wall so he
wouldn't see me. He got out in the drive and stood
listening to Enda singing for a minute before he opened
the front door. The music stopped suddenly, once the
door closed. But the tune was still going around in my
head when I went to bed.

Pinhead called for me the next day. It made it easier that
way, him calling to my house just as I finished my
cornflakes. It was like I hadn't seen him for a month and
we went out and sat on the Green, Jesse lying down
between the two of us and both of us talking at the same
time.

'You'll never guess, you'll never – '

'You'll never guess either, she's coming back, Time
Tunnel is coming on Thursday, she's – '

'My da might be getting tickets for the ... what? Time
Tunnel? Fuck off, Nod, fuck off.' His eyes were round
with not believing.

'Yeah. Coming to help my mam with the babies, can
you believe it? I thought we got rid of her for good. I
mean, she cried her eyes out over the knickers.'

'Jesus. She has some neck ... and some fuckin' mouth!'
he said and we laughed at that.

'So tell me. Tickets for what?' I asked as I rubbed Jesse's
ears. He wagged his tail when you did that.

'Tickets for the All-Ireland semi in Croke Park –
Limerick against Kilkenny,' he said, with a big grin on
his face.

'Lucky bastard. When is it anyway?' I asked, trying to
keep the jealousy out of my voice.

'Sunday week. He doesn't know for sure yet but he says

he'll try for three tickets,' he said and looked at me, half smiling.

There was more for him to tell, but I didn't ask, just rubbed Jesse's belly. The tail was doing ninety now.

'He said if he gets three, you can come because Diet doesn't like hurling, he doesn't want to go.' He was beaming at me.

My heart did a kind of hop, skip and jump in my chest, Croke Park with Limerick playing, I'd give anything to be there. But a whole day with him, with the father and after the piss and the pound and stuff. I looked away, over across the Green, trying to decide was it worth it. Croke Park won.

'Jesus, are you serious? I'd love it,' I said and looked at his face.

He had this curious look, like he was examining me, and I got the creepy feeling again that he could see into my mind. That he could look through my eyes into my head and he could see the pound note being waved in the pub and my hand reaching out for it and piss dripping off the seat on the bus.

'That's great so. He'll get the tickets, he always does in the end. Always.' said Pinhead.

8

She came in a thunderstorm. A real thunderstorm, like the one in *The Hound of the Baskervilles*, with sheets of white lightning and thunder so loud that it felt like the house was shaking, and Time Tunnel arrived right in the middle of it and I should have known then that she'd be even more trouble than last year.

The sky that morning was the colour of lead, clouds so thick and black that if you stretched up your hand, you could nearly touch them, as if the whole sky had dropped down just over the roofs of the houses. The boxroom was all ready for her and my dad had fixed a bolt on the door. Everybody remembered the knickers from last year.

The thunder started all of a sudden and first we thought there was a crash or something outside and we all ran to the front door and Colm and Brian ran under the kitchen table. They stayed there the whole day, even when the storm died down, and my mam had to give them their dinner under the table, they were so terrified. I loved it though. The lightning was the best, but my aunt said you weren't supposed to look at it or be near glass. I sat at my bedroom window and watched it for ages. It was as good as going to the pictures. The lightning first, silent and sneaky, and then the wait for the huge rolls of thunder.

And it was brilliant watching people out in it, fighting against the howling winds and everything blowing up in the air around them and the whole ordinary world in chaos. It reminded me of the atom bomb booklet and maybe that's why I loved the thunderstorm so much, that it made me less afraid. The atom bomb booklet happened a couple of years ago and started off grand, the kind of thing you wouldn't even think about. The Government sent every house in Ireland a booklet telling you what you should do if there was an atom war. It had pictures and everything and I saw it on the sideboard when I came home from school and glanced through it, just looking at the pictures really. That night I brought it up to bed and started reading it. By the end of the week I was convinced that we were all going to be blown up in an atom war, we were doomed and there was nothing we could do to stop the Americans and the Russians from blowing up the world.

And the worst thing was that I couldn't talk to people about it because they'd think I was mad or something and I might be committed to St Joseph's madhouse and that would be worse than being blown up by the atom bomb. Pinhead hadn't a fucking clue and he thought wars were great, but this wasn't just any war, this was the atom bomb.

The booklet was supposed to make us feel better and gave advice about what to do when it happened. Like, first you papered all your windows and you put wardrobes full of sand in front of them and then you got supplies of food, tinned was best, and you found somewhere dark, like under the stairs, to hide – I mean, everybody, the children and all – and you sat there while the atoms released from the bomb fell everywhere like red snow. That's what it looked like in the booklet, red snow falling on everything. You stayed indoors so it wouldn't fall on you and after about three days, maybe a week if it was a big bomb, you came out and washed the red stuff off everything and you would be grand then. Except Enda laughed at all of this, and said that the booklet was lying. He did science in the CBS, so he knew all about the atom and stuff.

I saw the booklet in Dodge's house, Enda had it in his hand, so I asked him about it because I knew he wouldn't think I was mad. He told me the truth about atom wars. That the red stuff was radioactive, that's the word he used, and that it would burn your skin to a crisp and it would make all the crops bad, and the cows and sheep and every single thing that lived or grew. And that an atom bomb would kill a whole lot of us, and if we did live, we'd have nothing to eat and we'd be better off to stand in the middle of the Green just as they dropped the bomb instead of hiding under the stairs or papering the windows. Enda said that was stupid. That the Government's great plan would never work.

And then he saw me crying. He knelt down in front of me and said, 'I'm sorry for scaring you, Nod, it's just sometimes you seem older than you are ... than your age. I'm sorry. Look, forget about the stupid atomic war, Nod. Listen to me now, they'll never do it because they'll have to blow themselves up as well. Come on up to Claughaun with me and I'll teach you the long puck.'

'But have they made it already, the bomb, is it stored somewhere ready to go?' I asked him.

I knew by his face that it was but he shook his head and said, 'No, come on now, Nod, forget about it.'

'But why if it's never going to happen are they sending us booklets about it?' I asked him.

And he said, 'Get your hurley, Nod, and forget about it.'

But I couldn't forget about it. I kept the booklet under my pillow for a while, so that if they dropped the bomb all of a sudden, like, I might be able to do something to save us all, even if it was just papering the windows. And in a way I was glad Enda had told me the truth at the start, that he liked me enough not to lie or give an easy answer. I thought then that I'd never get over the atom bomb, I couldn't get it out of my head, but it took the storm to remind me that I'd forgotten all about it. I didn't even know where the booklet was now.

I saw them coming in my Aunty Mary's car. The storm was really raging and the wind nearly took the doors off when they got out. And then I got my first shock. I mean, Time Tunnel was a woman. She was a skinny girl last year with a huge mouth and now she was a woman with huge tits. She had a wet-look raincoat on but you could still see the shape of her chest through it, bigger than Angela Walsh's, bigger than my mam's. I stood at my bedroom window looking down at them. I could hear my mam's voice at the front door.

'How are you, Marian? Isn't the weather awful? Is it as bad as this in Dublin? Show me your suitcase, love. I'll call Seán down now, he's looking forward to seeing you.'

Like fuck I was.

'Seán, she's here. Are you coming down to see her?' Mam called from the bottom of the stairs.

I took a deep breath and went down. She was in the kitchen, and my mam and my aunt were admiring her.

'Marian, you're so grown up and so tall. Beautiful, just like your mother, isn't she Mary? She's a Ryan for sure,' said my mam.

I stood in the doorway looking at her chest. You couldn't miss it.

'Nana is coming tonight for her tea. Wait until she sees you, Marian, she'll get such a shock,' said my aunt. But she never told Marian that Nana wouldn't have a fuckin' clue who she was.

'Hi Seán,' said Time Tunnel in a kind of husky voice. She wore a red miniskirt with a tight cream polo neck. She had matching cream tights on her. Long legs. Big chest.

'Hi,' I said, and gave her a Pinhead stare.

She was still Time Tunnel, even with the fancy clothes and the big chest, and I wasn't going to give her an easy time. Her mouth was still huge and she had lipstick on, not much but it was definitely there. And eye shadow. Blue eye shadow. Jesus, teenagers got away with murder in Dublin.

'So how's life in good old Limerick?' she asked, smirking at me.

'Great, spot on,' I said and smirked back at her.

She narrowed her eyes over the spot on bit. I smirked bigger.

'How are all the little boys in your gang?' she asked then, all innocence in front of my mam.

I said nothing, just did the stare. There a smell of perfume in the kitchen. Jesus, she was only a year older than me, I mean, Pinhead's age, and she was a woman.

'Go on up with your suitcase, love, and get settled in. The twins will be awake soon, and there's Colm and Brian under the table. Lads, say hello to your cousin. Do ye remember her at all?' my mam asked as she peered under the table at the two boys.

Then Time Tunnnel knelt down to talk to them and I could nearly see her knickers from where I was standing. I didn't see any polka dots though. And she caught me looking and smirked at me and bent down further. She did that on purpose.

The storm didn't die down until tea-time. It was lashing outside, so I was stuck indoors all day, bored stiff. I spent the afternoon avoiding Time Tunnel as she helped my mam with the twins and the washing and ironing. Mam loved having her around, and they chatted away. I could hear them downstairs, talking and laughing and cooing over the babies. And then Nana came with my Aunty Mary just as my dad arrived home from work.

Nana had her skirt on back to front and two odd shoes on her feet.

'Who's she?' she asked when Time Tunnel came into the kitchen to say hello.

'That's Marian, Nana, you know Marian, she's your eldest grandchild, she's Annie's girl,' said my mam, a twin in each arm.

'Who's Annie?' asked Nana, as she hitched up her skirt to scratch her arse.

I was trying to swallow my laugh by now and so was my dad. Pinhead would have loved this.

'Marian, this is Marian, Annie's daughter,' said Aunty Mary loudly, her mouth twitching with annoyance.

'Marian and Annie, never heard of them, that must have been before my time,' said Nana and she took up a teaspoon and the sugar bowl from the kitchen table and started shovelling sugar into her mouth.

We all sat down then around the table for our tea. Time Tunnel was like the perfect young woman, all manners and tinkly laughs. I could have sworn she was eyeing my dad, laughing at his dumb jokes and flicking her eyelashes at him.

Nana kept staring at her right through the whole tea, shoving food into her mouth and staring at her across the table.

'Who's that one over there with the hoor's mouth?' she said out of the blue.

I nearly choked on my rasher and let out a laugh. My mam thumped me in the arm and Colm said, 'Hoor hoor hoor', over and over. Time Tunnel was the colour of the tomatoes we had just eaten. It was too much, tears were running down my face now and my mam told me to leave the table and as I passed Nana she gave me a wink. Like she knew what she had just done.

Pinhead laughed the next day over the hoor's mouth

bit. He roared laughing at that on the Green and said, 'Don't worry, Nod, we'll sort her out, the oul bitch, the oul Dublin jackeen, we'll think of something even better than last year, just you wait.'

But nothing could have prepared me for what happened next. We were all on the Green by then, Dodge and Eyebrows and Deirdre and Libby Bourke. Pinhead was sitting on the Green, his back against the big willow. Libby was sitting between his legs, her blond head resting on his shoulder, her hand on his knee like she owned a piece of him. The rest of us were around them in a circle, Jesse had his head on my lap.

I saw her first coming towards us with Brian in her arms and Colm skipping along by her side, she had her head turned, talking to him. Then she looked over, straight at Pinhead and he looked at her. And I knew straight away. From that very minute I knew. There was something instant between them, like a connection or a wire that was invisible. I knew I wasn't the only one who could feel it, because Libby's hand on Pinhead's knee seemed to tighten. Time Tunnel just smiled and waved and followed after Colm, who was running down the Green towards the road. Pinhead kept looking, even when Libby spoke.

'Is that her? Your cousin? Her hair's gorgeous. I love that style with the top backcombed,' said Libby.

'Her clothes are fab, straight out of a magazine. You couldn't even buy clothes like that in Limerick,' said Deirdre. Deirdre, who always laughed at make-up and hairstyles. I couldn't believe this.

'She's a fuckin' ghoul with a hoor's mouth,' I said and got up off the damp grass.

Everybody looked at me as if I had just told a huge lie.

I walked off by myself, mad with the whole lot of them. It was the same fucking Time Tunnel, why couldn't they see that? And Pinhead, my best fucking friend in the world, a person I'd die for, and he couldn't see past my cousin's big tits. I hated her even more than last year.

I decided to call down to Karen's house. I hadn't seen her since the night of the slap and I'd a peace offering in my pocket – the Connemara brooch wrapped in toilet paper. Mam's brooch. I'd no choice really, because Colm and Brian found her rock and ate all the writing off it. I'd already given my mam the brooch and she wore it for a day and put it into her jewellery box. So I crept into her room and took it back, she'd hundreds of other brooches anyway, and then I wrapped it in the tissue paper. It was like I just bought it and Karen would know it cost a lot of money, so she'd know I liked her. I wasn't going to go right up and knock on the door, no way was I brave enough to do that. I'd wait instead at the bottom of the Well Hill for her to come out.

I waited for a long time but she came out in the end and jumped when I ran up behind her.

'Jesus, what do you want? You scared the life out of me.'

'I … I wanted to … well … I got you this from Salthill,' I said and handed her the little white parcel. I knew I should have said sorry about dropping the hand and stuff but it was too mortifying in broad daylight looking right at her face.

'Did you?' she said, but she didn't put out her hand for the parcel.

She started walking up the hill and I followed, still holding out the present. I had a reddener, I could feel my face burning. Her hair was tied into a long blond ponytail and it swung from side to side as she marched along. It was hard keeping up with her.

'I'm sorry about … you know … the other night,' I said then and it was like saying the magic words, the right spell.

She stopped her marching and turned around to face

me. 'Are you? Are you really sorry, Seán? Are you?'

'Yep.'

It was harder to talk when she was looking straight at me. I looked down at the ground and scuffed some dirt with my shoes.

'So what's that wrapped in toilet paper?' She laughed as she said this and took the present from me. 'It's lovely, thanks.' But she never put on the brooch, just dropped it into her jeans pocket.

A strand of blond hair had escaped from the ponytail and I wanted to reach up and touch it and then kiss her on the mouth again but I knew it'd be the wrong thing to do.

'I've got to go. See you around,' she said and walked away, the ponytail swaying behind her.

And that was it. She was gone. With my mam's five bob brooch. Maybe she'd have liked the rock better.

Uncle Pat did a runner two days later. Pinhead came flying into my house in the morning, saying, 'Come on, Nod, let's get a search party and find him, the dumb fucker. His passport and all is gone and my ma is going mad over it.'

Time Tunnel came to the door just as we were leaving. 'Wait for me, I'll help. I want to help find him, the poor old man,' she said and looked straight at Pinhead.

He looked at her with his mouth open, like a goldfish, staring at her tight blouse, the buttons stretched over her chest.

'Fuck off,' I said, and pulled Pinhead down the path.

My mam came out to the door then. 'How dare you speak to Marian like that, I'll sort you out later,' she said, but I didn't even look back.

We called for Dodge and Eyebrows and headed into

town. We went to Kelly's bar first and then we ran out of ideas.

'Where does he go usually?' I asked as we headed down Mulgrave Street.

'Jesus, I haven't a clue,' said Pinhead after a while.

'You must have some fuckin' idea what the oul man does all day,' I said.

Pinhead shrugged. 'Drinks in Kelly's, runs around balls naked in the middle of the night, how the fuck would I know what else he does?'

'We'll go to the railway station, he might have followed your da to work,' said Dodge, so we went there because we couldn't think of anything else.

The sun was getting warm, it was going to be a scorcher and we were supposed to be going to the Corbally Baths, except Uncle Pat changed all that, the dumb oul bastard. We were sweating by the time we got to the station and we saw Mr Duffy right away, standing on the railway platform talking with his friends. He waved at us and walked down the platform to the barrier. I hung back behind the others.

'What's up?' he asked Pinhead.

'Uncle Pat did a runner,' said Pinhead.

'What do you mean, did a runner? Arrah, he's only gone for a walk, he often does that,' said Mr Duffy, smiling at all of us.

I looked away, I just couldn't look him straight in the eye after the Mystery Tour.

'He took his passport, his hearing aid and his heart tablets, he doesn't often do that,' said Pinhead with a straight face.

I sniggered and Eyebrows laughed.

'Jesus Christ,' said Mr Duffy, 'look, search the pubs ... Flannery's and Kirby's ... and try the bus stop for Shannon. Jesus, I hope he isn't gone all the way to Shannon. Hang on, I'll come with ye, I'll just tell Mick.'

So Pinhead's da joined our search party and at least he had a few ideas about where to look. But Uncle Pat was hard to find. Not a sign of him anywhere, not in the pubs, not at the bus stop at Spaights. So Mr Duffy said, 'We'll look in Poor Man's Kilkee, lads, and then we'll try along the river by the Dock Road', and we all looked at each other and we knew without saying it out loud what it meant.

See, that's where people went to top themselves. Last year a man went to Poor Man's Kilkee and just took off his shoes and his jacket, he even folded his jacket, and then jumped in and drowned himself. Eyebrows' da saw it all but he couldn't do anything about it because he couldn't swim and by the time he raised the alarm the man was gone, swallowed up by the high tide of the Shannon. We found out later from Eyebrows' da that the man was happily married with two children and a good job with a pension and all. Pinhead said that he was just a fuckin' eejit, a nutcase, or else maybe he tripped. But I said, 'Why would he take off his shoes and fold his jacket?' And Pinhead said, 'That's it, you ghoul, sure he'd drown faster with them on.' And then he shrugged and said, 'Who gives a fuck anyway? Maybe his wife was frigid, who knows?' And we laughed.

'He won't be near the docks, he's probably sitting in Kelly's this minute drinking whiskey,' said Pinhead, but we turned down towards the Dock Road anyway.

There was no deserted bundle of clothes anywhere along the bank and the only person in Poor Man's Kilkee was a wino with a bottle, talking and fighting with himself. Even Mr Duffy was out of ideas now. So he said, 'One more look around the town and then we'll go down to the guards, lads.'

We were heading up O'Connell Street, just passing the

Royal George Hotel, when Pinhead let out a shout. We all turned around to see what was going on and Pinhead was pointing at the window of a big touring bus parked outside the George, and there was Uncle Pat sitting inside with a guard talking to him. A crowd was beginning to gather around the bus.

'Holy fuck, what is he doing?' said Mr Duffy, and ran onto the bus.

We watched them through the glass, Mr Duffy and the guard standing up talking to each other and Uncle Pat sitting on his seat, nodding and smiling at the onlookers. Pinhead was laughing already, before he even knew what happened. 'This is going to be good, Nod, this will be a howl,' he said, and he was right, it was good. Mr Duffy told us the full story as he walked us to the bus stop with Uncle Pat in tow.

'The mad bastard decided he was going home to Chicago for a few days. Jesus, can you believe that? Going to America for a few days, just dropping in for a cup of tea, like.'

'But why was he on the bus?' Dodge asked.

'The bus, that's the best part. He doesn't like travelling on his own, if you don't mind, so he barges onto a tourist bus and tells the driver that one more American grandpa won't even be noticed and would he head for Shannon immediately or he'd miss the plane to Chicago. I mean, can you credit that? Unbelievable,' said Mr Duffy.

I looked behind at Uncle Pat and he nodded and smiled. I didn't know if he was smiling at me or at what Mr Duffy was telling us. So we piled onto the bus with Uncle Pat and we were grand till we got near Kelly's bar and then he got up and rang the bell furiously, calling to the driver to let him off at Kelly's and telling him to have a real nice day. Pinhead was up from his seat like a shot and came back with the passport and the heart tablets and

Uncle Pat went for his whiskey.

There was still time for the Corbally Baths and I ran home in the blazing sun to get my togs and a towel and a few cuts of bread.

'Where do you think you're going?' asked my mam as I sneaked out the door, stuffing the bread into my mouth.

I shrugged and chewed away.

'Swimming, is it? Well, you can bring Marian with you. I was just saying to her that she needs a break, she's been minding the lads since she came. Are you listening to me, Seán?'

Fuck, that was all I needed. Another day ruined. Time Tunnel came out then in a top with no back on it and a bag over her shoulder. This was a balls.

We met up with the lads, there was a huge crowd of us, Enda and Diet and Deirdre were coming too. I never spoke one word to Time Tunnel but Enda did, even though I glared at him for it. Pinhead and me walked behind the gang. I was talking away to him and he was looking at my cousin's bare back. It was going to be a long day.

The baths were full, crowds of people all sitting along the banks, even the changing shelters were full. We changed into our togs with towels wrapped around us but the girls queued for the shelters. We were already in the water by the time they came out. And then I was really mortified. Time Tunnel had a swimsuit like you never saw before, a kind of knickers and bra thing. Everybody in the water, boys and girls, stopped swimming to look. I wanted to die. I could hear the girls' whispers as she jumped into the water. 'It's fabulous.' 'It's a bikini, that's what they call it.' 'I'd love one of those.' And the boys said nothing, just stared.

I swam away, right out to the middle of the river, but Pinhead didn't follow me, just stood there gawking, the dirty old bastard. But it was Enda she had eyes for and she swam straight over to him, her chest sticking out in front of her in the bra thing, like two white footballs. That minute I wished she'd drown, that the Shannon would take her and swallow her up and spit her out on some shoreline miles down the river.

I swam till I was exhausted, till sweat dripped down my face, even in the water, and then I lay on the grassy bank and let the sun dry me and lull me into a half-sleep. I was kind of dozing, drifting in and out of sleep and hearing everyone talking and splashing about. I needed to piss and had to get up when I couldn't ignore it any longer and I went over to the trees behind the baths, where you could piss in peace. It was cool in there and I shivered in my damp togs and bare feet and looked for a private place.

I heard the noises before I saw them. Grunting and sucking noises in the quiet woods. I noticed then how my bare feet crunched on the pine needles and I tried to be quiet as I followed the noises. I saw them then, a little blur of them, and I hid behind a tree and peered through the branches for a better look. I desperately wanted to piss.

She had her back against a tree, her eyes closed and her big mouth slightly open in a half smile. He had his back to me and had one of her tits in his mouth, sucking noisily on it, like the twins did to my mam. It was disgusting but I couldn't take my eyes off them. He stopped the sucking then and started kissing her. I leaned forward and saw him put his tongue in her mouth, saw him put his tongue in the Time Tunnel itself. My legs felt weak. She was a fuckin' hoor, my cousin. Then suddenly she opened her eyes and looked straight at me, right through the branches, and I knew she saw me. Her eyes smirked at me, and then I ran. I ran back to the bank where I left my clothes and dressed myself and never said good luck to the lads or anything and didn't even piss, just ran down the red path and all the way home without stopping once.

But I didn't go into the house. I couldn't arrive home without her, my mam would go mad, so I went up to Claughaun and sat down near the oak tree behind the goalpost. The field was empty, no hurleys or sliotars or boys calling out for the ball. Just me and some birds singing in the trees and every time I closed my eyes I saw Pinhead sucking her tit, heard the noise he made, over and over in my head, and saw her eyes smirking at me. And then it clicked. It all fell into place, perfect and right, like a hard sum that suddenly makes sense. She was getting us back, that's what she was doing, she was getting us back for last year and the knickers. I jumped up and did a little dance around the goalpost. She was getting us back and I had to warn Pinhead, warn him that she was only using him to get back at us, the sneaky oul bitch.

I called for him that night but he wasn't there. Deirdre answered the door in blue eye shadow. It was a holy show on her, so I just pretended I didn't notice it.

'Is Pinhead around?'

She fluttered her eyelashes at me, exactly the way Time Tunnel did. She must have been giving all the girls fuckin' hoor lessons at the baths. And hoor lessons for Pinhead too. She fluttered her eyelashes again. 'He's not here.'

'Thanks.' I walked out the path, glad to get away from those mad-looking eyes.

'Try Claughaun,' she shouted after me, 'or else the track.'

But I didn't have to search hard at all because I met Libby on the way to Claughaun. She looked funny, sick or upset or something.

'Have you seen Pinhead?' I asked before I copped the crying bit.

She sniffled and looked at me, her eyes wet, tears

spilling down her cheeks. 'He's a bastard, he is. He just called it all off, the bastard. Can you believe it? Why? Why did he do that to me, the bastard?'

'Do you know where he is now, though?' I asked, trying to ignore the crying stuff.

'Just dumps me out of the blue. Making a fool of me in front of everyone, the bastard.' She was bawling now.

'Where is he?'

'Calls it off for no reason and walks away, the bastard.'

'Is he out the track?'

'I'll get him back for this, I'll show him he can't make a ghoul out of me like that.'

I left her there and went up the road towards the track, that's where he always went with Libby, and I saw him then coming towards me, Jesse at his heels. He waved and grinned and ran to meet me.

'Where did you fuck off to today?' he said. 'We swam out to Thomas's Island. Jesus, I thought Eyebrows wouldn't make it, the ghoul. He did the dog's paddle the whole way and Enda had to half drag him back to the baths. It was a howl.' He leaned up against the wall and looked at me. 'What's wrong?' he asked.

'I just met Libby. What's up with her and you?'

He shrugged. 'Libby?'

'Yeah, remember her? I just met her in an awful state, bawling crying. She said you called it off.'

'It's none of your business.' He held me with his eyes, with that stare.

'This has to do with her, hasn't it? With Time Tunnel,' I said.

He shrugged again. Pinhead's fuckin' answer to any question he didn't like the sound of.

'She's using you. She's using you and me, she's getting us back for last year. She told you to drop Libby, didn't she?'

He bent down then and nuzzled Jesse. He stayed there fondling the dog, letting me do the talking.

'She's a bitch, a sneaky fuckin' bitch, and she wants to cause trouble, can't you even see that? Can't you see?'

Still no answer. He stood up and sat on the wall, looking back towards Claughaun. He started to whistle softly to himself, the tune from *The Virginian*. I sat on the wall beside him and let my legs dangle. Pinhead's legs nearly touched the ground. He was going to be a giant when he grew up. He kept whistling and I knew I had lost.

'Fuck her, Pin, she'll be gone next week,' I said then. And it was true. She would be gone and I wouldn't let her get between Pinhead and me. That's what she wanted but I would be cleverer than her.

He shrugged again and jumped off the wall. He punched me on the arm, smiling that smile that made his eyes crinkle at the corners. I smiled back, I just couldn't help it.

'We have business to do tonight,' he said. 'Can you get out? I mean, late, like. You'll have to sneak out. O'Riordan needs a paint job done.'

We cracked up laughing and walked home, Pinhead telling me his plan.

We picked the bright red paint at the back of Pinhead's shed under a pile of rubbish. I found a tin of pink paint but he said it might be traced back or his ma might cop it, since they'd just painted the bathroom that colour a while ago.

Mr Duffy came in while we were in the shed and waved something in the air. 'Gold dust, these are like gold dust, and we have three of them. Three beauties!'

The tickets, he got the tickets for the All-Ireland semi. Jesus, we were going to Croker!

'How much would you get if you sold one of them,

you know, outside the grounds?' asked Pinhead, but he was only joking, I knew by his voice.

His da beat him over the head with the tickets and laughed. 'Next Sunday it is, we'll have a great day. Hey, what are ye doing in here?' he asked then.

'We're just looking for something. We have a small job to do,' said Pinhead.

'Well aren't ye two great lads, the pair of ye,' he said as he left.

We looked at each other then and burst out laughing.

We didn't tell Eyebrows about the little paint job because he was a bit stupid and sometimes blurted things out and we couldn't take the risk. We told nobody and got the stuff we needed ready and hid it behind Pinhead's wall. We'd collect it later, in the middle of the night when everybody was asleep.

I thought they'd never go to bed in my house. They stayed up watching a film on the telly when the small lads went to bed. Time Tunnel sat with my mam and dad, throwing me a smirk now and again over her shoulder with her big hoor's mouth. I kept yawning so that they might start getting tired too, but it didn't work and finally my father said, 'Why don't you go up to bed, Seán? You must be very tired with all that yawning you're doing', and I just threw him a dirty look, a good one, like a dead man's stare.

I went to bed and lay under the blankets with all my clothes on, waiting for the house to fall silent, and boy did I have a long wait. I nearly fell asleep waiting and had to sit up in the bed and pinch myself to stay awake. Brian was asleep beside me. I could see the outline of his face in the dark, soft curls and roundy cheeks. He was sucking his thumb. I heard them then coming up the stairs, the toothbrushing and pissing and the flush of the toilet. And just as the house was settling down I heard the soft cry of one of the twins getting louder and somebody's bare feet on lino. Jesus, would they ever go to sleep?

I thought Pinhead would be gone. That he'd have waited and waited and then given up and gone off to do it on his own, but he was there with all the stuff on the footpath.

'Where the fuck were you? Bet you fell asleep,' he whispered.

'They took ages to go to sleep. And Time Tunnel took an hour to brush all the teeth in her big mouth,' I whispered back, and we laughed at that.

We walked down to St Patrick's Road, down to Dodge's house, and when I saw the shiny car in the drive, I started to panic.

'I don't want Dodge to get in trouble. We can't do anything that will get him in trouble,' I whispered. My legs were weak and my heart was thumping.

Pinhead was fiddling with a torch. 'I've thought of everything. Don't worry about Dodge, it'll be grand, you'll see,' he said as he opened the gate to O'Riordan's house.

I knew the plan, well some of it anyway, but I didn't understand how we could do it without Dodge getting into trouble. Pinhead hadn't gone into detail. He knelt down then by the side of the car and motioned to me to do the same. He gave me the torch to hold and opened the tin of red paint. It looked black in the watery beam of light. He took a small paintbrush from our stuff and started to write on the car in huge letters. I watched in terror and delight as Pinhead painted right across the side of the car.

'Now, isn't that grand?' he said when he finished the last letter, an R. I was laughing already, a kind of choking, whisper laugh, and he started too when he sat back and looked. I AM A STEAMER, it said, on the whole side of O'Riordan's pride and joy. Then Pinhead got up and went to the front wall of the house and started again, but a dog began barking next door and he had to hurry and I was no help from laughing and I dropped the torch, so when he finished, it said I AM A WONK, instead of I AM A WANKER, and then he did a quick PRICK across the back window of the car and we ran up the road skitting. He stopped four houses up and did UP THE GARRYOWENERS on the wall, asking me how to spell 'Garryoweners', and then I could see how Dodge would be all right and how Pinhead was the cleverest person I knew. We did one last one on the footpath, a big MOSSY WAS HERE, and we headed home laughing and punching each other and dying for the morning to come.

'Are you bleeding?' asked my mam at breakfast. I was standing up in my usual place eating my cornflakes.

'No, why? Is there blood on me?'

'On your neck, Seán, and your chin. Were you trying to shave yourself or something?' she asked as she buttered toast for the brothers.

I gulped down the rest of the cornflakes and drank the last of the milk from the bowl, then skirted up to the bathroom to look in the mirror. Red paint. A big daub of it on my chin and neck. I grinned at myself in the mirror and tried to scrub off the paint with soap and a sponge. Pinhead called to the door then, I could hear him talking quietly to Time Tunnel on the front step. I stood on the landing waiting to see if it was her or me he'd called for. I heard snatches of whispers about them meeting later, and then her voice calling me down.

'You're wanted at the door, little cousin,' she said as she walked into the house.

Bitch.

I wanted to go straight to Dodge's house, just to see if anything was happening, but Pinhead said that we shouldn't be seen, not yet, that we'd have to be careful, so we walked down and hid behind Murphys' shed. We had a good view from there and could even hear them talking when there was no traffic.

A squad car was outside the house and a crowd of neighbours had gathered. They were reading our handiwork and saying, 'Isn't it terrible? We never had any vandalism like this in our area', but some of the women were smiling too as they read Pinhead's masterpiece. Others had gathered up the road where the other stuff was written and a guard was standing with them looking at the writing and scratching his arse.

'Look at fucking Sherlock Holmes, he'd be better off looking up his itchy hole for clues,' said Pinhead.

Then O'Riordan came out of the house with another guard. We strained behind the shed to hear them talking.

'Ye better catch the little scuts that did it, ye hear? My car is ruined, ruined, and they can't respray it for a week. How am I supposed to drive to work in that? How will I drive around the town in it?' he said.

The guard was dead cute, he just kept nodding his head but said nothing. Dodge came out the gate and stood next to his da. He said nothing either but looked serious. O'Riordan put his arm around Dodge's shoulder.

'I pay my taxes, you know. I want ye to find the little scuts that did this. I'll write up my own report about it and I want something done, some answers,' he said. He wasn't shouting or anything, but his voice was hard and angry. His grip tightened on Dodge's shoulder. Dodge dropped his eyes and looked at the ground. I hated when Dodge did that. Pinhead was laughing quietly beside me.

'Sure we'll do our best, Mr O'Riordan. We're going down to interview that young fella in Garryowen now. 'Tis a lovely car and all,' said the guard.

'I'd be better off dealing with the little bastards myself. No bloody discipline, that's what I say. No control over children any more, they can do what they bloody well like. I'd straighten them out once and for all if I got my hands on them,' O'Riordan said to the guard.

The guard smiled away at him as if he was giving an account of the weather. He was cute all right. I was frightened though. There was something about O'Riordan's voice that was scary. Way scarier than my dad when he was mad. I wanted to go home but Pinhead, the brazen fucker, walked over to them. I stayed hidden behind the shed.

'Shame about your car, Mr O'Riordan,' he said and stood there only inches from him.

Dodge didn't know where to look. The guard smiled at everyone.

'Do you know something about this?' O'Riordan said, his voice deadly calm. Menacing.

'Only that somebody doesn't like you, Mister-O-Riordan, sir!' Pinhead drawled.

There was a look in O'Riordan's eyes, just for a second, a look of hate, and I knew if Pinhead was alone with him he'd beat him to within an inch of his life. Dodge stood like a statue, almost not breathing. The guard wasn't smiling any more. He could tell there was some mad thing brewing.

'We'll check it all out, Mr O'Riordan, don't you worry, we'll catch the scut who did this, sure we have a name and all,' he said and looked at his notebook, 'Mossy Sheehan, we'll interview him.'

'That was very convenient, the way he left his name for us,' said O'Riordan, never taking his eyes from Pinhead's.

'Wasn't it just? You're a lucky man, Mister-O-Riordan, sir!' said Pinhead.

I thought for a second that O'Riordan would make a go for him. His body tensed up and his fists curled. But he didn't. He just went into his house, pulling

Dodge along with him.

Pinhead's ma asked us about it later that day. She passed Dodge's house on the way to Mac's shop and Mr Mac told her what happened. She called us in then, her arms crossed and her eyes searching our faces for lies.

'Have we red paint in our shed?' she asked Pinhead.

'I don't know. Why?'

'You tell me. Tell me why I'd want to know that,' she said, never taking her eyes off his.

'I don't know. Maybe you want me to paint the front door red,' Pinhead said, dead serious.

'I don't know what I'll do with you. Trouble. Always trouble and too clever for your own good. Seán, what have you to say?'

'Nothing. I don't like red paint,' I said. It kind of popped out of me and Pinhead sniggered.

Mrs Duffy's face changed then and I thought she was examining my neck and chin. I hoped the paint was gone.

'He'll lead you astray, do you know that, Seán? He'll get you into trouble and you'll be caught and he won't. Too clever by half,' she said, and then she walked away without smiling or making a joke like she usually did.

I laughed. Pinhead didn't.

But I wanted more. More excitement, another plan, something like this to look forward to, but when I said this to Pinhead, he never even answered. And then I said, 'Let's do the marble thing again, that's the best laugh ever.' And he said, 'No, my da's on the dry a full week now. We might never be able to do it again. He has to be drinking for it to work, you know that.'

There was a huge crowd on the Green that night. The bigger lads were playing soccer and we sat and watched them. It was still warm, like the middle of the day, and we only had T-shirts on. Pinhead arrived in his Levi's, with the little red tag on the arse pocket, and the UCLA sweatshirt. He looked great, the oul fucker.

'Date clothes, Pin?' I said, and everyone laughed, except Libby, who was sitting a bit away from us with Karen and Deirdre.

Pinhead laughed too and Enda came over then and asked Pinhead to play. They were short a centre forward and Pinhead was excellent at soccer but he didn't play it much because his da said it was a foreigner's game with no skill. I would have loved a game myself but the big lads never asked unless you were brilliant. So Pinhead played, himself and Enda on the same team, laughing and joking with each other and passing and dribbling the ball between them like it was the easiest thing in the world.

I stole glances at Karen during the match but she never looked my way, not once. I was annoyed with her over that. I mean, I gave her a really dear brooch and all and you'd think she'd be delighted with me. But like all the other girls, she was too busy watching Enda and Pinhead. It struck me then, just as Pinhead scored a lovely goal from a header, that he was one of them now, one of the bigger lads. I mean, he looked like one of them, he had shot up all of a sudden and his shoulders were broad and straight. I couldn't remember noticing that before. It's like he went to bed last night and woke up almost a man, and we were still boys waiting for that magic to happen to us.

When the match was over, Enda and Pinhead stood together on the green, deep in conversation, their heads almost touching, Enda's long hair falling over his eyes, him running his hand through it, and then leaning closer to Pinhead, like they were whispering. I couldn't take my eyes off them, even when Dodge started talking to me.

'That was a right laugh, the car. I had to keep a straight face and when Pinhead came over ... are you listening, Nod?'

I looked at Dodge and smiled at him and then let my

gaze rest again on Pinhead and Enda. I wanted to know what they were talking about that could be so interesting and I wanted to know why Pinhead never talked like that to me.

'But you have to hand it to him, Nod. He's afraid of no one, Pinhead isn't. I wish I'd his guts, even half his guts would do,' Dodge said, watching Pinhead and Enda too now.

Time Tunnel arrived then. She didn't come onto the Green, she stood a bit away on the footpath and never called out or anything. She had on that red miniskirt again. And Pinhead knew she was there. He didn't look around, but you could tell he knew by the way he started showing off talking to Enda, the laugh a little louder, the back straighter, a hand waving casually in mid-conversation. Then Enda punched him in the arm and they both laughed together as if there was a secret between them and Pinhead walked over to my cousin with that special half smile of his and I wanted to kick him up the hole, a good, hard fong up the arse.

I felt sorry for Libby as Pinhead walked away with Time Tunnel. She was sitting there pretending not to notice them but I could see her sneaking glances. We all sat together then on the Green, me next to Karen, but every time she spoke, every time she opened her mouth, I wanted to put my tongue inside it and I had to force myself not to, I had to force myself not to look at her mouth at all. I'd look like a right fool if I did something like that in front of a big crowd and she'd really hate me then, so I went home instead.

He spent every night with her after that, Pinhead did. We'd meet up on the Green or in Claughaun and we'd have a laugh and stuff and make plans for the night and then she would come. Never right into the middle of us, always hovering near, not needing to call out to him, and he would just walk away and wink over at me or wave his hand as he left. I was counting the days for her to be gone back to Dublin, for Pinhead to be around again. I mean, even when he was with us, he seemed to be only half there and Eyebrows slagged him and said, 'You're in love, Pinhead, you big eejit, it must be the oul spotty knickers', and Pinhead gave him a stare and then got up and left without saying a word, so we knew not to slag him any more.

Once when Pinhead was missing for a whole two days, I thought, this is it, he's gone now and he'll ask somebody else to go to the semi-final in Croke Park, he'll ask Enda or even her, and I couldn't stand that, if he asked her. So I called one evening.

Mr Duffy was in the kitchen making scrambled eggs. 'Are you all set for Sunday, lad? It's an early start, mind, the trains will be packed.'

'I am,' I said, and looked at Pinhead who was sitting having his tea.

He smiled at me. I was still going.

I spent a lot of time with Dodge. He wasn't Pinhead but he was better than Eyebrows and he liked girls. Eyebrows still hadn't copped the girl thing. He was a bit slow, so he probably wouldn't like girls till he was really old, like twenty or something. But Dodge did and he stole one of Enda's magazines that he kept hidden under his mattress and we took it down to Dodge's shed and boy was it something. We nearly died of shock when we saw all the women with nothing on. I mean, you could see everything, every single part of their bodies. It was weird at first but the more you looked, the more you liked it, and Dodge tore out a big double-page spread for me to keep. Susie was her name and she was pin-up of the month but I wouldn't be able to pin her up, she'd have to stay well hidden under my mattress. So we got to know all sorts of things about women's bodies in Dodge's shed. A perfect shed, tidier than our house, with everything labelled and in its right place. Even the nail jars had labels on them.

9

'Get up, Seán, it's Sunday, semi-final day, come on, ye'll miss the train, there's two left Colbert Station already, packed to the gills, I heard it on the radio, come on, out of it,' said my dad, the morning of the match.

I jumped out of bed and as I brushed my teeth I could smell rashers and sausages frying, and my dad whistling above the murmur of the radio in the kitchen. I was full of excitement, it was bubbling in my stomach and I couldn't stop grinning at myself in the mirror.

'Get that into you now, you'll need it for the long day ahead. Your mother made you sandwiches for later on. The weather looks good anyway,' said my dad when I came downstairs.

'Hmm,' I said. That was my usual answer since he hit me. A kind of half yes and a half no, it answered everything but answered nothing too.

'I'd say it'll be a great match. Limerick are in form but Kilkenny will give them a run for their money, no better team, the Kilkenny cats won't lie down too easy. Did you find the flag?'

I knew he was trying to make it up to me and for a second it nearly worked. I mean, I was going off to Croke Park and all and I was in a great mood. But then I remembered the slap, the feel of it on my face.

'Hmm,' I said through a mouthful of sausage and toast.

'Paddy Duffy is great to be bringing you. I must buy him a pint in Kelly's when I see him.'

'Hmm,' I said again. I never told him that he was on the dry, probably forever.

A baby cried upstairs. Somebody got out of bed. The toilet flushed.

'That's Máire, I'd know that cry anywhere,' he said, as he put more sausages on the sizzling pan.

I was just finishing my breakfast when Time Tunnel arrived in her dressing gown with a baby under her arm. It was Máire and I noticed for the first time that she had dark eyes exactly like my mam's. She was lovely.

Time Tunnel should have dressed herself, parading around our kitchen in the short little dressing gown, not like my mam's pink furry one that went all the way down to the floor. And in front of my dad and all. Fucking hoor, no wonder Pinhead was like a dog in heat around the oul bitch. I grabbed my packed lunch and headed off.

'Wait, Seán, here's a few bob for you,' said my dad, rooting in his pocket for change.

'Hmm,' I said as I took the money and skirted out of the house.

She called me back as I reached the gate. 'Forgot something?' she asked, her head to one side, her big mouth in a little half smile, a little sneer. Máire was still under her arm and her other hand was behind her back.

'No. Fuck off,' I said and was just about to turn when she pulled out my green and white flag.

'There,' she said.

I made a grab for it but she held it close to her chest, so I was forced to go nearer. I stepped closer and grabbed the flag and as I did she caught my face with her free hand and bent her head and kissed me quickly on the lips, her tongue flicking mine just for a second.

'Give that to him for me,' she said then and laughed as I wiped my mouth with the sleeve of my sweatshirt.

'Fuck off hoor,' I said and ran down the path to Pinhead's.

The station was a sea of green when we got there.

Green hats and badges and flags all on the platform for the train to Dublin. Mr Duffy knew the railway men and they nodded and called out to him, so we got great seats with a table and all and it was a direct train, a special for the match, so we didn't have to change at Limerick Junction. There was even a bar on the train and a trolley that served tea and coffee and stuff.

It was noisy, though. Some of the men were drinking already and over the journey the noise grew louder, louder even than a pub. But Mr Duffy just had tea when the trolley came, he never went near the bar at all, and I believed Pinhead then about us never doing the marble thing again. Maybe we could do it to Uncle Pat, I thought, but that wouldn't be the same, he was too old for a chase.

'Have anything ye want, lads,' Mr Duffy said when the trolley came our way.

A young boy, smaller than Pinhead, with a white shirt and a dicky bow, pushed the trolley through the crowded train and we flipped a coin to see if he was a steamer or not and Pinhead said, 'Heads he's a steamer, and tails he's a steamer', and we laughed. The boy couldn't win. But we took Mr Duffy at his word and we had Coke and Taytos and currant cake.

The countryside flew by in a green blur and Mr Duffy read the *Sunday Press*, a fag in his brown fingers. The drinkers were singing by now and Pinhead did a great impression of a drunk, but his da told him to stop in case any of them thought they were being mocked. I never said a word to Pinhead, the whole way to Dublin, about Time Tunnel. And I never passed on her message either. No chance.

We walked to Croke Park. You didn't need directions, you just followed the seas of green and black and amber all going the same way.

'It's massive, isn't it?' said Pinhead as we walked through the streets.

You could feel the excitement in the air, like something alive that hovered over the throngs of people.

'It's brilliant! I'd love to live here,' I said as I tried to take it all in and walk at the same time.

'Yep, so would I, Nod, so would I.'

'Sure you might be soon, the way you're running after my cousin,' I said before I could stop myself.

'I'll give you a year,' Pinhead said, and then he laughed.

I didn't know what he meant but I pretended I did and laughed along with him. We had lost sight of Mr Duffy in the crowd and we ran to catch up with him.

The street near Croke Park was a huge mass of people and colours, and hawkers selling everything from chips and icecream to flags and badges. Some were selling tickets for ten times their original price. We made our way in through the turnstiles and towards the Hogan Stand. We found our seats halfway up the stand and Pinhead said he thought he saw the President of Ireland and he pointed him out, but it was just an ordinary man, so I didn't believe him. You had a great view of everything from the stands and didn't have to get up or anything or peer through people's arses.

When the Limerick team came out, I thought my heart would burst and we cheered and screamed till we were hoarse. But nothing was as good as the roar of the crowd and the first puck of the ball after we all sang 'Amhrán na bhFiann'. It was deafening, that roar, and it made my ears go funny and I thought I'd faint or die with pride and excitement. And Limerick didn't let us down, not for one minute in the first half. The game was so fast that if you looked around you at all, if you took your eyes off the game for a second, you'd miss something, a brilliant point, a great save or even a goal. Kilkenny were dirty players though, and when they tried to take the legs from under Pat Haran, Mr Duffy roared at the ref, 'Ye blind bastard ye, go and put on a pair of glasses!'

Every time Limerick scored, a sea of green and white flags would go up and it looked like a giant blanket being waved in the stand. We must win, we must win, I chanted in my head as Kilkenny rushed forward at the close of the first half, but Joe McCarthy had eyes in the back of his head and stopped them dead in their tracks and we gave a big cheer when the half-time whistle went. We were leading by two points.

'We'll win, won't we?' I said to Mr Duffy when the teams left the pitch.

'Two points is nothing in hurling. They should be well up on Kilkenny, they missed a pile of chances,' he said.

Pinhead was looking at a glamorous, big-chested woman in the seat across from us.

'But we'll win, we're better than them. Our hurling is better,' I said.

'We're better but are we hungry enough? That's what wins you the championship matches, hunger. The hurling comes after that,' Mr Duffy said as he lit up a fag.

The sun was hot and men had hankies on their heads for shade. Pinhead and me joined the queue at the drinks stand and missed the start of the second half. We didn't see the beaut of a goal from Eamon Grehan, the team captain, that set Limerick up for the game. I was never at a match before where you could relax knowing your team was going to win. It wasn't as exciting as other matches, where there's only a point or two in it and it could turn at any second till the final whistle, but there was a kind of luxury about it. To be able to think of the pleasure of winning before the match was over. The Limerick fans were celebrating for the last ten minutes of the game and we sang our hearts out as our team beat back Kilkenny time and time again.

Just before the end, Mr Duffy brought us right down onto the sideline. We waited there until the ref blew the final whistle and then we charged onto the pitch, thousands of Limerick fans, and the men carried the players on their shoulders. Then Mr Duffy grabbed our arms and hauled us through the crowd to meet Grehan. He was surrounded by people but when he saw us coming, he put his arms around Pinhead and me, one of us on each side of him. A photographer with a big camera snapped a picture as he hugged us. They carried the captain away then, high on their shoulders, and the photographer asked us our names.

Pinhead's da had to drag us away from Croke Park, we didn't want it all to end, but the crowds started to thin out and people were leaving in droves, and he said, 'Come on, lads, we'll find somewhere to eat before we get the train.'

When we got near the station, he said, 'We'll eat here, they do pub grub. There's tables out at the side and we can have our dinner there', and he went in the door of the pub.

Bourke's, it was called, Bourke's Inn, serving pub grub seven days a week. That's what it said over the door. We didn't follow him in, we stood at the door and didn't say anything, but I knew Pinhead was thinking the same as me – bars and Mr Duffy could be big trouble – and I swore to myself that if he had a few drinks, I wouldn't be sitting anywhere near him on the train home. Not within pissing distance anyway. So we sat outside at a wooden picnic table with an umbrella that said Harp all the way round it, Pinhead watching the door for his da.

'It was a great match, Pin,' I said to take his mind off it. 'I'd love to get that picture of us with Eamon Grehan.'

'Yep.' That was his answer. He never took his eyes off the door.

'I never had pub grub. I wonder what it's like?'

'Dunno.' He didn't even look my way.

And then he came, Mr Duffy did, with a tray of steaming food. Chips and steak-and-kidney pies and bottles of Coke and a big pot of tea.

'The queue in there was unbelievable. Everybody had the same idea as us – Bourke's is so near the station. Come on, help yourselves, it smells lovely, so it does.'

'Thanks, Da,' said Pinhead. 'It smells great and I'm starving. I'd eat a horse.'

Pinhead slept on the train home. I talked to his da for a while but his eyes started to drop too, so I sat there like a guard watching over the Duffys all the way back to Limerick. Pinhead was sitting next to me and his sleeping head had fallen on my shoulder. I could feel the warmth of his body and his breath deep and even. He smelled of sweat and chips and he had long curly eyelashes exactly like a girl's. I never noticed that before. They were black against his tanned skin.

I shook him awake as we came into Colbert Station. 'We're home, come on, you eejit, wake up.'

Pinhead was still half-asleep when we walked out of the station. Mr Duffy was ahead of us and stopped to talk to someone in the line of taxis outside. He turned back then and called us. 'Come on, lads, a taxi home for ye. We did enough walking today. Come on, in ye get.'

I climbed into the back seat, delighted with myself. I mean, it isn't every day you get to go home in a taxi. Pinhead sat in beside me and we waited for the father to get in the front but that never happened. Instead, he paid the driver and said, 'Good luck now, lads, I'm going to get the racing results. Christy will drive ye home to the door.' And then he was gone, just like that. Pinhead never said a word the whole way home.

There was bad news the next day. I saw the postman walking up our path whistling, a bunch of letters in his hands. I took the post and gave it to my mam and didn't know then that one of those letters would have very bad news for me. If I'd known, I could have kept it or burnt it and maybe that would have been the end of it, but I just handed them all to my mam and there was no going back then. I ate my cornflakes standing up as usual and I glared at Time Tunnel and mouthed fuck off at her like I always did when she said, 'Good morning, shrimp.' And then my mam came into the kitchen beaming. She had the letter in her hand. She was waving it in the air.

'Well done, I knew you could do it! You get it from our side,' she said to me. 'Your father will be so proud of you.'

I smiled at her. I mean, I had to with all this praise, but I didn't know what it was I was supposed to have done. I smiled and waited for her to tell me.

'You got in, Seán. You got the entrance exam to St Munchin's College. Imagine that! Isn't he great, Marian? It's very hard to get in there. Well done,' she said again and wrapped her arms around me.

My smile was gone now, well gone. I had forgotten all about it. About Burke, our teacher, telling me to sit the exam, about doing the fuckin' thing. I was going to the Tech with Pinhead. We were looking forward to it, going to school in town and doing metalwork and having a laugh. And spotting the Laurel Hill girls and getting one of their scarves to wear. They were like trophies, those Laurel Hill scarves. Enda had one. Pinhead had said, 'Just sit the exam, Nod, and make a balls of it and you'll keep them all happy and still go to the Tech. I mean, there's only steamers and rugby players in Munchin's, no hurling and no girls' school near you, so just fuck up the exam and you'll be flying it.' And that's what I was going to do till the exam was in front of me and I knew all the answers, easy stuff, and before I knew it, I had it finished and handed in.

'Seán, say something. You must be delighted with yourself!' Mam said.

I wasn't delighted with myself. I was sick to my stomach. I didn't want to go to a steamers' school and wear a uniform and play dumb rugby.

'I might be better off in the Tech. They do no metalwork in Munchin's, they do rugby instead of metalwork,' I said.

'Don't be silly! Of course they do metalwork. It's a very good school and I'm so proud you got in. I can't wait to tell your father,' she said and wiped floury hands on her apron.

The babies cried upstairs and I escaped out the front door and ran straight to Pinhead's. I thought he would be upset for me, that he'd understand and would think of a plan and everything would be all right, but he laughed. He doubled over laughing, tears coming to his eyes, and Uncle Pat came into the kitchen and he laughed too, though he didn't know what was so funny. And neither did I. Mrs Duffy came in then and Pinhead told her through bursts of laughing that I was going to a steamers' school, but she knuckled him across the head and said, 'Well done, Seán, you'll do really well, I know you will', and I got a reddener and was relieved when Pinhead said, 'Let's go fishing. We'll go on the bike, the two of us.'

The bike was under the stairs in Pinhead's hall because the tinkers were breaking into people's sheds and stealing bikes and saws and stuff. Mr Duffy's CIE jacket was thrown over it and his toolbox was on the saddle. We had no maggots but Pinhead said that we'd use other stuff or dig up worms when we got there. I carried the rods and

Pinhead cycled, and off we went out the Corbally Road to Clonlara.

St Munchin's College kind of sneaked up on us. One minute we were cycling along the road and the next minute Pinhead had swerved in through the gates and was pedalling up the long, tree-lined drive, laughing at my shouts to turn around.

It looked like a prison. A redbrick prison in the middle of nowhere, with hundreds of windows. Pinhead had stopped laughing.

'Jesus Christ, a jail. A fuckin' jail, Nod, look,' he said as we got off the bike.

'I know. Miles from town, no escape at all. How did I let this happen?'

'I told you what to do, you ghoul. Fuck up the test. Why didn't you?'

'I did, I thought I did,' I lied. I couldn't tell him that I enjoyed the exam. That it was a thrill to get stuff right.

'Then you mustn't be very good at fucking things up. You failed that test, you ghoul, how to be a good fucker-upper,' he said.

'So what do I do now? Any plans?'

'Nope. Can't think of a single thing to do. You went into that test and you had to show us all just how fuckin' clever you are, me and Dodge and Eyebrows, all of us. So you're so fuckin' clever now, you think of a plan all by yourself, wanker,' he said, dead serious all of a sudden. 'You'll have to practise being a steamer, that's all. A rugby-playing steamer.' And he climbed back on the bike.

I didn't believe him, though, that he had no plan. He always had a plan.

As we cycled home up St Patrick's Road, Enda called us from his gate. 'Hey hang on a minute, will ye?' he said and ran into the house.

He had patches on the arse of his Levi's and I said to

Pinhead, 'Jesus, he needs a new pair of jeans', and Pinhead said, 'You eejit, that's the fashion, they rip them themselves and sew on patches and stuff.' I thought that was a stupid thing to be doing, trying to make a grand new pair of jeans look old, but I didn't say so.

Enda came back waving a newspaper, a big smile on his face. 'Look lads, ye're famous!' he said.

And there was me and Pinhead on the front page of the *Evening Press*, with Eamon Grehan between us and a big headline, 'Limerick Rout Kilkenny', right across the top of the picture. We raced home with Enda's paper and we stopped at Pinhead's first.

'Ma, look at this, look at this! Da! Where's Da?' Pinhead shouted as we ran into the hall.

All the Duffy children had gathered around us and Mrs Duffy came out of the kitchen wiping her hands on a tea towel.

'What is it? Oh look at the two of ye! Isn't that great, right on the front page and all,' she said, taking the paper from me to have a closer look.

'Where's Da, is he still at work? He'll be over the moon!' said Pinhead.

'He must be doing overtime. He'll be home soon. God, it's great, isn't it?' she said.

We were standing in the hall right next to Mr Duffy's CIE jacket. One of the little Duffy girls was sitting on his toolbox.

'Come on, let's show them over in my house,' I said to Pinhead, and we ran out the door again.

My dad was standing in our garden with a crowd of neighbours. They were all looking at the front page of the *Evening Press*, which he held in his hand. There was a whole bunch of papers on the doorstep beside him.

'There they are now, the two stars. We'll have to ask them for their autographs next!' he said laughing. 'Look, I bought all the copies in Mac's shop. He had to ring to get more in. Here, Kevin, take a couple of copies for your house. We'll have to send this up to Dublin and over to Chester to your Uncle Matt, he'll love this.'

'It's a great picture, isn't it, Dad!' I said before I could stop myself. His eyes lit up for a second and I stopped smiling at him and ran past him into our house.

My mam was in the kitchen with Time Tunnel. 'I saw it, Seánie, the picture. You're so handsome in it and you too, Kevin, like two film stars, the two of ye. Aren't they, Marian?' she said.

Time Tunnel hadn't spotted Pinhead behind me until my mam spoke and she did the fluttery hoor thing with her eyelashes when she saw him standing in the hall. He did his half smile thing at her. I wanted to vomit.

'Come on, Pin, we'll show it to the lads,' I said and went out the door, not waiting for him to answer.

But Pinhead went missing again that night and I knew he was with her, even though I hadn't seen them together. I wanted him to share the fame with me, to hang around the Green and lord it over the lads, especially the bigger guys, but there was no fun doing it alone, so when my mam asked me to go to Mac's for two pints of milk, I didn't crib like normal. She gave me sixpence to spend on myself.

It had just stopped raining and Pinhead's dog Jesse followed me, jumping up and tripping me all the time. A man was coming towards us on St Patrick's Road and Jesse took off in a flying tear at him. First I thought the dog was going to attack him, but then I realised it was Mr Duffy and I ran after the dog to tell him about our picture, to see if he knew. As I got closer I saw that he was staggering a little, tottering on his feet and reaching out for the wall to steady himself.

'Mr Duffy, did you see it? Did you see the picture?' I

called out as I got near him.

He looked at me, stared right at me, but he might as well have been looking at the wall beside him. There was no recognition in his eyes, they were blank, and he turned his head away and concentrated on trying to walk. I stood outside Mac's shop watching his slow progress down St Patrick's Road, swaying from side to side and making a grab for the wall every few steps. Poor Jesse was in between the two of us, trying to decide which one to follow, but he came back to me in the end and licked my hand.

10

There was going to be some kind of party. I had only heard rumours, nobody asked me to go, but one of the bigger lads, Jamesy Moran, had a free house, his family were gone to Kilkee for the weekend. That's all I knew until Karen called to my front door out of the blue. I'm glad I answered because she had the marble brooch on and I didn't want my mam to see it.

'Hi stranger,' she said.

I was speechless and mortified, but I closed the door behind me and walked out the path with her.

'Did you hear anything about the free house tomorrow night?' she asked as we sat on the Green.

'No,' I said.

'Jamesy Moran, you know him, the tall skinny fella, well, it's his party.'

'Is that right?' I said, too embarrassed to look at her face.

'Want to come with me?'

'Yes,' I said too quickly.

She smiled, then narrowed her eyes. 'No funny stuff.'

'No funny stuff,' I said and laughed.

'It'll be great. Enda is bringing his guitar and you have to be asked, so the messers won't be there.'

'So who else is going?' I asked.

'Oh everyone really. Pinhead's going. Didn't he say anything to you? I think he's taking your cousin. I hate that bitch over what she did to Libby. A cow is all she is.'

Pinhead did stuff to Libby too, but I didn't want to point this out to Karen as I was back in her good books and wanted to stay there. And Pinhead was a shit for not saying anything about the free house.

'Will I call down for you so, tomorrow night?' I said.

'No, don't do that. Libby's going with us too and I don't want her to feel like a gooseberry. I'll meet you there around eight, is that OK?'

'That's grand,' I answered.

It wasn't grand. I'd have to walk in on my own with all the bigger lads there and Libby was coming with us. It wasn't grand at all.

I told my mam I was going to Dodge's. That his mother and father were going out and he had to mind the house, so I was keeping him company. She fell for it, but it helped that she had a baby in each arm and Colm and Brian in the bath when I asked her.

Time Tunnel spent the day getting ready for the party. I mean, it was just a free house, not a fuckin' proper party, but she didn't know the difference. The make-up was extra thick and my mam said she'd catch her death in that miniskirt, even though it was roasting out. I had to wait hours for the bathroom and then she smirked when she came out, and I said low, so my mam wouldn't hear, 'Fuck off hoor.' She just laughed at that.

I stood outside Jamesy Moran's house for ages, trying to work up the courage to knock on the door. I could hear voices and laughing inside and music on the record player. Then a crowd of fellas that I half knew came along, so I kind of sneaked in with them and hid behind them in the hall. Some were carrying bags and I could hear the rattle of bottles.

I followed the crowd into the sitting room and stood by the wall, trying to look invisible. People were sprawled everywhere, on the sofa and chairs and floor. Enda was in the corner playing the guitar and a group of people, mostly girls, were sitting around him. I could see Angela Walsh drinking a bottle of beer on the chair next to him.

And then I saw Pinhead. He was on the sofa with Time Tunnel and he pretended he didn't see me, I was sure of that. I was standing there like an eejit and then I realised that I was the youngest and that made me even more uncomfortable. I was just going to slink out the door when Karen came in with Libby.

We made space on the floor for ourselves and sat down and listened to Enda singing for a while. Then someone put a record on, loud rock stuff, and everybody got louder then, like the music was a signal. Most of them were drinking now and smoking fags and when Pinhead came over and offered me a bottle of beer, I didn't answer him. I pretended I couldn't hear him and got up to look for the jacks. I wanted to go home.

Enda and Angela Walsh were gone when I came back from the toilet and the noise from the sitting room was mad. The record player was blaring but it was the voices that were the worst, shouting and screaming above the music. A couple of fellas were drunk, and when Pisspot tried to stand up, he vomited all over the carpet and I said, 'Karen, I'm going home, this is stupid', and she said, 'Hang on another half-hour, it's a laugh, Seán, and anyway I can't leave Libby.'

At first I didn't notice that Pinhead was alone. I mean, sitting alone for a long time with no sign of Time Tunnel, and when she came back into the room, Jamesy followed her and they stood talking and whispering in the far corner. Fuckin' bitch.

I stole a glance at Pinhead to see if he'd noticed, but he was looking the other way. And then she did a lousy thing, the oul hoor. Jamesy and herself started French kissing right there in front of everyone and I got up straight away and said, 'I'm going, Karen', and she whispered fiercely into my ear, 'This is the good part, you fool. Libby wants to see this.' I looked over again and they were still at it, halfway down each other's throats now, and a hush had come over the room and the needle on the record player was making a noise over and over because it had run out of LP.

I was just about to leave when Pinhead got up from the sofa and walked out, shoulders hunched. He didn't run, just walked, trying to be casual, and I was glad about that. Karen grabbed me as I tried to follow him and said, 'Let him go, Seán, he deserved it, you came with me', but I shook her off and ran after him.

He was walking very fast and I was out of breath by the time I caught up with him. We walked together but never spoke or anything. We were turning the corner to our road when he stopped and grabbed my arm. There was a streetlamp overhead and I could see his eyes, black and angry in the yellow light.

'A fuckin' ghoul with a hoor's mouth,' he said. And then he started laughing and I laughed too. All the way home to the front door.

'Where were you till this hour?' my dad said when I went in. 'Where were you and don't tell me you were in Dodge's house because I called down there, you liar.' He was shouting now and I moved back a bit but looked straight at him. I wasn't afraid.

'And where's Marian? Your mother is worried sick. Jesus, it's quarter past twelve. Where is she?'

I shrugged my shoulders and turned away but he grabbed me by the arm as I tried to get past him.

'Answer me, you little scut, where's your cousin?'

'I don't know. How am I supposed to know?' I said and shook his hand away. I hated Time Tunnel but I wouldn't squeal, never.

My mam came into the kitchen then with a baby in her arms. Her face was all worry. 'Is she with Kevin? Tell us, Seán, it's very late,' she said, her voice soft and gentle.

I wanted to tell her then but I couldn't. I shrugged instead.

'I'll go over to the Duffys,' said my dad and went out the door.

'Go on up to bed now, go on, Seán. I'm sick and tired of this carry on, out all day and all night. I don't know what's got into you lately. Get out of my sight, up to bed,' she said. Her voice wasn't angry, just tired.

I felt ashamed. It would have been easier if she'd been shouting and roaring at me. But I wasn't going to bed. I wanted to wait up for the return of Time Tunnel. I wanted to see her squirm for a change, so I went upstairs and waited on the landing step.

They were ages and I knew then that Pinhead hadn't told either and that my dad had to go looking for himself. When I heard his key in the door, I nearly fell down the stairs trying to see what was going on.

My mam went out to the hall as they came in. 'You found her, thanks be to God! Where in the name of God were you until this hour, Marian? What would your mother say about this? You'll be on the first bus back home in the morning, mark my words,' she said, her voice now cold and angry and quiet.

I slid down another couple of steps for a better look. I could see them clearly through the banisters.

'A bloody party in Morans', and them gone away to Kilkee. The guards and all were called just as I got there. Bloody disgrace. Drinking and cavorting, disgusted I am,' said my dad.

Time Tunnel had her head turned to the side, towards me, and her big mouth was smeared with lipstick. I was grinning by now.

'She says Seán was there too but she's lying because Kevin said they were in his shed all night, fixing up a bike. He even showed me the bike, he did. Bloody disgracing us, you'll have a fine name around the place after this, young lady,' said my dad, his voice rising with every word.

He believed Pinhead and that was good. Pinhead was a brilliant liar. I nearly believed we were fixing up a bike all night myself.

'Bed, this minute,' said my mam, just as a baby started crying upstairs.

I scrambled up the stairs and when I heard Time Tunnel coming up and heading for the bathroom, I said, 'Fucking oul hoor' from behind my bedroom door and she nearly jumped out of her knickers with the fright.

So she left the next day. It was a Saturday and Pinhead called in the morning for me and I told him what happened when Dad brought her home. He was laughing, but quietly, to himself almost, and we lay on our bellies on the Green, watching my house. Time Tunnel came out. Dad was carrying her suitcase and a taxi was waiting to bring them to the station. We got up and stood at the wall, whispering and laughing as Dad put the case in the boot of the car. She was sitting in the back seat, looking straight ahead, and when my father went back into the house to tell my mam they were leaving, Time Tunnel rolled down the window.

'Come here,' she said to Pinhead.

Like a fool, he went over. She grabbed his face with her two hands and kissed him on the mouth right in front of me and the taxi driver. Then my dad came back and she rolled up the window and never looked our way, even when the car pulled off and my mam and little brothers were calling her and waving. 'Good riddance, hoor,' I said, and Pinhead looked at me with his half smile and touched his lips where she had kissed him and said, 'Nice.' That's all he said. Nice.

It rained for days after she left. Slow, steady drizzle that clung to everything and was wetter than if it had flogged down. By the end of the week I had forgotten what summer felt like, forgotten the fierce heat of the sun on your skin and milk going sour and the smell of tar melting. I was locked up in the house with all the babies. I tried to read, but I had lost the habit of reading and found it hard to finish even one page. Even of *Lord of the Rings*.

I called for Pinhead a few times but he always seemed to be in Dodge's house. This was strange because Pinhead would never call there if he could help it. So, on my third time calling for him, when Deirdre said, 'He's in Dodge's, tell him he's wanted for his dinner', I decided to call down to Dodge's to get him. O'Riordan's car wasn't in the drive. The mother answered the door when I knocked.

'Is Dodge ... I mean, James, is James there please?' I asked. I didn't want to ask for Pinhead straight away, seeing as it was Dodge's house, like.

She rubbed her thin pale hands together, like she was just going to say a few prayers, right there in the doorway in front of me. 'No, he's gone to his cousin's in Caherconlish for the day.'

'Oh,' I said, and stood there waiting for her to add more. Like where the fuck was Pinhead.

'I'll tell him you called but he'll be late getting home, so it's best not to call again till tomorrow,' she said, and folded her skinny arms across her chest, waiting for me to go.

I could hear Enda upstairs, playing the guitar. 'Thanks,' I said and walked out the path.

The door closed behind me and I heard Enda's voice laughing. And then I heard another voice, a voice I'd know anywhere. Then there was two guitars. Two guitars and I knew. I shivered in the damp, misty rain and a knot of jealousy kept coming up my throat but I forced it

down. I swallowed it back down. And then it just burst
out of me like vomit.

'Fuckin' sneaky cunts,' I said to the footpath outside
Dodge's drive. 'Fuckin' cunts,' I said again, but louder this
time, not afraid of the feeling any more.

I sat on the wall at the top of the road and waited for
Pinhead to come out of the house. I knew he wouldn't be
long because O'Riordan was due home from work soon.
And I was right. He came sauntering out after only a few
minutes and smiled and waved when he saw me. He
didn't even fuckin' care that he was a sneak. A fuckin'
snake in the grass. Well I cared and I wasn't going to hang
around with one and I'd tell him right to his face.

'I never knew you could be such a sneaky fucker.
Learning the guitar and not even saying it to me,' I said,
and the second I'd said it I was sorry.

He shrugged. 'What's up, Nod?' He looked at me in
shock, his eyes and mouth big circles of surprise.

I wanted to cry. And then he started laughing. First his
mouth cracked into a smile that grew across his face and
then the laugh started somewhere down in his stomach
and then he doubled over laughing. 'Oh Nod, you're
fucking mad, you are. A fuckin' madman!' he said.

I was smiling, but only because it's very hard not to
smile when someone is falling around laughing in front
of you.

Pinhead wiped tears of laughter from his eyes. 'Are you
jealous?' he said suddenly.

My face went bright red and the more I tried to stop it,
the worse it got.

'Jealous? Of you learning the guitar? I am in my hole,'
I said, but I knew my reddener was a giveaway.

'Are you a steamer?' he said then, his face serious
now.

I gave him one of his own stares. I held his eyes with

mine and he was the one that finally gave in. I'd beaten him for the first time.

He smiled at me, and swung the guitar case he was holding. 'I bought it out of my Salthill winnings and Enda's teaching me.'

'You never said anything.' I could hear the little whine of jealousy in my voice again and I knew he did too by the way he cocked his head to one side.

'I didn't see you and, anyway, I said it ages ago about wanting to learn.' His eyes examined my face.

'Where did you buy the guitar?' I asked as we started to head home.

'I heard Rasher Hanrahan was selling one, so I went down and bought it off him. Enda came with me and said it was a bargain.'

'Is it hard?'

'What?' he said, a sly grin on his face.

I laughed. 'Learning the guitar, you ghoul, is it hard?'

'Not too bad. Enda is fuckin' brilliant and a great laugh. I never knew that about him.'

'You never said a thing.'

'Do I have to tell you everything, Nod? Every fuckin' thing I do?' The laugh was gone out of his voice.

I didn't answer him and kept my eyes on the road in front of me.

'You know why I'm learning, don't you?'

'I don't. You want to join a band, something like that.'

'Nope. It's great for pulling the women. Enda agreed with me about that.'

'How?'

'Nod, you walk into a room and any oul fucker could be in the corner strumming a guitar and crooning and he'll have a gang of women at his feet, like bloody Jesus Christ!'

'So you want to be Jesus Christ?'

'No, smart-arse. Look, remember at Jamesy Moran's

party? Remember Enda and all the fucking birds sitting around adoring him? All of them, Libby, Karen, Deirdre, Angela Walsh. They loved him, so they did.'

'So you want to be Enda.'

'Fuck off, you bollocks.'

'So what are you going to do?'

'About what?'

'About your ugly face, that'll have to go for a start.'

'Bastard,' said Pinhead, but he was laughing as he turned into his garden, swinging the guitar in its black plastic cover.

The rain stopped the next evening just after tea and I went to Pinhead's, thinking we'd be able to go out for a while. I could hear shouting and crying as I walked down his path but I thought it was coming from another house. I was just about to knock the back door when I heard Mrs Duffy's voice inside.

'I'll send them down to Kelly's for their dinner, Arthur Guinness will feed them, God knows you've given him enough money this past few weeks,' she said.

I could see her standing inside the frosted glass of the door and Pinhead's da slumped down at the kitchen table. He had his head in his hands.

'You'll be the first person fired from CIE, the first person sacked. I'll have to go out to work myself at this rate. I need my wages and the children going back to school. Are you listening to me at all?' She was shouting at him now and I could see her shaking his arm. I stood at the side of the door so they wouldn't see me. I was too embarrassed to knock.

'You selfish bastard,' she said then, and went out of the kitchen and banged the door nearly off its hinges.

He never moved at all and then I copped he was sound asleep. There wasn't a child to be seen anywhere, so I went home.

None of the lads seemed to be around now. Dodge was in Caherconlish a lot and Eyebrows had to go working with his da on the milk van. And Pinhead. Well, Pinhead was a different story. He was with Enda all the time, learning the guitar, and I thought with all the fuckin' practice he was getting, he wouldn't need to go to the Tech at all. He could just walk straight into a job in a rock band. And when he wasn't at Enda's, he never called for me. Like he forgot about me, his best fucking friend ever. So, after calling for Pinhead loads of times, I decided that I had my pride too and I'd sit it out at home with all the pissy arses until he called for me again.

I only had to wait a couple of days, but it seemed much longer. There was Pinhead at my door, as brazen as you like, as if he had seen me only five minutes ago. I wasn't going to go out, I was going to tell him I didn't feel like it and to call back tomorrow. But he was there in front of me with that huge grin on his face, a grin that promised the world. A baby cried upstairs and that decided it for me.

I could have sworn he had grown a whole six inches in that few days and I knew there was something different about his face. It took me a while to realise he was getting a moustache. I mean, you would have to examine him closely to see it – very light and hard to notice with his dark skin, but definitely there all the same. I was jealous and never said anything to him but he saw me looking and knew and gave me that smile.

We headed for the Green with Dodge's soccer ball. The bigger lads were there already but they had no ball and they had to let us play with them, which was good, except they put me in goal. I hated doing goal. I mean, if you were stupid in goal, everybody could see, but at least I got a game. The girls came during the match. I could hear them laughing behind me as Pinhead made a run on my goal. He scored too, the bastard, and smirked at me when Enda said, 'Well done, Pin, good shot.'

After the match we stood around for a while and it wasn't till everyone said, 'See ya, Nod, good luck' that I copped what was going on. Karen and Deirdre walked off arm in arm, throwing me dirty slitty-eyed looks as they passed me. They were best friends now and I was on their hate list. Sometimes I detested girls, they just never made sense, and no matter what you did, you couldn't win unless you were Pinhead or Enda and had the magic that girls loved. Libby, the fool, was hanging out of Pinhead again. I was standing there like a spare prick and they were all walking off. I went home then by myself and swore to God I would never like a girl again for the rest of my life. They weren't worth the trouble.

I didn't believe it would happen until I was standing in Denis Moran's shop on Friday. I thought right up to that minute something would stop it or Munchin's would send a letter saying it was all a big mistake. Or that Pinhead would come up with a plan. But I stood in Moran's with my mam hovering around me and the new uniform on me, the shirt collar stiff and choking and grey pants that only a steamer would wear.

'It's lovely on you. Perfect. You're so grown up in it,' she said, and I thought for a second there were tears in her eyes. Spare me.

'I'm not going there,' I said, but she just looked at the shop assistant and both of them laughed.

'I'll take socks and a couple of vests as well,' she said to the salesman.

'I'm not going to a steamers' school. I hate rugby. I'm not going and you can't make me. I mean it. I'm not going. That's it. End of story.'

'Watch your mouth, Seán, there's no need for language like that. I'll take another shirt. I'll need the two,' she said.

The salesman nodded in agreement.

I gave her hell after that. She brought me to O'Sullivan's to get new school shoes and I cursed and swore while the woman there was measuring my feet, and when she came out with a pair of ugly black brogues, I said, 'What the fuck do you think I am, a fucking culchie?' and my mam gave me a stare better than any I had ever done to the Sacred Heart. But like the uniform, the shoes were bought too and I knew then the more we bought, the more certain it was I would be going to school in Munchin's. Our last stop was O'Mahony's bookshop and that was the final nail in the coffin, I knew it and my mam did too. I didn't say another word the whole way home, not even when she stopped to buy me chips at the Golden Grill.

I called for Pinhead later that night. I was rehearsing what was going to say as I knocked on his back door because I wanted to make him feel bad for letting me down after the soccer match. His mam answered the door and brought me into the kitchen.

'He'll be down in a minute. He's going to the shop for me,' she said as she washed dishes in the sink.

Pinhead came in then and I knew by his face and how quiet he was that something big had happened. He had his nail jar in his hand, the one he kept his life savings in. The top of it was jagged where it had been smashed open. He looked hurt and I knew that if he was younger or on his own, he would be crying. The jar was almost empty, all the notes were gone and the silver and copper was down to a few half-crowns and pennies. I couldn't bear to look at him, so I looked away, out the small kitchen window, as if nothing was happening.

'Ah Jesus, not your money box, he didn't have a go at your money box,' said Mrs Duffy and reached out to him.

He shrugged her hand away and put the broken jar on the table. 'Eggs and milk, is that it?' he asked her, and put his hand into the jar for a half-crown. 'Right so, Nod?' he said to me and we left.

I never said a word to him about his life savings. I never said a word because you just didn't with Pinhead, but I knew this was the worst thing that had happened to him, even worse than Mossy Sheehan killing the birds. That Friday night walking to the shop it was the worst thing that could have happened. But that was only true until Monday. Everything changed on Monday.

11

The mushrooms were out. We knew because we saw old Baldy O'Brien with a Besco bag full to the brim on Sunday. We should have known they would be out after the week of rain but we slipped up somehow. You could make great money off mushrooms but you had to be in there first supplying Balls of Flour. That Sunday night the four of us played cards in Pinhead's shed. We were playing for money, not matches, and you kind of knew Pinhead wasn't going to be poor for very long and that he must have got a new nail jar, because he was cleaning us out.

'Four o'clock tomorrow morning,' Pinhead said as he pocketed the last of his winnings.

We all looked at each other.

He laughed. 'Four o'clock. We'll meet at the railway gates then and head out the Bloodmill. Baldy O'Brien said the mushrooms were great there this morning. I hope the old wanker didn't pick them all.'

'Jesus, why are we going looking for mushrooms in the middle of the night? We won't be able to see them if it's still dark. Seven o'clock is plenty time,' said Dodge.

'Four o'clock sharp. I know where the best fields are and we'll have a long walk. I'm leaving at four, are you on, Nod?' he asked turning to look at me.

'Yeah, first come, first served. They'll all be out tomorrow after seeing Baldy coming home. A crowd saw him on their way back from early Mass,' I said.

Dodge threw his eyes up to heaven but he knew it was agreed. Four o'clock.

I never woke in time. I spent half the night in bed worrying about not waking and then I must have gone into a really deep sleep because I woke with a fright to stones being thrown at my window. There was Pinhead below in the garden, his pockets stuffed with Besco bags. It was dark outside, except for the yellow light of a streetlamp. I grinned at him and dressed myself without switching on the light, careful not to wake Colm and Brian. I brought Pinhead into our kitchen and we both ate a bowl of cornflakes, skitting at the effort of staying quiet. We were just heading towards the railway gates when we heard a noise behind us and there was Jesse after getting out somehow, tail wagging, tongue hanging out, delighted that he'd found us. Pinhead went mad.

'Fuck off home, you ghoul. He'll frighten the cows. He'll chase them and the farmers will kill us,' he said, pushing the dog around to face home.

Jesse cocked his ears and then licked Pinhead's face and ran off ahead.

'He'll be grand, leave him, it'll take too long to bring him back home now,' I said.

All the houses were silent and dark around us. The moon was out and it was going to be a good day, you could tell from the sky smattered with stars. The air was still, no wind at all, and warm for the middle of the night.

Dodge and Eyebrows were waiting for us at the railway gates. We were all whispering as we headed out the Bloodmill Road and that was stupid because there was nobody around and no houses as we left the streetlights behind and walked into the pitch black night. I could just make out the goalposts in Claughaun. If I had've been alone it would've been scary, but we were full of the day ahead and the thrill of finding a big crop of mushrooms and the money we could make.

'It's very dark,' said Eyebrows as he pushed himself in amongst us. Pinhead pinched my arm, I pinched Dodge's, and then we took off, running down Singland Hill, with Jesse streaking ahead of us and poor Eyebrows standing there on his own calling us, 'Ah lads, come back, will ye? I can't see my hand in front of me.' We hid behind Danahers' wall and waited, trying not to laugh, the Besco bags rustling in our pockets. But dumb old Jesse gave us away. He stood on the wall barking, the oul eejit, and Eyebrows knew we were lying in wait for him and he threw himself over the wall right on top of us and we all cracked up laughing.

So we walked the Bloodmill and I saw my first sunrise ever. A line of light in the black sky that broke into a hundred shades of yellows and oranges, and the sun, shy and wary at first and then just taking over the whole show. I stopped in my tracks to look and the others stopped too. Nobody spoke, we just stood there, all of us, near Groody, mesmerised by the sun. Then Dodge farted, a long rouser, and we all cracked up. And suddenly, without any warning at all, a flock of birds swooshed into the sky above our heads, hundreds of them, maybe even thousands, turning the orange sky black again. Their noisy cries filled our ears and we could hear their wings beating out a kind of rhythm in the half-light.

'There's fucking ghosts around here,' said Eyebrows as the birds flew away. 'There's something spooky here, lads, I swear it'.

'Nope, Dodge's fart woke everyone, that's all. Woke the birds and probably the Living Dead as well,' said Pinhead, smiling.

Eyebrows smiled back but you could tell he was scared.

At Groody we left the road and crossed through the fields towards the old mill. The minute our feet were on the damp, dewy grass, our heads went down searching for the first signs of a crop of mushrooms, the little white heads that popped up like magic and made your heart somersault at seeing them, like finding treasure.

But there wasn't a mushroom in sight. We'd crossed five fields and not a mushroom anywhere, and Jesse was giving us hell with the cows.

'We'll turn back after this field,' I said as we climbed another ditch.

'Yeah, I'm starving, I am. I'd no breakfast,' said Dodge.

The sun was getting warm and we had our jumpers tied around our waists. My shoes were covered in cow shit. For the first field or two I had tried to avoid the big green splatters of dung but then I landed on one, the hard black crust breaking as my shoe sank in, the green liquid filling up until my sock was covered. So I just walked in them after that, all of us did, and our feet were slimy green and stinking.

'Fuck this, we'll turn back,' I said, after the next field came up empty. 'That wanker Baldy O'Brien must have cleared them all yesterday.'

'There's no going back without the mushrooms, no way,' said Pinhead, stopping on the top of the ditch and looking straight at us with that look that meant it was all decided already, that there was no changing your mind. I could hear Jesse barking in the next field. He was giving the cows a right doing but they deserved it for shitting everywhere.

'We'll try the next two fields and then that's it,' I said, holding Pinhead's eyes with a stare of my own.

'What's up with you, Pin? With the fuckin' money you won from us last night, you could buy a lorry-load of mushrooms,' said Dodge, and we all laughed.

'I don't even eat the fuckin' things,' said Eyebrows.

'We'll go home when we find something,' said

Pinhead, and he turned his back on us as he scrambled over the ditch.

'Yeah, ye'll find me dead from the hunger,' said Dodge under his breath.

And then we saw them. A whole field of them over the ditch, so many that the grass seemed white and when we jumped down we smashed some under our feet. There was so many that you couldn't walk without trampling on them. We all jumped around then, shouting and roaring and waving the plastic bags in the air like victory flags. Jesse even deserted his cow chase to join our celebrations, and then he chose the biggest mushroom he could find, the size of a dinner plate it was, and lifted his leg and pissed on it.

'Jesse found a grand one for your da,' Pinhead said to Dodge, and we laughed.

And then we worked. No talking or laughing or anything, we worked and worked until our backs were sore from bending.

We stopped for a rest at the old mill, lying on the grass in the hot morning sun and Dodge's stomach was talking to him from the hunger. There wasn't one cloud in the sky.

'We'll make a fortune with these,' Pinhead said, nodding at all the bags of mushrooms on the grass around us. 'We'll go straight to Balls of Flour, he won't be gone delivering yet if we're lucky.'

'We might as well go home now so, we don't have any more bags left anyway,' I said and got up off the grass.

Dodge and Eyebrows got up too and started picking up the bags of mushrooms.

'Here,' said Pinhead and reached into his pocket. He pulled out another pile of Besco bags and waved them in the air. He was laughing.

'Fuck off,' I said, and we all laughed then.

But we did head home, weighed down by the bags of mushrooms. We couldn't have picked any more even if we'd wanted to.

The road seemed longer on the way back. There was loads of fields between us and the Bloodmill and we were tired from walking and everyone was starving. Even Jesse didn't bother to chase the cows now and lagged behind us with his pink tongue lolling out of his mouth. When we got to the road, Jesse ran straight into Groody and jumped around in the water. The four of us slouched our way up the steep hill. I could feel the effort of it in the backs of my legs. We were too tired to talk but it was a good tired, the kind of tired that you almost enjoy. When you stop, that is. The dip in Groody had revived Jesse and he made a lunge at running up the hill, leaving us behind.

Just as we reached the top the birds did that thing again, they swooshed up suddenly and we all stopped as the sky turned black and noisy.

'Fuckin' ghosts,' said Eyebrows.

Nobody answered. And just as the birds circled and headed off into the morning sky Jesse came back, whimpering and slinking behind Pinhead.

'The fuckin' dog knows. He smells them. Fuckin' ghosts,' said Eyebrows.

'Ghosts have no smell, you ghoul,' said Pinhead, with Jesse still hiding behind his legs.

'Those fuckin' birds. It's a sign. A sign of ghosts,' said Eyebrows. His eyes darted from the bushes to trees at each side of us, as if he expected a corpse or a skeleton to jump out.

'Come on,' Dodge said, marching up the road with the bags of mushrooms swinging out of his hands. 'I'm starving, let's go home.'

We all followed Dodge up the Bloodmill and we knew we were nearly home when we smelt the slaughter house, a sickly, clinging smell in the warm morning sun. Jesse was still glued to Pinhead's heels and nobody talked.

Pinhead saw it first just as we passed by Claughaun.

'What's that?' he asked, looking over the hedge towards the playing fields. He shaded his eyes from the sun. I couldn't see a thing, just spots in front of my eyes from the blinding glare of the sunshine.

'Nothing there, come on lads. I could drop down dead this minute from the hunger, let's go,' said Dodge.

I blinked and then I saw it too, swaying gently on the goalpost, and my stomach did a little flip. Pinhead was over the hedge like a shot, still clutching the bags of mushrooms. Jesse sat in the middle of the road howling. I ran after Pinhead, mushrooms flying everywhere as I tried to catch up with him. I could hear him saying 'Jesus fuckin' Jesus' over and over as we raced towards the goalpost. The others were behind us. I could hear them but they seemed very far away, like they were in another part of the day altogether. Jesse's howls sounded far away too.

I was just behind Pinhead now and if I'd reached out my hand, I'd have been able to touch him. Someone was swinging from the goalpost, we couldn't make out who it was but I could see blue jeans and a red T-shirt and I could hear Pinhead saying, 'It's a fuckin' joke, this is a joke, what bastard would think this was funny?' and we stopped then and I made myself look straight at the goalpost. Pinhead dropped his mushrooms, I could hear the bags rustling as they hit the ground.

There was a body hanging there, Adidas sneakers with a red stripe, blue jeans, red T-shirt, hair falling down, covering the face, orange rope around the neck, like the rope on our clothesline. It was swinging slowly from side to side and I thought I saw the hands twitching. It was a joke, the head would rise in a second, the hair would fall back from the face and the face would smile a fooled-ye smile.

I stood perfectly still, unable to move. Then Pinhead let out a roar and lunged towards the goalpost, screaming and roaring, 'You fuckin' bastard, Enda, you bollocks, get the fuck down, you bastard, I'll fuckin' kill you, I will, you bastard you.' My legs wouldn't move and I stood like a statue watching Pinhead screaming and belting the body with his fists. He could only reach the top of the legs and as he beat and shook them the head fell to one side, and I could see him then, Enda, but not Enda, more a Hallowe'en Enda, with bulging eyes and a huge tongue. The skin on his face was purple.

I could hear the other lads right behind me and I turned to look. Dodge had this awful smile on his face and Eyebrows was talking rubbish, like baby talk, and all the time Pinhead's voice shouting, 'Bastard bastard fuckin' cunt bastard.' Then he started to climb the goalpost and I made my legs move, I forced them to, and I ran to Pinhead and said, 'We need help, Pin, get the fuck down.' And I grabbed his leg and tore him down and he landed on the brown earth where the grass was worn from the goalies standing there. A swaying Adidas sneaker was inches from his face. He was crying and held his penknife in his hand, grasping the bone handle in a tight grip. I took it off him and said, 'Get Dodge away, get up and get him the fuck away from here, I'm going for help, get up.' And he did and wiped his face with his jumper and he stood for a second there in front of the goalpost with Enda swinging behind him and then he said, 'Dodge.' But Dodge didn't hear, he just stood there with a big frozen grin on his face, smiling at his brother. Eyebrows was still jabbering, but now he was running around in circles like a dog. Pinhead screamed, 'Dodge, we're going now', like it was an order or a command, but Dodge didn't move, so Pinhead grabbed him by the arm and made him turn his back on Enda.

I ran across the field towards the road. My heart was thumping in my chest and I had a bad stitch in my side. I couldn't think over the roaring noise in my ears, so I stopped at the gate of Claughaun and hung over it just for a second, and when I looked up, I knew what to do and I talked to myself out loud as I did it to stop the pictures in my head, stop the pictures of swaying shoes and bright red T-shirts and orange rope. Out loud I said, 'Walk don't run to the railway house they have to have a phone over minding the railway gates walk there and knock on the door and say there's something wrong in Claughaun call the guards and then go back and find Dodge poor Dodge stop thinking about Dodge there's the door now knock.'

A man opened the door in his vest and long johns and said, 'Jesus Christ' when he saw me, 'Jesus Christ, what's wrong, what happened to you?' A woman stood behind him in a pink dressing gown like my mother's. I wanted my mother.

'I … there's something … in the field … the goalpost … we need the guards … will they save him?'

'Where? What field? Claughaun, is it? Jesus, get my shoes, Mags, Jesus, what happened? Save who? Was there an accident?'

'On the … goalpost … the hands twitched though … so it could be fine if they hurry …'

'Mags, ring 999, tell them, go on, it's not a trick. Look at the state of the lad, he pissed himself and everything.'

The man flew past me on a black bike, his shirt open and flying behind him like a white shroud. I didn't run, I walked and I talked out loud again. 'Go back now go back and find the lads and pick up the mushrooms.' The woman's voice was calling me, 'Come back, the guards are coming, stay with me and Paddy will sort it out.' But

I kept walking, the sound of my own voice filling my ears and my head, repeating over and over the things I needed to do.

The man was with them when I got back to Claughaun. He had them halfway up the field with their backs to the goalpost. He had his arms around Eyebrows and Dodge. I walked towards them without looking at the goalpost, with my face turned sideways.

There was vomit on the ground near Eyebrows. Pinhead stood a little bit away from the others, head down, his hands in his pockets. I could hear the man saying, 'It's all right, take it easy now, lads, the guards will be here in a minute.' And then he made all of us, even Pinhead, sit on the grass with our backs to the goalpost and he talked and talked about hurling and telly and fishing and I couldn't follow the half of it but the sound of his voice made everything stop in my head and that was good.

The guards came then and crowds of people and an ambulance. The man from the railway house talked to the guards in a low voice and nodded over at us. I stole a glance at Dodge and he still had that smile on his face. Pinhead kept his head down and his back to me.

A guard came over and crouched down in front of us. 'I know this is awful lads,' he said, 'but we ... I need to find out who he ... the boy ... do ye know him?'

'Is he ... will he be all right?' I asked.

'Enda O'Riordan, 22 Lilac Terrace, St Patrick's Road, that's his brother there,' said Pinhead in a low, tight voice. The voice he used when he was really mad.

'Ah Christ no, ah Jesus, is there any God at all?' said the guard and covered his face with his hands.

Dodge started to laugh. A weird, high, girl's laugh that caught in his throat and turned to crying.

Pinhead got up and walked towards the goalpost, his

head still bent and his shoulders hunched. I followed him and so did one of the guards.

'Come back here, now, you've no business going over there again, come on …'

'Fuck off,' said Pinhead, and he kept walking. 'Fuck off and leave me alone, just fuck off, do you hear me?'

The guard grabbed him by the arm and then he lost it. Pinhead did. I knew it was coming because his face was red and he was all wound up and tight like a spring. He just lashed out at the guard, kicking, head-butting, belting. The guard put his two arms around him from the back but it was like trying to hold down a wild animal or something. I just stood and watched.

Pinhead stopped all of a sudden when he caught sight of me, of my face. 'Don't cry, stop it, will you? Don't, Nod, don't,' he said. He was completely still now and the guard held him lightly by the shoulders.

I put my hand to my face and felt wet tears. The salt taste was in my mouth and nose and I could feel my trousers wet and clammy between my legs. I started to sob, long, shuddering sobs that came from right inside me and made my body shake.

Pinhead shook his head at me. 'You fuckin' eejit, shut up, will you? Shut the fuck up,' he said. He tried to hold me with a stare but I looked away. I wasn't able not to cry. He came towards me then and when he put his hand on my shoulder, and I fell into him, into his body, rigid still with anger. 'Stop it, d'you hear me, you fuckin' ghoul? Stop it and cop yourself on,' he said, but he put his arms around me, not tight like I wanted but around me all the same. I let my head rest on his shoulder and my breath slowed down until it matched his.

I heard the guard behind Pinhead saying, 'That's it, lads, it's OK', but he was crying too, I could hear tears caught in his voice.

Then I thought I heard my dad's voice, 'Seán, Seánie, are you all right? Ah Seánie', and I lifted my head from Pinhead's shoulder and there he was right in front of me. I threw myself at him and he scooped me into his arms and hugged me and kissed the top of my head, and I started sobbing all over again.

'Let it out, go on, cry your heart out, let it all out,' he said, stroking my hair.

Pinhead was gone when I looked up again and the front of my dad's shirt was soaked with tears.

'Dad, we have to catch up with him … come on,' I said, and ran after Pinhead. I could see him near the gate.

We walked home together, me, my dad and Pinhead. My dad walked between us, an arm around each of our shoulders. He never asked us anything about what happened. I was glad about that. People were standing at their gates and when we passed, they whispered and nodded towards us. We were nearly home when the ambulance drove by, silent, no sirens. A Garda car followed with Dodge and Eyebrows in the back seat.

Our house was crowded, but my dad told everyone to leave the sitting room and he brought me and Pinhead in there and then he went into the hall. We could hear him whispering orders to people,

'Get Paddy Duffy, call down and get Paddy, call to Kelly's if you have to, or get Ann Duffy, I don't care, just get one of them … Tea … they need something to eat and some tea. Don't mind getting the Parish Priest to talk to them, he doesn't know his arse from his elbow. I'll talk to Seánie myself. Go on now … shh, shh, they'll hear you asking.'

He came back into the sitting room and pulled a chair over to face us on the sofa. I noticed for the first time that the clock on the mantelpiece had a very loud tick.

'I saw his hands twitching, did I tell you that, Dad? His

hands were twitching.'

'Ah Seánie.'

'Do you think it was an accident? That's what happened, it was an accident.'

'It's all right, Seánie, it'll be all right.'

'But they might save him. Pin, did you see his hand moving? Maybe they'll save him in the hospital.'

Pinhead never answered, he just sat there on the sofa with his fists clenched tightly on his lap. A baby cried somewhere in the house and my mam brought in a tray of tea and stuff. She looked at me as she put the things down on the table. Her eyes were red and watery. She reached out her hand and stroked my face.

'His hands twitched,' I told her.

'Shut up, shut fucking up about it. About him and his stupid hands,' Pinhead hissed, never turning his head.

My father put four spoons of sugar in each cup and stirred them for ages, and made us drink the hot sweet tea. The ham sandwiches looked nice but tasted of nothing and after I finished the second one, my stomach started churning and my head went dizzy. I ran to the jacks and vomited my guts up. I liked the vomiting, it gave me something to do.

I went back down to the sitting room and sat on the sofa, close to Pinhead, so close I could hear him breathing. My dad had his head in his hands.

'I'm going home, good luck,' said Pinhead and stood up.

'Sit back down now, your dad will be here soon, you're not going home to an empty house, now sit,' said my dad, putting his hands on Pinhead's shoulders and easing him back into the seat.

Then Dad held both my hands in his and I wanted to tell but it all came out together, mixed up with tears.

'We went for the mushrooms … we found a whole

field of them, Dad ... and ... the dog knew, Dad ... I think Jesse knew, and we nearly didn't see it but Pinhead did, you saw it, Pinhead, and we were nearly home and all. He was wearing his Adidas sneakers, Dad. I wanted a pair of sneakers like that ... Why did he do it, Dad, why?'

'Nobody knows, son. Here, push over and let me sit down between ye. There, it's better that you talk about it. He was a great fella, Enda, but nobody knows what goes on in a person's head. He seemed a happy enough lad, everything going for him, but something must have been on his mind.'

'But you wouldn't do that, no matter how sad you were, you wouldn't do that fucking thing, you wouldn't ...'

My dad had his arms tight around me now and I had my head buried in his chest. The tears wouldn't stop and I let the pictures back into my head. All the pictures, even the ones of Enda's face.

'It was orange rope, like our clothesline, orange rope and he ... he was just swinging there with his shoes on ... and Pin wanted to cut him down but I stopped him, Dad, over Dodge, see ... Dodge was standing behind us, I think he was behind us, and I made Pinhead stop ... and he might have been able to save him or something ...'

My sobs took over then and my dad stroked my hair and said, 'It's OK, Seánie, I'm here, you'll be all right, that's it, let it all out.'

I sat back up then and wiped my eyes.

'He's gone.'

'Yes, but he's in a better place now.'

'Not Enda, Dad, Pinhead. Pinhead's gone.'

My dad ran out to the hall and opened the front door with me following. 'Jesus, there's no sign of him. Did any-one see Kevin leave?' he asked the crowd in the kitchen.

'There was nobody in his house when I went down

there except the uncle. Leave him be, Tom, he needs to come to terms with it himself,' said my mam.

'He needs his bloody father, that's what he needs,' said my dad as he closed the door.

Pinhead came back at tea-time. He stood there at the front door grinning, with his hurley and sliotar in his hand. 'Hey, are you on for a game?' he said.

'I don't know … I …'

'Get your hurley, go on, get it.'

So I got my hurley from the shed and my mam said, 'What are you doing? You're not going out, are you?' And my dad looked at her and shook his head and said, 'Off you go, lad, see you later.'

But I didn't think we'd go back there. To Claughaun. First I thought we'd play on the Green and all the little fellas stared at us as we passed and even the girls, Karen and Deirdre and all, were whispering and staring, and only then did I realise we were kind of special because we found a dead body on a goalpost. If we hadn't known the dead body, we maybe could have enjoyed this. But we went past the Green, just the two of us and our hurleys, and up towards the Bloodmill. I stopped near the railway gates, near the house that I called to for help, but Pinhead kept walking, whistling softly under his breath, and I followed.

Claughaun was deserted and I knew before we went in that Pinhead would choose that goalpost to play in. And he did, never glancing up once. He was the goalie and I took frees against him. I rose the sliotar onto the hurley the way I'd been taught, the way Enda had shown me, and I pucked it long and low and hard and even Pinhead was surprised at the bullet of a goal I produced.

'You'll make the team next year if you keep that up,' he said as he sent the ball back to me, whizzing it right over my head, so that I had to walk miles to get it.

We played like that for ages, taking turns at goal, pucking harder and harder, and then we played against each other with an invisible goalie until the light started to fade and the midges came out looking for blood. We lay on the damp grass behind the goalpost then, covered in sweat. I could see pieces of white mushrooms scattered around the goalmouth, trampled and broken after all the traffic of feet during the day.

'Where do you think he is now … you know … where is he gone, like?' I asked Pinhead after a while.

'Dunno, you have to die to find that out.'

'I hope he likes it though, the new place he's in.'

'Would you like it if you were dead?'

'I mean … heaven and all that.'

'You wouldn't be able to like anything if you were dead, simple as that,' he said.

'Yeah, but your soul and stuff would be alive, wouldn't it?'

'Dead is dead is dead. Come on, I'm starving, let's go home. Where's the sliotar?' he asked as he got up from the grass.

I didn't want to leave and that surprised me. I hadn't wanted to come in the first place and now I didn't want to leave.

My dad cycled all the way into Donkey Ford's for us and he came back with bags of chips and battered sausages and even a big bottle of Coke and we all sat at the kitchen table eating the chips straight from the bags – they tasted way better that way. My mam said that Pinhead should sleep in our house and she'd bring Brian into their bed, so there would be room for him. My dad went to the Duffys' house to ask if it was all right for Pinhead to stay. So we went to bed with our bellies full of chips and sausages and my mam said, 'Good night, lads, ye'll sleep better on full stomachs.'

We undressed in the dark and left on our T-shirts and jockeys. I lay awake listening to Pinhead tossing and turning beside me and then I thought of something.

'Pin, Pin, are you awake? What happened Jesse? Where did he go after ... you know, after it happened?' I whispered into the dark.

I thought he was asleep, he took so long to answer.

'We'd have made five pounds and six shillings from those mushrooms. I added it up in my head. That much money,' he said, and then he yawned and turned his back on me.

12

They laid him out in the parlour, the Sacred Heart scowling down at him. This was the first time it happened in our estate. The first time a body didn't go to the dead house but stayed at home until it was time for the burial Mass. Everybody talked about it, on the street corners, in Mac's shop, whether it was right or wrong to keep a body in the house. I asked my dad what he thought about it and he said that people always did it in the past, and he thought it was right if Enda's family wanted it. But Pinhead said Dodge wouldn't be too happy with a dead body in his parlour, even if it was his brother.

We all gathered outside the house on the evening of the wake. Nobody planned to do this, to gather in silence outside the house, it just kind of happened that way. First Eyebrows and Pinhead and me, then some of the Claughaun team and towards the end the Garryoweners and all were there. A big gang of us, talking in whispers, wanting to show Enda how much we liked him. I was mad to see Dodge, I hadn't seen him since it happened, but my mam had said not to call, to give him time.

O'Riordan opened the door when it was time for the viewing, that's what they called it, looking at the dead body, they called it a viewing. I didn't want to go in but I knew I had to, like this was the end part of all the stuff with Enda.

We saw Angela Walsh going into the house with her father. She was crying. All dressed in black and tears streaming down her face ruining her make-up and making her eyes black too. Her father held her tightly around the waist. Everybody was dead silent when they walked up the path, no one even sniggered when she stumbled in her platform shoes as they climbed the steps to the front door.

Crowds came then and there was a queue going in the front door and I wanted to go home. To go home and watch *The Man from Uncle* and have Nana to tea and play with the small brothers.

My dad came then and said, 'Come on now, lads, we'll go in together. I'll go first, so ye'll know what to do. Come on, it'll be grand.'

So we followed him in. Pinhead first, then me, then poor Eyebrows, his face white and haunted. He wasn't able for this, looking at dead people in houses. The hallway was crowded but there was just the low murmur of voices. I could smell roast chicken.

We followed the queue into the parlour. The men stood at the side of the coffin and the women were sitting down in a row. I couldn't see the women but I knew it was them in the corner because of the crying. I searched for Dodge but the men standing in the black suits blocked my view. As we got near them I watched to see what my dad was saying and doing, so I could copy him when it was my turn. I never looked once at the coffin. At what was in it. My dad shook hands with the row of men and then he stopped at the last one.

It was O'Riordan, standing tall and straight, his eyes fixed on my dad. I waited for Dad to shake his hand and move on to the women, but he stood there just looking at O'Riordan. Then he nodded at him, and shook his hand fast, and walked over to Dodge's mother. He bent and whispered in her ear, his hand on her shoulder. She wiped her eyes with a pale, yellow hanky.

O'Riordan stared at my dad, still talking softly to Dodge's mother. Then it was Pinhead's turn.

They stood there looking at each other. I was standing

next to Pinhead and I could feel all the anger curled up inside in him, waiting to escape. He finally stuck out his hand and O'Riordan hesitated, like he expected a head in the face instead of a handshake, but then he took Pinhead's hand and shook it. Pinhead leaned in close to him and whispered something. I nearly died when I heard it.

'Fuckin' steamer.' Only a whisper, a breath, but I heard it. Pinhead walked away and left me there with O'Riordan, who looked like he couldn't decide if he'd heard it or not.

'I'm sorry for … you know… it,' I said then and caught his hand and shook it like a madman.

He nodded at me but his eyes followed Pinhead.

I looked back and there was poor Eyebrows turning tail and running out the door before he even got a glimpse of the coffin. I followed my dad and circled the coffin. I tried to keep my eyes on the picture of the Sacred Heart on the wall above the crying women but I looked when my father bent into the coffin and kissed Enda, Jesus, poor Enda, his face covered in make-up, and he said, 'God bless you, son.' I stared at Enda's face then and it was all right because it wasn't really Enda, just something left over from Enda.

Dodge was standing next to a little table covered with pictures of Enda. Enda as a baby, Enda as a toddler with fat legs in a cowboy suit, Enda making his First Communion, Enda making his Confirmation, Enda smiling in the Claughaun jersey, with the League cup held over his head.

And that's what made me cry. Not Dodge's stricken face, not the cute baby pictures or the body in the coffin. It was the picture of Enda in his glory, because that made you see how sad it really was. Tears ran down my face and I looked at Dodge and looked back down at the picture and sobs were coming and my dad steered me out the door.

In the hallway and the kitchen other people were crying too, so I didn't feel bad about it. Angela Walsh came over to me and put her arms around me and hugged me tightly. So tight I could feel her chest right up against mine, and when I opened my eyes, Pinhead was there winking and grinning at me and giving me the thumbs up. I was laughing and crying all at once then, and knew I'd remember this for a long time. The feel of her chest pressed up against me.

We hung around outside the house while the grown-ups drank tea and whiskey and stuff in the kitchen. Someone brought out a crate of lemonade for us and bags of crisps and we sat on the wall watching people going in, with Pinhead giving a running commentary.

'There's oul prick face Burke. Jesus, I didn't realise how fuckin' small he is, I'm bigger than him, so I am. And Balls of Flour. His wife is a fine thing, nice arse,' he said.

Libby was with him now, leaning her body into his and laughing at everything he said. Karen was there too, with Deirdre, and they came and stood next to me.

'Hi Nod, you OK?' asked Deirdre, her dark slitty eyes searching my face. Karen said nothing, just examined me as well.

'Fine, I'm grand. Why wouldn't I be grand?' I asked, looking straight at them.

They dropped their eyes but nudged each other.

'Well, if you ... you know ... if you ever want to talk about it or anything, I'll ... we'll be there for you,' said Karen, shaking her blond ponytail.

I got it now. They couldn't help Enda, so they were going to save me instead. Fuckin' girls, all concern when there was a big drama. I hated every last one of them. Except for Angela Walsh. I felt sorry for her.

'Thanks, girls. I'll call ye so. One of ye can hold the goalpost for me and the other one can hand me the rope, thanks a lot,' I said, my voice low and steady and mean.

Pinhead was laughing softly on the wall.

'Prick,' said Deirdre, and she walked away with Karen. They were like the terrible twins now and I could imagine the talks they had about me and what a bad kisser I was and what a ghoul I was. They deserved each other.

Pinhead was laughing out loud, shaking his head and saying, 'You mad bastard, Nod', but the minute I said the thing about the goalpost I was sorry. It wasn't funny at all.

It was late when Pinhead's parents came. Diet was with them and Uncle Pat. He hadn't a clue what was happening, Uncle Pat. He was rubbing his hands together and asking people were they going to Kelly's for a jar, like he was at a hurling match or something. They came just as the coffin was being closed and the priest was saying prayers. We'd all piled back into the house for this. Mr Duffy's voice sounded loud and happy in the quiet parlour. His face was bright red, like it had been in the pub in Salthill the time of the pound. Pinhead moved away, almost out the front door, and I wanted to tell Mr Duffy to shut up and keep his voice down, but I gave him a stare instead. He just smiled and waved when he saw me.

Enda's mam cried as they put the lid on the coffin. Long hoarse cries that filled the house and gave you a pain in your heart. The crying drowned the priest's blessing. When they brought the coffin out, the Claughaun team stood guard of honour outside the door. Some of the senior team shouldered it, and all the girls were crying now, and the women. Black funeral cars were waiting at the kerb and the women climbed into them. We all lined up behind the hearse. O'Riordan was right in front of us, his hand tight on Dodge's shoulder.

So we walked behind the hearse, all the men and the boys, and when Diet asked could he walk with us, Pinhead said, "Course you can, no need to even ask.' That was a first for Pinhead.

I slept badly that night. Dreams came but I couldn't remember them, I just woke up trying to scream but no sound came out of my mouth. When I told my mam, she said, 'Sleep on your side, you dream more if you sleep on your back.'

It rained for the funeral the next day. Wet rain in nonstop sheets and we had to search the house for umbrellas. I found a Harp one but my mam said black was best. We walked behind the coffin again after the Mass, the rain beating down on a sea of black umbrellas. We made our way slowly to Mount St Laurence's graveyard. Dodge and O'Riordan were at the front, just the two of them, his big hand on Dodge's shoulder again. As we made our way through the graveyard, I read the headstones. 'In Loving Memory of Lily Byrne who died 17th November 1962, aged 2 years.' 'In Loving Memory of John Higgins, who died 6th July 1967, aged 13 years.' My age, that boy died at my age. I wanted to know what happened him, but the headstone didn't tell you that.

We came to Enda's grave all of a sudden. There it was in front of us, a freshly dug hole, the earth wet and dark. No headstone. I never took my eyes off the hole, all through the priest's prayers and the crowd's mumbled answers, and I watched as they slowly laid the coffin into the black earth. That made my heart do a somersault. I watched as they shovelled earth into the hole, I heard it drop on the coffin, I heard the hollow sound it made and the sound of rain dripping onto umbrellas and trees. Our feet crunched on the wet gravel as the crowd drifted away and I took one look back at the grave. His grave. It looked lonely.

We saw another funeral on our way out. Solemn faces and dark clothes standing around another open grave and there in the middle of the mourners was Uncle Pat, the big eejit, at the wrong funeral. Even my dad laughed at that. Eyebrows walked home with me and Pinhead. The crowd headed for the pubs, the Munster Fair Tavern and Kelly's bar, and my mam said, 'Come on back to our house, lads, and I'll make a big fry-up.' We let Diet come too, even though we knew there wouldn't be a spare sausage with him around. But Pinhead said, 'Let him come.'

It was three days before I saw Dodge again. My mam said to let him be for a while. And everyone was talking about it still. About Enda dying and what a pig O'Riordan was and that it was all his fault. I overheard my dad tell my mam that, but they stopped talking about it when they saw me standing at the door. There was no way I was calling down to that house if I could help it. So I was glad in a way when I saw Dodge at my door. He looked different, kind of tired. I hadn't a clue what to say to him, so I just said, 'Hi, Dodge. Come in.'

'I can't. I'm not supposed to be out at all,' he said, and scuffed the step with his sneaker.

The silence was deadly, so I said the first thing that came into my head. 'How's it going?'

He looked right at me then, with dark circles under his eyes and that beaten-up look like he had in the squad car after robbing Woolworths.

'They cleared out his room today. They got a tea chest and filled it with his clothes and things ... his guitar.'

I couldn't look at his face any more, so I looked down at my feet instead. I could hear my mam upstairs singing to the small brothers before they went to sleep.

'It's like he was never here at all. I can't even say his name in the house,' he said. I could hear tears in his voice.

'And do you know the worst part? We'll just forget about him. Like we forgot about Victor.' He wiped his face with his sleeve without looking at me.

I had to think of something.

'We won't forget him, Dodge, don't be stupid,' I said, but in my heart I knew that he was right. Like when you get a really deep cut in your hand and the pain is awful and you can't imagine it ever getting better. But it does and it's like it never happened at all. Not a mark where that cut was. I didn't tell him that though. 'We'll remember him ourselves, Dodge. You and me. We'll go to the graveyard every week, every day if you want, and we'll tell him all the news. How about that?'

Dodge looked at me. 'Would you do that, Nod?'

'Yeah, I swear it. We'll start tomorrow if you like. First thing.'

'Really, you'd come with me?'

I nodded my head.

'Tomorrow?'

I nodded again.

'I'll call up for you so,' he said and gave me a small smile before he turned to leave.

I was still in bed the next morning when Dodge called for me.

'Are you ready? Look what I have for him, his sliotar, his best one. If I leave it on the grave though, somebody might steal it. He loved that one,' he said as he held the ball out for me to see.

I was standing in our kitchen rubbing the sleep from my eyes and searching for cornflakes. 'Yeah,' I said as I poured out cereal. The lino was cold under my bare feet. The house was quiet for once, the babies were still asleep and my dad was gone to work, his breakfast dishes were in the sink.

'I got this for him too, his plec from the guitar. He

has … he had loads of them. I'll leave that too, what do you think?'

'Hmm,' I said through a mouthful of cornflakes.

We didn't call for Pinhead. I wanted to but Dodge said that he wanted to keep it between the two of us. So we headed off towards the graveyard, passing Dodge's house on our way. The curtains were closed in all the windows and Dodge's black cat was stretched on the mat at the front door.

'They're selling the house,' Dodge said.

'What?'

Dodge kept walking and didn't look at me when he answered. 'I heard him saying it last night. We're moving.'

I stopped dead on the footpath and Dodge stopped too.

'Moving where? Somewhere in Limerick?' I asked.

He shrugged. 'Caherconlish. It's in the county but it might as well be on Mars.'

'And he said this for definite?'

'My uncles live there and my dad said it'd be a new start.' Dodge shrugged again and started walking.

'Fuck sake, Caherconlish? Jesus, Dodge, that's lousy. Did he say when?'

'No, but I know him. Once he says something, it'll happen.' He looked at me then and his eyes looked old and sad somehow.

We got lost the minute we went in to the graveyard. Paths crisscrossed all over the place and Dodge said he knew which way to go and I wanted to go in the other direction, but we were both wrong. We were looking for a grave with no headstone and loads of flowers but suddenly there were piles of graves just like that, like Enda's, freshly dug. I was smiling because it was funny really – here we were after making a promise to visit him every day and we couldn't even remember where the grave was. But Dodge didn't smile, he was running now, up and down the gravel paths, his face pinched with panic.

I saw the little girl's headstone then – 'In Loving Memory of Lily Byrne' – and I knew if we walked straight past it, we'd find Enda. And there it was in front of us, flowers piled on top of black earth.

I hunched down and read some of the cards, one from Claughaun GAA Club and one from Angela Walsh. The flowers she sent were shaped in a heart. The card said 'My love, Angela'. That's all it said.

Dodge was kneeling beside me with the sliotar in his hand. 'Who left that? Jesus, somebody was here already, Nod, look at this.' He held up a red plec, a different colour to the one he had brought.

I looked at the plec in Dodge's hand and watched as he put it back down on Enda's grave. It lay on the dark earth like a tiny pool of blood.

There wasn't a sound in the place, except for some birds and the leaves rustling in the trees, no other sound, not even a far-away car or a dog barking. Dodge knelt there, not saying anything, just holding the sliotar in his hand.

'Go on,' I said, 'put the ball in under the flowers so it won't be stolen, look there's a grand space there.'

'But I wanted to … you know … say something … talk to him, like.'

I remembered Pinhead's words in Claughaun and just then they seemed true. He was right, dead was dead was dead. I couldn't see the point of talking to a bunch of wreaths and cards, but I nodded at Dodge. 'Talk so, come on, I told Pinhead I'd call for him.'

'I … all right,' he said and he put the sliotar under Angela Walsh's heart-shaped flowers and stood up and dusted the earth off the knees of his trousers.

'The plec, you forgot the plec that you brought.'

'That's for tomorrow,' he said and looked straight at

me, held me with his eyes better than even Pinhead could.

'Right so,' I said, and we headed back down the gravel path.

We walked in silence for a while, the only sound was the crunch of our feet on the gravel.

'He was right, Pinhead was,' said Dodge as we reached the Ballysimon Road.

'About what?'

'That day ... the thing I remember the most, all the time going around in my head, was Pinhead screaming, you fucking bastard cunt bastard. And do you know something?'

We'd stopped to cross the road and he put his hand on my arm. I didn't like the sound of this, so I didn't answer him.

'That's what Enda was, a fucking bastard. Because only a fucking bastard would do it.' His voice was angry and I didn't look at his face because he might have been crying.

We walked the rest of the way in silence.

I didn't call for Pinhead. We got to his house and I was just opening the gate when I heard the shouting. Mrs Duffy's voice first, high-pitched and angry, and then his voice, the father's, booming and scary. You couldn't make out what they were screaming at each other, not the exact words anyway, and Dodge said, 'Let's call back later or he might call for us', and I said, 'That's grand.'

I looked up at Pinhead's bedroom window as we walked away and one of the tiny sisters was there, her head cocked up to see out the window. She smiled when she saw me and waved.

I knew Pinhead would call for me. Since Enda died, he called for me all the time. He came at tea-time. It was Nana's birthday and my aunt was just bringing her up the path when Pinhead arrived. We were having a cake and stuff, but I thought that was dumb. I mean, she couldn't remember what day it was, never mind her birthday. My mam made Pinhead stay for his tea and Nana kept staring at him and I nearly wet myself laughing when she started winking at him.

'Who's that handsome fella?' she asked as she sat down opposite him at the table.

'That's Paddy Duffy's boy, you know, Paddy Duffy, in CIE,' said my mam as she buttered thick slices of cottage loaf.

Aunty Mary with her face like a hatchet was sitting right next to Pinhead. Brian had his hand in the butter.

'Don't ever marry,' said Nana to Pinhead as she stuffed black pudding into her mouth. Then she ate two spoons of sugar.

Aunty Mary tut-tutted and I kicked Pinhead's legs under the table.

My dad came in from work then. He washed his hands at the sink and sat between Colm and Brian, the two of them chattering away at him together.

'I have a bit of a surprise for ye,' he said as he started eating his tea.

Nana leaned over and took a sausage from Pinhead's plate.

'We're getting a car – isn't that a fine bit of news!' said my dad. He was grinning from ear to ear.

We all started talking at once then, when and what colour and can we go for a spin and you can't drive. Nana was laughing really loud.

'Sshh will ye? We'll have it soon. I went to the bank for a loan and all. So what do you think, Mam?' he said.

'Can we afford it?' she asked as she poured tea into his cup.

'It's grand, it's all sorted. I'm having a look at a few tomorrow and Dick Halpin – you know, Dick, the mechanic down the road – he's keeping an eye out for me as well.'

'But you can't drive, Dad,' I said then.

He laughed. 'That's the easy part, anyone can drive, even Colm here could drive, couldn't you, lad?' he said as he ruffled Colm's hair.

'Beep beep, vroom, vroom,' said Colm, standing up on the chair with a pretend steering wheel in his hand.

Everybody laughed, even Aunty Mary.

'We can visit Dodge if we get a car,' I said then.

They all looked at me.

'They're moving to Caherconlish. His da told them last night,' I said.

'Dodge'll be a culchie,' said Pinhead.

'Bastard,' said my dad, 'that poor young fella.'

'Tom,' my mam said, giving him a look to be careful what he said in front of us. 'Here, I'll go and get the cake.'

She brought out the cake then, white with pink writing on it and we all sang happy birthday to Nana, and Nana said, 'Who's she? Who's Nana?' and Pinhead and me cracked up. And then she winked at Pinhead again and fluttered her eyelashes and asked him was he going to the Matterson's dinner dance and my dad fell about laughing.

We sat on the Green later, just Pinhead and me, Eyebrows had some kind of bug again, something you could catch off him, and Dodge didn't show up. I was glad Dodge wasn't out. I told Pinhead about the graveyard.

'He wants me to go back with him tomorrow. Jesus, I know it was my idea but I just said it for something to say. I mean, there he was first thing this morning.'

'Don't be there in the morning, be gone when he calls, he'll get the message. It's easy,' said Pinhead, with that lazy smile. He definitely had a moustache, I could see it clearly now above his smiling lips.

'I couldn't do that to him. You come with us, will you?'

'I'm going swimming with Libby tomorrow, just the two of us,' he said, and he winked at me and laughed.

I played with a blade of grass and tried to split it in two in one long tear. 'There was something strange up at the grave today.'

'Yeah?' said Pinhead. He stretched his long legs out in front of him and looked away up the road, like he was bored.

'Yeah. There was a red plec just lying there right on top of the grave.'

'Is that right? Hey, I'm starving, let's pool our money and go to Mac's,' he said and smiled at me as he got up off the grass.

'Will you give it up, now? The guitar?' I asked.

He shrugged as he walked away.

13

Two things happened the following Friday. We hadn't seen Dodge for a few days and nobody would call for him any more. Even the smaller fellas wouldn't go near the house now because their mothers had them all warned to stay away. Pinhead and me were passing Dodge's on Friday morning when we saw the big removal van pulling up outside it.

'They must be moving today,' said Pinhead. 'Good fuckin' riddance.'

'That's lousy, what about poor Dodge?' I said.

Pinhead shrugged. 'It's lousy for him, all right, out there in the sticks, but I'm glad that cunt is going.'

'I heard my dad talking. He said the guards should have been on to O'Riordan after Enda died,' I said.

Pinhead laughed. 'Cunts like him could beat the living shit out of you and get away with it. And anyway, Enda killed himself, remember?' Pinhead looked at me as if I was stupid and then punched me in the arm. 'Race you to Mac's,' he said, and took off down the road.

Then we sat on the wall opposite Dodge's with a bag of sweets each. Eyebrows had come too and a few of the others. We all sat there watching the removal men loading wardrobes and chairs and beds into the back of the van. There wasn't a sign of Dodge. I saw Enda's guitar sticking up out of a tea chest and I knew that was the one that held all his clothes and things. The one Dodge had told me about. Then I saw Dodge's bike being put in and somehow that was sadder than Enda's stuff. Tears pricked my eyes and I blinked them away before Pinhead or the others noticed.

They didn't come out until the removal van was pulling away. O'Riordan came first, shouting instructions to the driver, and then Dodge came, holding his cat in his arms. He waved over at us and climbed into the back of his da's shiny car. Then the mother and father got in and they reversed out of the drive and pulled away down the road. I could see the shape of Dodge, sitting there in the back seat and I willed him to look back. A last look, a goodbye. He never looked at all.

My dad brought the car home that evening. Pinhead and Eyebrows and me waited on the front wall for him to come, and we let Diet wait with us. The girls waited too and fussed over the twins who were sitting in their pram in the garden. Colm and Brian were like two little madmen running around making car noises. Then we saw it coming, Dick Halpin in the driver's seat and my dad beside him with a big grin on his face. Some of the neighbours were coming out to their gates to see the great event.

We spent the whole of Saturday on the Green watching my dad learning to drive and Dick Halpin's terrified face teaching him. It was better than a hurling match. First my dad came out and examined the car, opening the bonnet and looking at the engine. You'd have thought he was great with cars the way he nosed around it but, boy, did things change when he got behind the wheel. The very second the key was turned in the ignition he changed into some kind of mad, half rally driver/half kerb crawler, and you just had to laugh, even though it was your father and everybody was laughing too.

They drove round and round the Green, Dick Halpin

snow white in the passenger seat and my dad with his head turned, chatting away, not looking at the road at all. And then, all of a sudden, my dad would speed up and Dick's eyes would bulge and you could see him shouting, 'Slow down! Slow down!' And my dad would drop down to a crawl and all the small kids would race the car.

It was hysterical. Pinhead was crying from laughing so much and Eyebrows said it was the best laugh he had had in years. But it wasn't funny when they nearly hit the lorry parked outside the empty house at the end of our terrace. We all ran down to see.

'Jesus, there's a new family moving in and your father nearly killed them,' said Pinhead as we raced down the Green.

My dad was joking with the lorry driver. Dick Halpin was holding himself up against the wall, saying 'Fuck me pink' under his breath, his face white and sick-looking. The new family came running out of the house to see what was happening. A tall boy kicked a football in the garden. He never looked up from the ball.

'Are you all right?' asked the father in a funny accent.

'English,' whispered Pinhead.

The wife was all glamour, shiny jewellery and stiff, perfect, blond hair.

'Hi, I'm Tom Hickey, welcome to the neighbourhood. I'm sorry for giving ye a fright, I'm just learning, see, it's my first day out in the car,' said my dad, and he stuck out his hand.

Then they were all chat and introductions and we knew that they were from Liverpool and the father was starting work in the airport. And they had three boys, Nick, Marty and Don. We started laughing when we heard the names but my dad silenced us with a glare from hell. The boy in the garden never looked at us at all.

We saw the boy on the Green that night. We were

kicking a ball around, Eyesbrows was in goal and the girls were on the sideline giggling and whispering. I looked across to see what they were laughing at and there was the English boy a bit away from us kicking a football. He was taller than Pinhead and that was tall, and he was looking the other way. But he knew we were watching him because he started doing tricks with the ball, brilliant stuff that you'd only see the best footballers do on the telly.

Pinhead asked him did he want a game. So we played football with Nick from Liverpool and I hated his guts straight away. Too tall, too good-looking, too good at football, all the stuff, the magic stuff, that girls loved. Pinhead and him were the best footballers on the Green, so that gave them a reason to get on and at the end of the game they sat together on Nick's wall chatting. The girls hung about admiring them both and I went home. I just couldn't compete with that.

I went to bed early and I could hear them all still out on the Green. Pinhead's voice laughing and joking and the English boy answering him and laughing a low, deep laugh. I shut my eyes tight and put my head under the blankets. It sounded like the day I heard Enda and Pinhead in Enda's bedroom. And now Pinhead didn't really give a fuck at all that Enda was dead because he had a new friend who could kick a football. A bollocks was all he was, Pinhead. An oul bollocks.

My dad took us for a short drive the next day. I didn't want to go. My mam sat in the back with the babies in her arms and Colm and Brian sat next to her. I tried to get into the back too.

'Seánie, you sit in the front with me. I like the company,' said my dad as he straightened the mirrors and stuck the key in the ignition. The car shuddered to life and then died. Ten minutes later we were still outside the house, but now a crowd had gathered. Pinhead was playing football with Nick the Prick on the Green and they were laughing. I was mortified in the front seat and pretended I was looking for something on the floor of the car.

At last it started and off we went at full speed down the road. I gripped my seat in terror as we came to the turn for the Ballysimon Road.

'Jesus, stop, Dad, stop and look,' I shouted. 'Just edge out, Dad. Christ!'

'I know exactly what I'm doing, just stop shouting, you,' he said, but he was looking straight at me and going onto the Ballysimon Road at the same time. A car screeched to a halt and another coming in the opposite direction swerved and a horn blared.

'Mother of Divine Jesus, he'll kill us all, turn back, turn back now this minute Tom, before you kill the lot of us! You told me you could drive,' screamed my mam.

The twins were roaring and the boys' lips were quivering. I wanted to die. We were stopped right in the middle of the Ballysimon Road. I probably would die.

'I can't,' said my dad in a quiet voice.

'What do you mean, you can't? Just turn the car and go home. Now!' shouted my mam.

'I can't,' said my dad again. 'I don't know how to reverse.'

I started laughing then and I wasn't mad any more, I just felt sorry for him, and then we were all laughing, even my mam. In the end another driver had to reverse the car for him and point it up St Patrick's Hill.

'I'll drive it to work for the week, I'll be flying it then,' said my dad as he stopped the car at our door and we tumbled out onto the street.

My mam almost ran into the house, a baby in each arm. She looked like she had been to hell and back.

'Do you know what we'll do next Saturday, Seánie?

We'll take the car for a long spin, just us, just the boys. That's a great idea. You can ask the lads to come too. We'll have a great day.'

'I ... we might be busy ... Pinhead said we might go swimming.'

'I'll bring you swimming. We'll go to Ballybunion or Kilkee maybe. And we can fish for mackerel if you want. It'll be a grand day out before you all go back to school. I'm dying to take the car out on the open road. Look, it's settled so.'

'But Dad ... the open road might be too much ... what I mean is ... it's too far and you might have to practise a bit more, maybe for a year or two before you go on the open road.'

'You're a gas card, Seánie. I'll be flying it by next week, you'll see,' he said and whistled then as he walked up the path.

Pinhead loved the idea of going on a trip with my father. We were sitting on the Green the next evening. Nick was kicking a ball beside us and every girl in the place was admiring him. He knew it too, the prick.

'We'll have a right laugh, your da will be fine, we'll have a crack,' said Pinhead. He was lying on the grass with his head in Libby's lap. Nick bounced the ball near his stomach and they both laughed. 'Who's going anyway?' Pinhead asked.

'I don't want to go at all. Jesus, you didn't see him on the Ballysimon Road, he nearly killed the lot of us,' I said, watching Karen and Deirdre watching Nick.

'It'll be a scream. Can Nick come?' Pinhead asked.

Nick stopped kicking the ball but kept his back to us.

'Em ... I don't think there'll be enough room,' I said.

Nick started kicking the ball again and looked at Pinhead and smiled. Bastard, Liverpool bastard.

'So who's going?' asked Pinhead.

'Ah ... Eyebrows ... and ... you know, the usual,' I said, looking straight at him.

He smiled at me. Libby stroked his hair. In front of everybody. She was worse than Time Tunnel lately around Pinhead.

'Hey, come on, shall we have a proper game of footie?' asked Nick, and the girls giggled at his English accent.

'You playing, Nod?' Pinhead said, but he was up and gone already, himself and Nick dribbling and passing to each other.

I stood watching for a while. Then I had an idea. 'Let's have a game of hurling, there's training in Claughaun, so we're sure to get a game,' I shouted over to Pinhead.

They both stopped kicking the ball and looked at me.

'Yeah, that's a great idea. We'll play too,' said Deirdre. Pinhead looked at Nick. 'Can you hurl?' he asked.

'No, but I'll come and watch,' said Nick.

I wanted to say to him, don't bother your arse, but I said, 'Come on so.'

It was a great game. Deirdre was a brilliant hurler, fast and brave, as good as any of us. Eyebrows played too, his first time in Claughaun since the day we found Enda. He was nervous about it, you could see that, but he never mentioned it. Nick stood behind the goals like a spare prick and I enjoyed smiling over at him as we tore into the game. He didn't smile back.

'I like that game, hurling. Will you teach me?' he asked Pinhead, when we were sitting around after the game.

'Sure. We'll get you a hurley and I'll teach you. It'd be a laugh if you made the team. Imagine that, an English fella playing for Claughaun. Playing for Limerick even. Up in Croke Park. That would be some joke.'

Everybody laughed at that.

It was still early when we walked home. The girls had to go for a babysitting job or something. Eyebrows headed home, so that just left me, Pinhead and Nick.

'Do you want to come to my house to see my Liverpool poster? It's the new team one. My uncle sent it over,' Nick said.

We were standing in front of my gate, but he was only asking Pinhead to go, I knew that.

'What are you doing, Nod? Are you going in or what?' Pinhead asked me.

I wanted to thump Pinhead right in the mouth. I wanted to thump Nick even more but I just acted casual and said, 'Right so, see ye', and opened our gate.

'See you, Nick,' said Pinhead then and he followed me down our path.

I could have kissed him then and there, hugged him, but I didn't do anything. I didn't even turn around. I just opened the front door.

14

'I haven't had wages for three weeks, Rita, three weeks without a penny from him and he'll be sacked from CIE. He hasn't been to work, I know that because I called last Friday. I thought if I caught him before he went to the pub, I'd get my money, but his foreman told me he was out sick. I don't know where to turn,' said Mrs Duffy to my mam.

It was the night before my dad was taking the lot of us for the drive in the car. I was just about to go into the kitchen when I heard Mrs Duffy's voice. I knew I shouldn't be listening outside the door like that but there was something fascinating about it at the same time. I wanted to hear it.

'Did you try talking to him? You should sit down with him when he's sober. Sit down and talk, Ann,' said my mam.

I could hear her pouring tea into cups. I could hear Charles Mitchell in the sitting room telling the news to nobody. My dad was out in the car. The others were in bed.

'He's never there to talk about it. And when he is, he's like a dog, waiting to go back out again. I've uniforms and books to buy for school next week and they've no school shoes. I can't let them back to school in plastic sandals. I'm at my wits end, I swear it, I am.' She was crying. I could hear sniffles and rustling as my mam gave her a tissue.

'Come on, Ann, it won't last. Look, he's gone on binges before and then he stops and everything is grand again.'

'I know that. And when he's not drinking, he's the best in the world. He never raised a hand to me, drunk or sober.'

'I know, Ann, I know.'

'I went to the welfare office but they can't help. He has a full-time job, that's what they said. And me with no bloody wages.'

I could hear louder sniffles and I wanted to walk away but I couldn't.

'It'll be all right. And they mightn't need shoes straight away. The weather is gorgeous. Remember last September? We had to leave them back to school in their summer clothes over the heat.'

'You're right, Rita. And I didn't get a chance to look at the uniforms yet, they might be grand. And I've Balls of Flour. He's great, he told me not to worry about paying him. He's a great fella.'

I heard my dad's key in the lock then and I stumbled in the kitchen door with the fright.

'Seán, what are you doing?' said my mam.

'Nothing ... I ... I was looking for a drink,' I said and opened the fridge.

'Are ye all set for tomorrow? Did he say where he was taking ye yet? It's like another Mystery Tour,' said Mrs Duffy. She smiled but her eyes were red and puffy.

My dad was up at the dawn packing the car. I could hear him whistling as I lay in bed. Brian was asleep beside me, his tight little body curled the way a cat curls in the sun. I was dreading the trip and hoping against hope that my dad's driving had really improved in the past week.

Eyebrows was first to come. 'I brought my da's fishing rod and a bottle of Cream Soda,' he said.

I was eating toast in the kitchen. My mam was buttering slices for the brothers.

'I don't want to go,' I said to Eyebrows, loud enough

for my mam to hear.

'You don't know how lucky you are, going off for the day and the sun shining. Ye'll have a great time, so ye will,' she said.

Eyebrows was nodding his head in agreement.

She stopped the buttering. 'Dick Halpin says your dad's driving is much better. It'll be fine, love,' she said and smiled at me.

Pinhead came just as we were all piling into the car. He talked to Nick, who was kicking a football by himself around the Green, and then he sauntered over to us, all smiles.

There was no way I would sit in the front seat, so my father said, 'Go on so, Kevin, you sit there, you're the biggest, you're as big as myself.' I sat in the back with Eyebrows. I always thought it'd be great to have a car, to be able to just take off somewhere on a Sunday like the Bourkes and the Mulcahys. But their dads could drive, that was the difference.

Dad started off grand this time. He took off without the car shuddering once and we all waved at Nick. He waved back and I knew he could see there was plenty room, but I didn't care. I gave him a big grin as well as a wave.

We set off through town and out the Ennis Road.

'Spanish Point,' said my dad.

I hoped Pinhead wouldn't answer him in the front seat.

'Where's that, Mr Hickey?' asked Pinhead.

'Jesus,' I said.

'Stop swearing.' My dad turned right around to say that to me.

'Jesus, mind the road,' I said. The car had veered over the white line in the middle of the road.

He straightened up the car and answered Pinhead. 'A great place for fishing, Spanish Point is. I'll show you the best fishing spot in the country.' He looked at Pinhead as he talked and I felt like skelping the back of his head. The car now veered towards the ditch, and a lorry behind beeped furiously at us.

'Don't answer, Pinhead, don't talk to him, he'll crash the fuck ... he'll crash,' I said, with my hands over my eyes.

'If you swear once more I'll stop the fuckin' car and let you out on the side of the road.'

I peeped out through my fingers. He was looking straight in front of him and that was good. I started to relax a little as the car gathered speed. My dad was getting better, no question about it.

We fished off the cliffs with the seagulls screeching above us and the waves crashing against the rocks below. My dad was an expert and had a mountain of mackerel beside him in no time. I could see Pinhead and Eyebrows looking at him in admiration. And the swim was great too, with big waves that carried you right onto the shore.

He swam with us, my dad did, and lifted us up and threw us back into the sea. And we chased him and tried to throw him, all three of us together pitching our weight against his. He fought us off and then he slipped and went under and we laughed. But I think he did that on purpose, he slipped to make us laugh. Sitting in the water, he looked years younger than he was at home, almost like a boy, like us.

We ate our picnic on the beach and I couldn't believe it was time to pack up and go. The day had flown by. All of us were tired on the journey home and I felt myself dropping off to sleep, the smell of fresh mackerel and our bodies mixing together in the warm car.

I woke up with a stone wall rushing towards me. First I thought I was dreaming but then I heard my dad saying, 'Jesus, where did that wall come out of?'

'Swerve! Swerve, Dad!' I screamed, but the bang as we

hit the wall drowned out my words. I shut my eyes tight and I could feel my body being jerked forward and Eyebrows' head banged off mine. Then there was a kind of silence, a weird kind of silence, and I opened my eyes and the wall was gone. Just disappeared like magic. Gone.

'Is everyone all right? Answer me,' said my dad as he examined us for injuries. 'Are you all OK? Jesus, where did that wall come out of at all?'

Pinhead had a cut above his eye, it dripped blood down his face in a straight line. People had come out to see what the commotion was about. I opened the door of the car and stumbled out onto the road. Then I recognised where we were, the top of St Patrick's Road and we had demolished Reddans' wall. The car was sitting in the middle of Reddans' front lawn. We were spitting distance from home when he decided to drive through a wall.

'Jesus, I slept through it, Nod. Imagine that, I slept through the whole thing,' said Pinhead as he stood beside me.

My dad was talking to Eyebrows, who was still sitting in the back seat. He was crying, I could hear small sobs and then he came out of the car, but he was fine, not hurt at all. It was a miracle really that we were all walking around grand and I went to look at the front of the car. The bumper was smashed but otherwise you'd never have thought it had just been driven through a stone wall.

'As long as all of you are all right, that's all that matters. We can fix walls and cars, we can buy new ones even, but as long as you're safe, that's the main thing. Jesus, where did the wall jump out of though?' said my dad.

Someone in the crowd sniggered and I didn't blame them because everyone knew that the road narrowed just before Reddans' house and that their wall jutted out. The way my dad said it, you'd swear the wall just decided, hey here's the Hickeys in their new car, I'll just move a few feet across the road so they'll crash into me.

Pinhead was laughing and I knew he was thinking along the same lines as I was about the walking wall and I started laughing too and Eyebrows. And my father started then, leaning against the car laughing a big laugh that came right up from his belly. I could hear someone in the crowd whispering, ''Tis the shock, they're all in shock. They should go to the hospital', and we laughed even more at that, my dad slapping his thigh and pointing to the person that said it.

But in the end we did go to hospital, my dad said it was best to be checked out and Pinhead might need a stitch or two in his head. Mr Reddan drove us to Barrington's, which was very nice of him, seeing as we'd just knocked down his wall.

We weren't long in Barrington's and the crash was nearly worth it when the nurse came to examine Pinhead.

'And you, young man. Were you in the car when it crashed as well?' she asked as she knelt to examine Pinhead's cut.

Pinhead looked at her, dead serious, eyes and all. 'No. I was sitting on the wall,' he said, and we all cracked up.

When we arrived home, my mam met us at the door. 'What in the name of God happened, Tom? Jesus, look at Kevin's eye. I didn't know a thing till someone brought the car home, Pa Reddan's son it was, and he told me you were gone to the hospital,' she said.

She looked worried and glad at the same time, but I had a feeling my dad was in for it. He knew it too, so he went out to the boot of the car to get the mackerel. He was going to make us a feed.

'Sit down, sit down, lads, I'll cook something for you,' my mam said as she rattled pots and frying pans.

'We're having the fish. Dad is cooking the fish for us. He promised,' I said.

'And he promised me he'd drive carefully and he nearly killed the lot of ye.'

'He didn't, Mam, I swear he didn't. He was careful, wasn't he, Pin? It was just the bit with the wall at the end. He was good for the whole day, I swear he was,' I said.

My dad came in then with Eyebrows' ma behind him. You could smell the fish already, even before he opened the bag.

'Are ye all right?' asked Eyebrows' ma, standing close to him. She was the skinniest mother I had ever seen. For a second I thought she was going to kiss him or hug him or something, she reached out her hand towards him but dropped it before it touched his face. She stayed and sat at the table with us and had two whole mackerel to herself and two mugs of tea.

Pinhead nearly missed the feed. My mam sent him home to tell them he was all right. She was worried they might have heard about the crash. He took ages to come back. His mackerel were getting cold on the plate and Eyebrows and me were eyeing them, one each and we'd split the third, but my mam said, 'No, wait for Kevin, he'll be back for his fish.'

Eyebrows and his ma were gone when Pinhead came back. He had that look, like someone had hit him or something, and I knew it wasn't just me imagining it because my mam noticed too.

'Hey, sit down and have your fish. What happened, did something happen?' she asked as she put the plate of food in front of him.

He sat down and started to eat but he kept his eyes on his plate. Mam poured him tea. She looked at me then and gave me the eye to leave the kitchen but I pretended I didn't understand her and I sat there avoiding her looks. I was his best friend and if something happened, I wanted to know. But he never said a word. He ate his fish in silence and drank his mug of tea and he got up then and said, 'Good luck and thanks. I'll see you tomorrow, Nod.'

My mam followed him to the door, with some mackerel in a bag for his mother. I could hear her voice low and soft talking to him for a while. I never heard his voice at all.

I woke up the next morning staring at the St Munchin's school uniform. It had been there every morning since the day Mam bought it, hanging on the back of the door. But that morning was different, like the uniform had grown sure of itself during the night and was there now saying, look at me, Nod, time is running out and I'm going to be a part of your life whether you like it or not. And it was true. I sat up in bed and eyeballed the uniform, gave it the Sacred Heart stare, willed it away to the back of my mind, where it had been for the past few weeks. But it wouldn't go away and I realised then that summer was nearly over and that there would be no plan to rescue me from Munchin's. That the uniform would have to be worn and that everything would change. I clutched the blankets around me and sat there thinking how I could stop it happening, but Brian woke up beside me then. Opened his eyes and sat up in the bed and said, 'Seán.' As clear as that, he said my name for the first time, and I laughed and ruffled his hair.

We went to Groody that day. Just Pinhead and me. We got the bike and headed off down the Bloodmill, me cycling and Pinhead on the bar. The sun was shining but there was a bite in the air, an edge of coldness that slapped you around the face as you cycled. I couldn't shake that feeling from earlier that morning and the cold nip in the air added to it.

We lay on the bank of the stream watching the water rush by. The grass felt damp beneath me even though the sun was high in the sky. I watched the trees swaying overhead. The leaves were losing their bright green colour. I felt odd, strange, not myself. I knew better than to say this to Pinhead, but he beat me to it in a way, he took me by surprise and beat me to it.

'I want to leave school.' He said it out of the blue. The two of us were lying there on the bank looking up at the sky, thinking our own thoughts, and he says this, makes this announcement.

'You can't leave school, your ma and da will kill you.'

'You can leave when you're fourteen. I'm fourteen. I want to leave and get an apprenticeship or something. I'm not a kid any more and when you're at school, you'll always be treated like one.'

I flipped over onto my belly and looked at him, at his eyes, to see if he was pulling my leg. He turned and looked straight at me, dark eyes locked to mine, a tiny smile on his lips. He meant it. I knew that by the smile.

'You have to do your exam first. You won't get an apprenticeship without it. You have to go to the Tech and get your Dayvo, you ghoul.'

'No I don't. I'm dead serious, Nod. I don't want to be treated like a kid any more.'

'Fuck off. You're only a year older than me. Fuck off.'

I turned away from him before I hit him a belt. I was mad with him, the maddest I had ever been and I didn't know why. Just that this was the last thing I wanted to hear and the uneasiness that had started this morning was eating now at my gut, growing as the day went on. I should have stayed in bed. I sat up and started throwing pebbles into the stream, slowly, one after the other, lining them up on the grass beside me and aiming them into the water. I never looked at him at all and held the silence, wanted the silence. I was afraid to speak, afraid of what I might say.

'I could get a job tomorrow with Balls of Flour. He

offered me a job, you know, if I left school. But an apprenticeship would be better. That's what Nick said.'

'What the fuck does Nick know? Is he leaving school? In his arse he is, but he's telling you to leave, the fucker is. Why would you listen to him? Why would you even ask him?' I shouted at him then.

I really wanted to belt him and I tried to control the rage inside me. I couldn't understand him telling Nick, trusting and confiding in him. He should have told me first, the bollocks, he should have told me first. I threw a rock into the water, a fierce lob that ended with a huge splash.

'Relax.'

'Fuck off.'

'What's up with you?'

'What's up with you, acting the prick, the big man? So what did your ma say? What did your da say? Same as Nick was it? I doubt it very much.'

He stiffened beside me. I wasn't looking at him but I could feel him tense up like an elastic band stretched too far, beyond its limit. I held my breath. He caught me by the arm, a tight iron grip, and shoved his face in front of mine so our eyes met. 'Look at me. Look at me, Nod. I couldn't give two fucks what my da thinks, he's the very last person I'd ask. Do you understand that? Is that clear?' His voice was steady and quiet, it was a lid on something big that wasn't going to be let out through anger, like I would do it. You had to admire him for that. For perfect control always. Nearly always.

'I just don't think it's the right thing, leaving school. That's all. It's not the right thing to do. If Enda was here, he'd …'

'Enda isn't here, and anyway he was only a bollocks.'

'You shouldn't talk about him like that, it's not – '

'I'll talk about him any fuckin' way I want, Nod. You

still don't get it, do you? Enda was only a cunt, that's all, a cunt. A fucking coward.'

'Stop it. Shut up.'

Pinhead laughed. A mean, hollow laugh. 'Grow up, will you.'

I turned my face away from his and blinked back tears. There was silence for a minute.

'I'll try the Tech for a few weeks until I see about an apprenticeship. Or a job might come up.'

He smiled then, that smile that I loved, that only he could produce, and I smiled back. Him going to the Tech for a few weeks was better than nothing, he might even like it. I punched his arm and said, 'Let's go, we've training tonight in Claughaun and I'd eat a horse I'm that hungry.' But all the way up the Bloodmill Road I couldn't shake that feeling in my gut, that feeling I couldn't give a name to.

15

'Puck it over to Nick, you ghoul, he can score from there, go on, for fuck's sake,' screamed Pinhead from the back line. We were training with the senior team and Nick had turned into Mick Mackey overnight.

'Puck my hole,' I shouted at Pinhead with a big grin and then I rose the sliotar and whipped it over towards Pisspot, who hadn't a hope of scoring from where he stood. No fucking way was I making Nick the Prick look good on this field.

'Well done, Nod, well fuckin' done, you bollocks. We could have beat the senior team,' said Pinhead as we stripped behind the trainer's car after the game ended.

'It's not about winning, its about playing the game and enjoying it. Relax, Pin, enjoy it for its own sake,' I answered, with a big innocent smile on my face.

Eyebrows and Pisspot sniggered, and even Nick smiled.

'Fuckin' bullshit,' said Pinhead, his face going red, his eyes narrow and mean.

'Temper temper, you don't want to have a little tantrum here with all the girls looking at you,' I said.

I had my back to him as I pulled on my trousers. The others were laughing now. I was feeling pleased with myself. Until he dived on my back and dragged the trousers and jockeys off me. I stood there like a spare prick groping for the trousers, down round my ankles. He pushed me then and I landed flat on my face, in front of the car, right opposite the girls who were sitting across the way waiting for us to get dressed. My arse was sticking right up in the air. Everybody was cracking up laughing and I knew the best way out of it was to join in. I laughed and waved at the hysterical girls and crawled backwards behind the car.

'Bollocks,' I said to Pinhead as I pulled my trousers up around me.

'Yeah. That's what we saw, your bollocks,' he said, and everyone hooted with laughter again.

'So you run around now trying to catch a glimpse of a fella's bollocks? We've a name for that. It's steamer,' I said as I zipped my fly.

People sniggered around me. Pinhead narrowed his eyes and stood there staring at me and for a second I thought he was going to kill me, that he was just going to beat the shit out of me, like he did to Mossy Sheehan over burning Eyebrows' dog. Instead, he walked right up to me and a kind of hush fell around us. He was smiling, looking straight at me, right into my eyes. He stretched out his hand towards me and I was just about to duck but then he stroked my face. 'Darling, I love you,' he said and went to kiss me on the lips.

We all cracked up then, the girls and all, and I said, 'Come on, Pin, I'll buy you something in Mac's.'

We sat on the Green with our haul from the shop, Taytos and lemonade and penny biscuits. Pinhead loved penny biscuits.

'Hey, where are you going to school, Nick?' Eyebrows asked through a mouthful of crisps. Deirdre had to translate for Nick.

'The Tech. I'm starting next Monday,' said Nick.

'Same as me, it's grand there,' said Pisspot. 'There's a couple of fuckers to watch out for but I'll fill you in, don't worry. Pinhead and Eyebrows are starting there too, aren't ye lads?'

I looked at Pinhead and he smiled back at me as he answered Pisspot. 'Yeah, next Monday. Hard to believe the summer's over,' he said.

'Do you know what's hard to believe? That St Patrick's is over. You know, we'll never walk down that hill to school again, never. Jesus I'm starting to feel old,' said Eyebrows with a grin.

'But Irish, Nick, what will you do about Irish?' asked Deirdre then. It was a good question, something I hadn't even thought of.

'An exemption or something like that,' said Nick with a shrug of his shoulders.

Deirdre looked at him with big adoring eyes, like he just said the most brilliant thing. He could talk a pile of horse shit for the night and the girls would still be hanging on to his every word.

'Wonder what Munchin's will be like, Nod? I mean, do you know anyone that's going there?' asked Eyebrows.

'Nope, and I don't know the first thing about rugby either, except Pinhead says it's a steamer's game.'

'No fuckin' way,' said Nick. 'Rugby is a brilliant game. You'll see, Nod, you'll see. It's the best.'

I thought he was pulling my leg, rising me, like, but he was dead serious. I examined his face for smirks or sniggers but he was nodding his head furiously. He meant it. The wonderful Nick, brilliant at everything, including girls, liked rugby. Pinhead was wrong about Munchin's and rugby, and from that second on a tiny bit of hope grew inside me and I realised a part of me, only a small part though, was looking forward to school next Monday. I smiled at Nick and offered him a slug of my Cream Soda.

'Three more days of freedom, I can't believe it. I can't believe we'll be back in our uniforms,' said Karen. Her lovely ponytail swung as she talked.

'And the nights will be getting darker. And cold. No more sunny days,' said Deirdre.

'No more swims in the Forty Foot.' That was Pisspot.

'No more trips to the beach. And no fishing.'
Eyebrows.

'Ah shut the fuck up the lot of ye, you'd swear we were
all going to die. It's not like we had a brilliant summer or
anything. Fuck all happened really,' said Pinhead.

I stared at him. A lot happened. Enda died and that
wasn't fuck all happening, whatever Pinhead said.

They bought me a brand new bike for St Munchin's. I got
up on Saturday morning and my mam wouldn't let me
out until my dad came back from town. She wouldn't say
why, so I just played with the babies for a while. God,
they were big already. They were sitting in the pram, one
at each end, propped up by pillows. It was a tight squeeze.

'They're squashed into that pram,' I said to my mam, in
case she hadn't noticed, like. 'Ye'll have to get a new one,
a bigger one. Do they make prams for two? You know,
for twins?'

The babies stared up at me with round brown eyes, two
pairs of eyes, exactly the same.

'We'll get a twin go-car soon, they'll get another month
out of the pram. You're getting so big, aren't you, my
gorgeous girls?' Mam smiled over at the twins and then
turned back to the dishes in the sink. 'We'll have no babies
soon if you keep growing like that. I'll have to think about
getting you a little brother or sister, so I will,' she said.

'Mam cop on!' I roared but I could see her shoulders
shaking from laughing, and I joined in.

My dad came back then with Colm and Brian in tow.
'Hey Seánie, I want you to look at something in the
garden, tell me what you think,' he said. His face was
excited and he pulled me out of the kitchen by the arm
and through the hall to the front garden. And there it was

propped up against the gate, a brand new Raleigh racer, the one me and Pinhead had seen weeks ago in the front window of the bike shop in Broad Street. I couldn't believe it was mine.

'I love it! Thanks, Dad! I love it, I swear,' I said as I got on the bike. Five speed, Jesus it was great. I went straight to Pinhead's house.

His da was walking out the path as I was going in. He was all cleaned up, shaved and all, with Brylcreem in his hair. 'Hello young man, isn't that a fine bike, a lovely machine that. Go on in there and get him up out of his bed. Some of us have to be up early, some of us have to work,' he said laughing. He went off down the road whistling and I knew one thing for sure, the last place he was going was CIE.

The little girls answered the door in their nighties. One of them got Pinhead for me. I heard him getting out of bed and pissing in the bathroom. Their kitchen was up in a heap, I'd never seen it like that before. I sat down at the table covered in cornflakes and spilled sugar. Deirdre came in the back door then, carrying an empty laundry basket.

'I got a new bike, Dee, a racer, five speed, do you want to see it?'

'In a while, Nod, I have to make Uncle Pat's breakfast and feed that lot. Is Pinhead up yet?'

'Yeah, he's getting dressed. Where's everyone?'

'What do you mean, everyone?' She narrowed her eyes when she said this, like she thought I was trying to catch her out or something.

'You know, your mam, Diet, everyone,' I said.

'Didn't Pinhead tell you? My mother is working. She got a job cleaning in Barrington's. And Diet got a job too in Kelly's bar but only on Saturday mornings,' she said as she cleaned off the table.

Milk dripped down the side of the tablecloth onto the

lino. She scrubbed at the sugar that was stuck to the cloth and the more she scrubbed, the more the milk dripped. I got another dishcloth and started helping her. The three little sisters screeched around the sitting room. Deirdre ignored their racket. She kept scrubbing the sugar and knocked over the jug. A sheet of milk slid onto the floor like a white waterfall.

'Fuck,' said Deirdre and she threw the cloth on the table. There were tears in her eyes, I could see them, but she turned away from me and went to get the mop.

'It's all right. Show me the mop, I'll help you.' I took the mop from her.

She blinked back tears. 'Oh Nod.' That's all she said.

We could hear Pinhead coming down the stairs. I cleaned up the milk and she got bowls out for the breakfast.

'Bollocks,' said Pinhead when he saw me. I looked at him, his eyes still swollen from sleep, a tiny smile at the edge of his mouth. He ran his hand through his hair. 'Bollocks, big ugly bollocks. You got it, the bike,' he said as he took one of the bowls Deirdre had put out for the girls and filled it right to the brim with cornflakes.

I said nothing. I didn't want to gloat or show off or anything. He would have had that bike if he still had his life savings.

'Well wear, Nod, at least one of us got it. We'll go for a spin in a while,' he said then and grinned at me.

'You're supposed to help. Mam said I wasn't to do everything, you're supposed to help, she said so,' Deirdre said. She faced Pinhead with her hand on her hip.

There was an unmerciful scream from the sitting room and she ran in to see what was happening.

'Let's go,' said Pinhead, and he gulped down the last of his cornflakes.

'But …'

'Let's go, come on, we'll go for a spin,' he said, and took his bike from the hall.

There were more screams from the sitting room as Deirdre tried to break up a fight. Uncle Pat was calling from his bedroom.

Deirdre followed us out to the front door. 'Come back, Pinhead, come back. I'm telling, so I am!' she screamed. 'You have to go to the shop, we've no eggs.'

That was a first, the Duffys having no eggs, that was like no hurleys in Claughaun or no bras in Angela Walsh's house. We got on our bikes and cycled like hell down the road.

There was nobody around that night. It was the last Saturday night before we all went back to school, so Pinhead and me were hoping for a grand finale or something. What we got was the two of us sitting on our wall in the rain. Nick was having a bath – how that could take all night, I didn't know – and the rain put off the others.

My mam called us in when it started pelting down. 'If it clears up at all, you can walk down to Donkey Ford's for fish and chips. Or your dad can drive you. Would you prefer that, Seán?' she said.

'No, Mam, we'll walk, it'll clear soon.'

'We'll walk, Mrs Hickey, we'll be grand walking,' said Pinhead. He pinched my arm as he spoke and I laughed. No way were we getting into that car, no bloody way.

The rain did stop and my mam gave us money for fish and chips and a drink too. I didn't want to go the shortcut through Garryowen and meet a big gang of Garryoweners with only two of us. I wanted to walk down Mulgrave Street.

'We'll go the long way, Pin,' I said as we were heading across the Green. 'It's getting dark and there's more light this way.'

'No we won't and no there isn't.'

'Come on, we'll go down Mulgrave Street, there's a full moon tonight, we'll hear all the looneys howling when we pass St Joseph's.' I slowed down as we came to the turn off through Garryowen.

'Nope. We'll walk home that way. There's a girl I like. Jesus, she's lovely, Nod. Big tits, gorgeous arse. She likes me. I know she does. Lives near the Markets Field, come on.' He stopped under a streetlight and was smiling at me. A smile that would have melted even old Hatchet Face and I nodded agreement at him. He winked at me. If I was a girl, I would like him too. No, I'd probably love him.

'What about Libby?' I asked as we headed down Garryowen.

It was dusk but there didn't seem to be too many people around. No gangs of Garryoweners lurking at corners waiting to kill us and that was good.

'What about her?'

'You know, won't she be mad with you if she finds out?'

He laughed at that and looked at me as if I'd said the dumbest thing ever. 'Nod, you're a howl sometimes. Jesus, I've so much to teach you. Won't she be mad! A howl that is.'

'Why?'

He just laughed again.

'No, answer it. Why?'

'Because that's it, Nod. That's what it's about. Having one and if a better one comes along, one you like more, a sexier one, then you drop the first one and move on. Simple!' He laughed like he was half-joking but I knew he wasn't.

We were coming up to the Markets Field. There was a short row of terraced houses just before it and I could see three or four girls at the gate of the last house. So could Pinhead.

'So why did they build the Munster Fair Tavern right in the middle of the road, the last place a pub should be? I asked Uncle Pat to find out for me, he drinks there sometimes,' Pinhead said then.

We were walking right past the girls now and I copped that he was saying this to make us look casual, no, even more than that, to make us look like we didn't even notice the girls were there. I couldn't help clocking the big tits, though, out of the corner of my eye. But I was learning from Pinhead. Casual was the best way.

'So did he find out?' I said and jangled our money in the pocket of my trousers.

We were just past them now. I could get an awful stink of perfume. Jesus, it'd knock you over.

'No, not really. He said he asked and the whole pub cracked up laughing.' He grinned at me and gave the girls a quick once over, still smiling.

I could hear giggles and sighs behind me. His magic was working, the bastard. He could never teach me that magic, you just had to be born with it.

'Did you see her?' he asked when we were well out of earshot.

'No, just her tits, you couldn't miss them.'

He laughed and punched me in the arm. We were nearly at Donkey's. I could see the lights on and people queuing inside the damp, foggy window.

'Don't look now, but they're right behind us. Following us, I'd say. See how easy it is! Ignore them now if they come in after us, just let me do the talking,' he said and winked at me as he pushed the door of the chipper open with his shoulder.

But they didn't follow us in, they waited outside on the wall. I could hear their tinkly laughter every time the door opened. We got our grub and bottles of Coke and went out and sat on the wall, well past the girls, and ate our fish and chips with our backs to them.

'Any chance of a chip?' one of them shouted down to us.

Pinhead winked at me and turned around and shrugged at the girl who spoke. It was Tits, there was no mistaking her.

'If you like,' he said and held out the bag.

The three girls came down and sat with us, all giggles and whispers and rotten perfume. I prayed they couldn't see my reddener in the streetlight. Tits sat down right next to Pinhead, as brazen as you like, and they were chatting and laughing together in no time. I sat there with the other two girls, like a spare prick, eating my chips. They were chatting away too. But not to me.

'Are you right, Pin?' I asked then. I wanted out of there fast.

'Yeah, sure,' he said, and whispered something into Tits' ear.

She laughed and nodded her head at him. 'We'll walk home with ye. We're going the same way, aren't we?' she said and jumped off the wall.

'No we're not, we've to go somewhere, do something. See ya,' said Pinhead and we walked away towards Mulgrave Street, both of us laughing.

'Get anywhere?' I asked as we crossed the road at St John's Cathedral.

'Of course.'

'Well?'

He smiled and punched my arm.

'Well, come on, tell me, get on with it, you ghoul. She said no, that's it, isn't it? She said no!'

He laughed out loud at that. 'Next Saturday night outside the Horse and Hound. Eight o'clock. Her name is

Tina. Isn't that a great name? Tina. You'd kind of know someone called Tina would have big tits.'

'And a fine arse,' I said, and we cracked up.

'You too, Nod,' he said.

We were turning on to Mulgrave Street. You could hear the bingo in the pavilion, all the sixes sixty-six.

'Me too what?'

'You've a date too, with her best friend, Trisha, the dark one, the one with the tan and the platform shoes.'

'Jesus.'

'Nope, just Pinhead looking after his friend. Hey look, if you don't want to go, I'm sure Nick will be interested. He's mad for the women, that fucker is!'

I didn't want to go, not after the last time with Libby and Karen, but I didn't want Nick to go either.

'Does she like me though? She wasn't very friendly outside Donkey's.'

'She likes you enough. Jesus, she's not marrying you or anything. It'll be a laugh, I swear it, Nod, it'll be a crack.'

I had heard that one before. But Saturday was a long way off, a whole week, and I had Munchin's to go through as well, so that made it seem even further away. A lot could happen in a week.

It was dark now and the full moon was right over St Joseph's madhouse. We stopped opposite it for a while but we heard nothing, no howling or screaming, no looneys running around, no sound at all.

'That's spookier,' said Pinhead as we started walking again. 'No sounds, nothing, not a car going in or out, or nurses going for fags. Weird that is, maybe they're all dead in there. Hey let's go in, we'll sneak in the back way, by the Jail Boreen, come on, Nod.' He had turned already to cross the road.

'No, I can't. My mam will send my dad out in the car for us. It's too late,' I said, and kept walking home. I didn't want to go into the madhouse. I wasn't scared or anything, I just didn't want to go.

'Chicken, come on, yellowbelly, cluckcluckcluck,' he shouted at me.

I kept walking and he crossed the road towards the Jail Boreen. I walked faster and never looked back at all.

I was at the Fairgreen when it happened. I heard a noise and just as I turned around someone jumped on my back and put his hands tightly across my eyes, howling like Jesse did when the bitches were in heat. I staggered around blindly yelling, 'Get off, you fucker, you cunt!' I couldn't see and the weight of him on my back was dragging me down. His hand moved lower and when it did I sunk my teeth into it, full force like. He fell off me screaming.

'You bollocks, Nod, you ugly bollocks, look at my fuckin' hand, look, you bastard, look!' Pinhead stuck his hand under my eyes. It was bleeding at the side.

I started laughing then, relieved it was Pinhead. I was sure it had been a Garryowener or a looney. He was skitting now too and the two of us got into fits of laughing, holding on to each other with the effort of it. Tears streamed down my face.

'Mad bastard, you are,' said Pinhead, when the laughing had dwindled into odd bursts.

'Mad bastard you too'

'Well met, that's what Uncle Pat says about us, you and me, that we're well met. I don't really know what it means though, probably some dumb thing he picked up in America. They have loads of dumb sayings there.'

The moon was gone, hidden behind black clouds.

'Come on, we'll get home before the rain if we hurry,' I said and began walking.

'Wait, I know what we'll do, we'll go up and say hello to Enda. I wasn't up there for a while, come on, it's only around the corner from here.' He stood there with the pleading eyes and did his little smile thing. But it didn't work on me any more.

'Nope,' I said. 'I'm going home. Are you coming, or are you going to piss around for the night?' It started to rain.

'I hope I'll be coming next Saturday night. Hey, you ghoul, I was only joking about going to visit Enda. I'll wait till Saturday night to do that. The perfect date, what do you think, Nod? Break it to her gently – I hope you don't mind if we drop in on a good friend of mine for a few minutes, just to say hello, he's not very talkative at the moment but don't take it personal, he's like that with everyone!' he said and laughed.

'Not funny, not funny at all. But it wouldn't surprise me, you bringing someone to a graveyard on a date, mad fucker. I'll be visiting you in St Joseph's in another few years, wait and see.'

We turned up St Patrick's Road. Pinhead found a can and we kicked it to each other, to and fro, nobody missing. The rain stopped again and you could see stars dotting the sky.

We were just passing Ryans' house when Pinhead thought he heard a noise. 'Ssh, did you hear that?'

'Hear what? I can't hear anything.'

'Something, in Ryans' garden, I think. There it is again. Come on, let's see what it is. Sounds weird.'

'Not more piss-acting, Pin. I'm going home.'

And then I heard it too, a soft choking noise, over the hedge in Ryans' garden. Pinhead had worked his way through the thin hedge already.

'What is it, hey wait for me, what the fuck is it … Jesus Christ Almighty!'

I could see clearly now. The moon was out again and it threw a path of silver light across Ryans' vegetable garden, across the neat rows of carrots and leeks, and across the drunk stuck in the middle of the cabbages, with his bare arse in the air. The eejit of a bowsie was on all fours and still making the choking noise.

'Fong him, Pin, fong his bare arse. His arse is just asking for it,' I whispered to Pinhead.

I could hear him laughing softly.

'Who the fuck is it anyway? It's Joe O'Brien, I bet, he's always langers on a Saturday night,' I said, louder than before.

The drunk turned around then, his glassy, drunken eyes seeing nothing. Mr Duffy's eyes. Pinhead's breathing got faster. I wanted to say something to make it all right but Mr Duffy started vomiting thick black ropes of vomit that stank of Guinness. Pinhead stood there like a statue. I couldn't see his face, his eyes, and I was glad about that. Mr Duffy started the choking thing again but much worse than before. He fell down on his back in some kind of fit, his tongue hanging out like a snake trying to leave his body. This was serious.

'Come on, help me, fuck, he's having a fit or a heart attack, Jesus, move Pinhead, call an ambulance!' I screamed and knelt down next to Mr Duffy. His eyes were rolling in his head now. My knees were wet and sticky. I was kneeling in the black vomit. 'Do something!' I screamed again.

Pinhead stood there and looked at us, gave me and his father one of his stares.

'For fuck's sake get help.' I looked up at Ryans' house to see if they heard the racket but there was no lights on.

'Let's go,' Pinhead said then, his voice quiet and steady.

'Jesus, we can't just go.'

'I said, let's go. He'll be fine, he'll sleep it off.' Voice as cold as ice, dead calm.

'Fuck it, he's having a fit, he's twitching now, for fuck's sake, look, will you, his fuckin' eyes are disappearing.'

I got up and started to run for help. Pinhead put out his leg and tripped me. I fell in more vomit.

'Jesus, what did you do that for?' I got up and walked backwards, facing him.

'I said he's fine, no ambulances, no fuss, do you hear me?' His voice was low and calm but his eyes were deadly, he was ready to pounce at me if I moved.

I put out my hand to calm him. 'We'll get my dad. He'll know whether to call an ambulance or not, come on, Pin, look at him. He's not even moving now,' I pleaded.

'He's fine. The old bollocks will just sleep it off. I know him, you don't. Let him be. I mean it,' he said and walked over to his father, never taking his eyes from me, then he spat on the ground beside him.

Mr Duffy never moved, his eyes were open and staring, his tongue lolled in his mouth, just like Enda's on the goalpost.

I turned and ran for help. Pinhead knocked me to the ground almost straight away, took an almighty leap from where he stood right onto my back, knocking me onto the road. I cracked my head on the tarmac. He started beating me with his fists. He sat on top of me and beat my face and my chest. I heard somebody crying, bawling like a small kid, and I copped then that it was me. I didn't fight him. I just put my hands up to protect my face, then curled in a ball with my hands around my head, like he had shown me years ago. I let him beat me and after a minute it stopped hurting. I stopped feeling the thump of his knuckles on my face and body. He talked to me while he hit me, his voice low and menacing, 'I thought you were my friend, I thought you were my friend, I thought you were my friend, just another bastard, just another one.'

He stopped suddenly and burst out crying. He rolled off

me and sobbed. I never saw him crying like that before and I got up on unsteady legs and knelt beside him on the road. Blood or snot or both dripped down my face and I wiped it with the sleeve of my jumper. I reached out and nearly put my hand on his shoulder.

'I am your friend,' I said to his back.

His shoulders shook with sobs and I stretched out my fingers the last inch and let them rest on his shoulder.

'Go fuck yourself, Nod, go fuck yourself in hell,' he said in the low deadly voice and pushed my fingers off his shoulder. He turned around and looked straight at me. Then he got up and raced like a madman down St Patrick's Road.

I ran for my dad then and he called the ambulance and I showed him where Mr Duffy was in Ryans' garden. By the time the ambulance came, all the neighbours were standing huddled in groups, whispering and pointing and shaking their heads. Somebody had fetched Mrs Duffy and she stood there surrounded by women, but she wasn't crying or anything. She wore slippers on her feet.

I sat on the wall with my dad, he had his arm around me and I watched as they checked Mr Duffy's pulse and lifted him onto a stretcher. Nick was there and Eyebrows too and I could hear them all whispering, 'It's Pinhead's father, it's Pinhead's da, so it is. Jesus, will he die? I think he's dead already. No he's not, somebody said they found a pulse. What's a pulse?'

I realised then that I couldn't care less whether he had a pulse or not, whether he lived or died. I didn't care at all.

16

It might have been worth it if he had died. If Mr Duffy had taken his last breath that night in Ryans' garden or maybe in the hospital surrounded by doctors and nurses fighting to save his life. It might have been worth it if he was dead and I was right and Pinhead was wrong. But it was exactly like Pinhead said it would be. He had some kind of fit all right and then he slept for two days and sat up on the third day and ate a huge fry-up. There was nothing dead about Mr Duffy.

And me. My face was a mess on my very first day in Munchin's. He'd broken my nose, the bastard, and I looked like a boxer, a bad boxer, my dad said. I cycled out that Corbally Road, though, and up that long drive to the main doors of the school and I walked in there like I was Errol Flynn. It worked too. Even the older fellas nudged each other and whispered behind their hands and pointed at me on lunch break. They thought I was a hard man. I loved the idea of that. And it was great because nobody there knew me, so I could tell lies if I wanted to, but I did a Pinhead thing instead. I said nothing about it and let them make up their own lies, much better lies than I could ever tell.

I got used to life without Pinhead, like you get used to having only one hand when you break your arm. You still try to use the broken one, see, you keep forgetting about it. And that's exactly the way I was when I discovered rugby. Nick was right — it was the best game in the whole world and nothing, not hurling or soccer or Gaelic, could ever come near it. And I wanted to tell Pinhead. I wanted to go straight to his house after school and burst in the door and say, Pinhead, we had it all wrong about rugby, it's the opposite to a steamer's game, Pin, you can go out there and ram into people and do anything for the ball, well almost anything, and the ref won't give soft frees all the time, and it's all about strength and pace and skill, and you'd love it, I know you would, it's brilliant. And my bike seemed to have a mind of its own and nearly took the turn-off at the top of our road that would have brought me to his house. But I went home, just caught the bike as it tried to sneak around the corner. I went home and told my dad about rugby instead.

Nothing was the same. I had new friends all right, Joey and Ralph. Joey was great. He was on the junior rugby team for Shannon with me. Ralph was in my science class. He was a laugh, kind of mad, with a weird country accent. We called him Turnip. They were grand friends but not the kind you would have outside of school, you know, not the friendships that just happen all by themselves, like breathing or eating or pissing.

Sometimes I saw Pisspot at the shop or at the bus stop on a Saturday heading into town. At the start I wanted to ask him about Pinhead, about Claughaun and hurling and stuff, but I didn't because I was afraid he'd tell Pinhead that I had asked and that Pinhead would think I cared. I didn't care.

Pisspot told me about Eyebrows. He left school and was working with his father as a milkman, well milkboy really but maybe you were a man once you had a job. They needed money badly because of the thirteen children, so it made sense that he was working. I met him at Christmas in town. They were delivering milk to the Stella restaurant and I was just passing at the same time. He jumped down off the van when he saw me, all smiles, eager to talk. But after the how's it goings and do you see Pinhead at all now – he asked that, not me – there was an awkward silence. We had no more to say to each other. I knew nothing about milk and he knew nothing about rugby.

And once last February I saw Enda. Or I thought I saw him anyway. Heading into the Wimpy with a gang of friends, hippie friends with beads and patches on their clothes and long hair. Sometimes you couldn't tell if they were boys or girls. My dad said that, that they all looked the same. Hippies thought they were different but they all looked the same. I was sure it was Enda though. I saw him talking to his friends, leaning into them talking, his long hair flicked behind his ear, like I'd seen Enda do a hundred times. I crossed O'Connell Street and just saw a glimpse of his face as he went into the Wimpy. Enda's double. I liked the idea of that.

And Nick, I bumped into him a few times and we just nodded at each other. We didn't stop and talk or anything but then we never really were friends as such. I mean, we just had a friend in common, that's all. He was hurling for Claughaun now, he made the team. I saw him against St Patrick's and he was good, right enough.

My sisters can walk. It's funny seeing two little identical people stagger around our house. They chatter to each other all the time like they have a language of their own. They say that about twins, you know, but I think it's just baby talk. Colm is starting school in a few weeks, I can't believe that, and Brian can say fuck me pink, I can't believe that either. I think Nana taught him. My mam blames me but I know it was her, she taught him arse and bullshit too, he told me she did. The house is very full but it's nice, I like it. But enough is enough and I worry sometimes and check my mam's belly, but it's flat, well kind of flat anyway.

Dodge's mother got the big C. My mam heard it in the hairdresser's. She had to have an operation and all and my mam talked about going out there some Sunday to visit but it never happened. She was never really pals with Dodge's mother and, anyway, I have rugby training on a Sunday.

I saw Mr Duffy yesterday. It was a Saturday and he was heading into Kelly's bar. He was all jolly smiles and Brylcreem and waved back at me, but I think he didn't know me. I mean, it's ages since I saw him. Not since that night and I saw more of his arse than his face then. The old bollocks. I hate him now. But it's not a mad hate, where you want to bash him or kill him or something, it's more a cold, icy hate that you mind inside yourself and take out and think about now and again. The kind of hate that will keep for years.

And right after that, I saw Pinhead. Life is like that, full of little surprises that make sense really – you know, you've just met the father, so now here's the son. Something like that. He was across the road, I was heading into town, he was coming out. He stopped for a minute, long enough for me to see his face, see his eyes. My stomach did a somersault thing, the kind that usually happens when you see a girl you like, and my heart thumped so hard in my chest I thought he'd be able to hear it right across the road.

For a split second I was sure he was going to come over, he half-raised his hand and took a step towards the kerb. My mind was full of all the stuff I wanted to talk to him about, all the rumours and half stories I'd heard. Like, he ate the bowl of fruit they were supposed to be sketching in art class in the Tech on his first day and that he gave the metalwork teacher a head in the face and left after a week. That he got his apprenticeship in the cement factory and that every girl in Limerick was in love with him. That he was captain of Claughaun. And that he missed me, like I missed him. I made that one up, that rumour, that lie.

But I waited for him to make the first move. And he did, he waved and smiled that perfect smile and shrugged his shoulders very slightly. I waved back, trying to be casual, like, but my arm shot up too quickly and I grinned from ear to ear. He stepped back from the kerb and shrugged again and walked away. I stood there for a minute and shouted after him, 'Pinhead wait', but it came out a whisper. He didn't hear it. I walked away too, with my hands in my pockets and tears stinging my eyes.

Some things are just … well, just over. That's it. Over, done with, gone forever. Like a great summer or Christmas or a good game of rugby. It will never happen again, no matter how much you want it to, it will never be exactly the same. So you have to think of all the good summers that will come, or the great Christmases or the brilliant game of rugby that might happen as soon as next week.

There's one thing I'm glad about though. The marble thing only ever happened once. It was the best laugh of my life so far. Even now when I think about it I still laugh. In the whole history of mankind there was only one time for the marble thing. And I was there. With Pinhead. I was there.